INVISIBLE
HELIX

ALSO BY KEIGO HIGASHINO

INVISIBLE HELIX

KEIGO HIGASHINO

MINOTAUR BOOKS
NEW YORK

First published in the United States by Minotaur Books, an imprint of St. Martin's Publishing Group

INVISIBLE HELIX. Copyright © 2021 by Keigo Higashino. Translation copyright © 2024 by Giles Murray. All rights reserved. Printed in the United States of America. For information, address St. Martin's Publishing Group, 120 Broadway, New York, NY 10271.

www.minotaurbooks.com

Designed by Gabriel Guma

Library of Congress Cataloging-in-Publication Data

Names: Higashino, Keigo, 1958- author. | Murray, Giles, translator.
Title: Invisible helix / Keigo Higashino ; translation, Giles Murray.
Other titles: Tomei na rasen. English
Description: First U.S. edition. | New York : Minotaur Books, 2024. |
    Series: Detective Galileo series ; 5 | "Originally published in Japan
    under the title Tomei Na Rasen by Bungeishunju Ltd."—
    Title page verso.
Identifiers: LCCN 2024034944 | ISBN 9781250875563 (hardcover) |
    ISBN 9781250875570 (ebook)
Subjects: LCGFT: Detective and mystery fiction. | Novels.
Classification: LCC PL852.I3625 T6613 2024 | DDC [FIC]—dc23
LC record available at https://lccn.loc.gov/2024034944

Our books may be purchased in bulk for promotional, educational, or business use. Please contact your local bookseller or the Macmillan Corporate and Premium Sales Department at 1-800-221-7945, extension 5442, or by email at MacmillanSpecialMarkets@macmillan.com.

Originally published in Japanese under the title Tomei Na Rasen by Bungeishunju Ltd.

English translation rights arranged with Bungeishunju Ltd. through Japan UNI Agency, Inc.

First U.S. Edition: 2024

1   3   5   7   9   10   8   6   4   2

CAST OF CHARACTERS

Professor Manabu Yukawa, a.k.a. "Detective Galileo": Professor of physics and occasional unofficial consultant to the Tokyo Metropolitan Police Department

Director Mamiya: Head of the homicide division, Tokyo Metropolitan Police division, Tokyo Metropolitan Police

Chief Inspector Kusanagi: Leads the investigation, college friend of Professor Yukawa

Detective Inspector Kishitani: Part of Kusanagi's team

Detective Sergeant Kaoru Utsumi: Part of Kusanagi's team and a longtime acquaintance of Professor Yukawa

Sonoka Shimauchi: Daughter of Chizuko, girlfriend of Ryota Uetsuji, works in a flower shop

Chizuko Shimauchi: Raised in an orphanage, single mother of Sonoka

Ryota Uetsuji: Video producer and boyfriend of Sonoka

Nae Matsunaga: Children's book author and longtime friend of Chizuko

Hidemi Negishi: Owner and mama-san of VOWM, a hostess bar

NOTE

One million yen is approximately equal to 7,000 U.S. dollars.

PROLOGUE

Three years after the end of the war, a baby girl was born in a small village in Akita Prefecture. She had two older brothers who were later joined by a younger brother and sister. Being from a farming family, although not well-off, they grew up healthy and vigorous.

Many of the girl's contemporaries were sent off to find work in the city after graduating junior high school, as soon as they could. She, however, continued on to the local high school. When she graduated, she found a job at a textile mill in Chiba, on the outskirts of Tokyo. She told her family that she wanted to help them financially when, in fact, she just wanted to put the poverty and hardships of country life behind her. Hosting the 1964 Olympics had endowed Greater Tokyo with an irresistible luster in her eyes.

Unfortunately, her textile mill was out in the suburbs and both it and the all-female dormitory next to it were surrounded by nothing but fields and rice paddies. Still, on her day off, she would head into Tokyo. Parading in her miniskirt through the lively parts of town—that simply did not exist where she came from—was an exhilarating experience.

Life was fun and the time rushed by. She almost never went

back to her hometown. The first year she went home for New Year and for the Obon summer holiday. She found it dreadfully dull and she was disgusted by the way her siblings would shamelessly try to squeeze her for money. She gradually started making up excuses to not go back.

In this way, around two years passed. She'd gotten used to life in the big city and learned to have fun in all sorts of ways. And now that she was over twenty, she was allowed to drink.

It was a Sunday when it happened. She was looking into the display window of a boutique not far from Ginza when a shadowy figure came up behind her. She was just about to turn around when her handbag was grabbed and torn off her. She yelled but it was too late. The man had already run off. A purse snatcher!

Yelling "Thief!" she launched herself in pursuit. In her high heels, she was barely able to run. The other people in the street did not seem to grasp what had happened.

She stopped and stood frozen to the spot, overcome with the shock of it, before sinking down into a squatting position. She felt demoralized. Her brain was a blank. She had no idea what to do. Her wallet was in the bag. She wouldn't even be able to get back home.

She noticed a shadow on the sidewalk followed by a pair of black leather shoes. She looked up. A man in a rather flashy shirt open at the neck was standing there. He was young but probably older than she was, she reckoned.

"This yours, miss?"

She caught her breath when she saw what he had in his hands. It was the bag that had been snatched just a moment or two ago! She pulled herself hastily to her feet and took it. She opened it. Her wallet was still there!

"I let the fellow go. Handing him over to the police is more trouble than it's worth. You got your stuff back, and that's what counts, right, miss?"

"You . . . you ran after him and caught him?"

"Nah. I was just walking along minding my own business when the guy comes charging across the street. He was holding a woman's handbag. Right away I was like, 'This guy's got to be a purse snatcher.' I just stuck out my leg and—*crash*—down he goes. He dropped the bag and was too stunned to pick it up again. He just took off, so I picked it up and was walking this way, wondering who it belonged to, when I saw you."

"Thank you. You saved my life." She bowed deeply to show her gratitude.

"You need to be careful. There's bag snatchers on bicycles and motorbikes too." The man was already moving off as he said this, but spotting a hole-in-the-wall tobacconist a few meters away, he stopped at the counter. "A pack of Highlights," she heard him say.

The girl dashed up to him, pulling her wallet out of her bag as she did so. "Look . . . Let me pay for those."

"What? Why?" There was an expression of surprise on the man's face.

"It's my way of saying thank you. It's the least I can do."

"You don't need to."

"I can't help it. It's something my parents drilled into me: if somebody does you a good turn, you've got to show them you're grateful." She turned and looked at the old woman behind the counter. "How much for the Highlights?"

"Seventy yen," she said.

The younger woman hesitated. Was that too little to properly express her thanks?

The man burst out laughing. "Okay, okay, I get it. Fine, then, go ahead and pay for them."

She felt her cheeks reddening as she handed over the money.

"I think that gives me the right to do something for *you*. What would you say to having a cup of coffee with me?" the man said as he dropped the cigarette packet into the chest pocket of his shirt.

"Oh, I couldn't possibly . . . I mean, coffee costs more than a pack of cigarettes."

"It's okay. Really. The cost price of coffee's less than seventy yen."

"The 'cost price'?"

"Yeah. Come with me. You'll soon see what I mean."

He took her to a bar on the third floor of a modern building. It was closed, but he unlocked the door. There was a counter on one side and four tables in a row on the other.

The man went around to the inside of the counter and started preparing some coffee. He sometimes served it to people who didn't want anything alcoholic, he explained.

He introduced himself. His name was Hiroshi Yano and he worked behind the bar here. The place was closed because it was a Sunday.

She told him her name.

"Where're you from? Sounds like the northeast to me."

"I'm from Akita. . . . It's that obvious, is it?"

After two years in Tokyo, she liked to think that she'd gotten rid of her accent, but people often commented on it.

"It's nothing to get upset about. I think it's rather sweet. I'm an out-of-towner too."

Hiroshi was from Nagano Prefecture. He'd come to Tokyo as part of a group who had moved in search of work. When the factory he and his cohort were working at shut down, he'd started working at the bar. As well as tending bar, he was also a general drudge, doing the unglamorous jobs like cleaning and tidying before the place opened for the night.

They went on to discuss their interests and enthusiasms. She'd never had such a long conversation with a man outside of her workplace. If truth be told, at work, conversation was kept to a minimum, and she wasn't much good at it anyway. As she chatted away with Hiroshi, she felt relaxed and comfortable. At the same time, her whole body felt burning hot. It was a strange feeling.

She wanted to stay longer, but she needed to get back to the factory dormitory before it got too late. As she was getting ready to leave, Hiroshi said, "Fancy getting together again some time?"

"I'd like that. . . ."

"How about next Sunday? Will you be back in town?"

"Probably . . ."

"Good. Same place, same time?"

"Fine by me."

"It's a deal, then. If there's any problem, give me a call." Hiroshi slid a book of matches across the counter with the bar's phone number on it.

They started meeting at the bar every Sunday. They would go out for a meal or occasionally go see a movie. She felt miserable when it was time to say goodbye. In the train on the way home from Ueno Station, she would often sing, "I love him and I'll never forget him," quietly to herself. It was a song from Pinky & Killers' *The Season of Love*, which had been a big hit the year before.

They'd been seeing each other like this for around three months when she went to Hiroshi's apartment for the first time. It was a single room with a small kitchen area. The futon almost completely covered the floor. It was on that futon that the two of them made love. It was her first time.

Instead of meeting Hiroshi at the bar on Sunday afternoons, she started going around to his apartment on Saturday night. She would head to the station as soon as work finished for the day and catch the train for Tokyo. Sometimes she would cook up a simple dinner for them both. She started keeping toiletries and a change of clothes at his place.

After a while, she noticed that something was not quite right. She wasn't getting her period. Initially, she wasn't too worried; it was irregular at the best of times. Only when she was late by over a month did she really get concerned. She went to the hospital. "Congratulations," the doctor said. "You're already into the third month."

She simply couldn't accept it. She couldn't believe what was happening. She shared her confusion with Hiroshi, who just burst out laughing.

"You're pregnant? Thought you might be. No big surprise when we've been screwing like rabbits week in, week out! Besides, people say that the pullout method doesn't really work."

"What should we do?"

"Simple enough. You're going to quit your job and I'm going to have to do enough work for two. No, make that enough work for *three*, for when the baby comes along. It won't be easy, but what other choice have we got?"

"What are you saying? What am I supposed to do after quitting my job?"

"Move in here. Let's live together. It's not the biggest place, but we'll just have to make do for the time being. As soon as I start earning more, we can move somewhere bigger."

As soon as Hiroshi said that, the gloom that had been enveloping her like a fog instantly lifted. He was pleased at the news. He even went a step further and took the opportunity to ask her to marry him.

She wrapped her arms around his neck.

They still had one problem to deal with. She had not told her parents about Hiroshi. She knew for a fact that they would be furious to discover that she was pregnant out of wedlock. On top of that, as country people, they had a powerful and instinctive prejudice against the nightlife world in which Hiroshi worked. They were hoping that their daughter would find herself a respectable husband.

They talked it over and decided that the best thing to do was to pay a formal visit to her parents after the baby had been born. Surely when her parents saw the baby's little face, they would forgive her on the spot!

She handed in her notice the following month. She moved out of the factory dormitory and into Hiroshi's little apartment, bringing as few things with her as she possibly could.

Alongside his job at the bar, Hiroshi got himself a part-time gig delivering newspapers. He would work until the early hours of the morning, then head straight for the newspaper delivery office. He got home at around 7:00 A.M. and slept through to the afternoon. He was able to keep up this routine because he was physically robust and capable of holding his liquor. Hiroshi always said, "It's for our family. I'll do whatever it takes."

She made a doll for the baby she was expecting. Not knowing if it was going to be a boy or a girl, she kitted the doll out with a blue-and-pink-striped sweater and gave it longish hair. With all the Japanese pop groups copying the Beatles, plenty of men had started growing out their hair too.

Even if they were not well-off, they were happy. They weren't expecting anything bad to happen to them.

Then, on a Friday morning the month before she was due to have the baby, the janitor knocked on the door of their apartment. "Phone call for you," he said.

Hiroshi had collapsed while he was out delivering papers.

She rushed to the hospital. She almost fainted at the sight of Hiroshi laid out in the ward. Someone had placed a white cloth over his face.

It was a cerebral hemorrhage. The doctor wasn't sure what had caused it. He said that overwork could have had something to do with it.

She cried for three days and three nights. After her tears finally dried up, she sank into deep despondency. She didn't want to do anything and she just stayed in bed all day.

That was when she unexpectedly went into labor, almost a full month ahead of her due date! She dragged herself on all fours to the janitor's room, where the startled man called an ambulance.

She had a baby girl weighing roughly five pounds. Holding the little body against hers, she felt joy and bewilderment in equal measure. How was she supposed to go about her life now?

She had barely any money. She had no way of paying next month's rent. And she couldn't very well go out and work now that she had a baby to take care of.

At a loss what to do, she delayed registering the birth. Throwing herself at the mercy of her parents back home wasn't an option.

One day, she fainted in the apartment. In addition to not eating properly, a lot of her energy was being diverted to the baby in the form of breast milk. She was lucky she'd had the attack indoors. It could have been much more serious. She shuddered when she imagined what would have happened if she'd been holding her baby daughter at the time.

I can't go on like this. As she looked down at the baby sleeping peacefully, she made a decision. She couldn't bring up the baby by herself. In the long run, it would be better if she gave her up.

She could only think of one solution. There was an orphanage not far from the textile mill where she'd been working. She had no idea how the place was managed, but she did remember seeing the children when they had come to visit the textile mill on a field trip. They had all looked healthy and happy. *She'll be well looked after there*, she thought to herself.

Autumn came. On a slightly chilly day, she left the apartment. She was holding the baby in her arms and had a basket in the crook of her elbow. It contained a few spare clothes, a blanket, and the doll she'd made herself.

She took a train and then a bus. When she was close to the

orphanage, she got out and sat down in a park a certain distance away, waiting for night to fall. She ate a sweet bun and breastfed the baby. The knowledge that this was the last feeding she would ever do made her weep uncontrollably.

When it got dark, she went into action. She wrapped the baby in a towel and placed it in the basket. She slipped the doll in beside her before putting the blanket over them both. If they took off the doll's clothes, the people at the orphanage would find what she'd written in Magic Marker on the doll's back. It was the name she and Hiroshi had planned to give their baby. They had thought of it together. It was a name, in kanji, that would work equally well for a boy or a girl.

When she reached the orphanage, she stopped in front of the waist-high gate and examined the place. It was a cluster of solid-looking buildings. There were lights on in the windows.

She glanced around. There was no one nearby. If she was going to do this, she would have to do it quickly. Her plan would fail if anyone spotted her hanging around.

She went up to the gate and placed the basket on the ground next to it. Although she'd promised herself not to take a second look at her baby, she couldn't help herself and turned back the blanket slightly.

The baby's round white face was illuminated by the moonlight. It was asleep, breathing peacefully, and its eyes were shut.

She touched one of its cheeks with her fingertips. *I will never forget the feel of her skin as long as I live*, she thought.

She felt the tears coming. Fighting them off, she pulled the blanket back up over the baby's head. She was hoping that the orphanage staff would find the baby in the morning.

She got to her feet and walked away. *Don't look back*, she told herself. Imagining that she could hear the sound of whimpering behind her, she struggled for breath.

She had no idea where she was going. Eventually, she found herself sitting on the train without knowing how she'd got there. Looking at the darkness outside the window, she wondered what the point of going back to Tokyo was.

1

Sonoka Shimauchi popped into the grilled chicken joint after emerging from Ayase Station with all the other commuters and before heading to her usual bus stop. Today was her day to make dinner, but she'd let her mother, Chizuko, know that she would be picking up chicken takeout. "Cutting corners again, eh?" Chizuko had joked. Since she actually liked grilled chicken, she didn't mind really.

Sonoka frowned as she looked up at the menu. *The quails' eggs were sold out.* What should she do? There was another shop she liked, but it was a bit of a walk away.

She pulled out her phone and called her mother. They both adored quails' eggs. She didn't want her mother to give her a hard time for having given up too easily.

No one picked up. Chizuko had said she was doing the early shift today. She should be home by now.

Sonoka waited for a minute or two, then called again. Once again, no answer.

Oh, what the heck. She decided to buy something else at the same place. They could get quails' eggs another time.

She bought a couple of mixed chicken grills and caught her bus. The smell of chicken wafted out of the bag on her lap.

The sun had now set fully. She contemplated the city going by as she rocked along with the motion of the bus. It was a succession of gas stations, big electronics stores, and car dealerships, with small stores, private houses, and office buildings filling up the spaces in between. It was a cityscape she knew well. In a day or two, it would be four years since they moved to this part of Tokyo. The time had gone by so quickly! They were living somewhere new, but living together with her mom, just the two of them, was as much fun as ever. Sure, they fought from time to time, but they had never had a serious falling-out.

When Sonoka was a child, most of the children at the place where Chizuko worked had *no* parents, rather than just one. As a result, Sonoka didn't feel that she was different. She had a vague idea that her father was dead.

It was only after she'd been at primary school for a while that she started thinking about him. Most of her school friends had two parents. She was eager to discover what her father had been like.

Chizuko couldn't bring herself to lie.

"Your father worked at the same place where I was working. It's a long time ago now. Circumstances prevented us from getting married. Mommy wanted to have a baby anyway, so I had a baby with him, and that baby was you."

That was the explanation Sonoka got the first time she asked. She kept on asking the same question over and over until she finally learned the truth. It was simple enough. Her father already had a family of his own. When he found out that Chizuko was pregnant, he didn't want her to have the baby and told her that if she went ahead and had it, he would refuse to acknowledge it. That was when Chizuko had made the decision to bring up the child as a single parent. She broke up with Sonoka's father and never contacted him again. That was why Sonoka had never met him.

None of this came as any great shock to Sonoka. When she asked Chizuko what sort of man he was, she was told that he was "very kind, very nice." That was good enough for her.

She was still sunk in these old memories when the bus reached her stop. She climbed down onto the sidewalk, the bag of grilled chicken in her hand.

She walked along the road for a few minutes. There was the two-story wooden apartment building off on the left. The place was called Dolphin Heights. Both she and her mother had liked the name and it was one reason why they had decided to live there. There were four apartments on each floor, with an outdoor staircase leading up to the second floor. Chizuko and Sonoka lived in the apartment at the end of the second floor closest to the stairs and the road.

Sonoka took her key out of her handbag as she made her way up the stairs. She could see light seeping through the cracks around the door. Chizuko was home after all.

She unlocked the door and pulled it open. "It's me. I'm back," she said.

Normally, her mother was quick to respond with "Welcome home." This time, there was nothing but silence. Closing the door behind her, Sonoka slipped off her shoes. What was going on? Her mother's shoes were right there below the step, meaning she *should* be at home.

She looked around the living room. There was no Chizuko, but the tote bag she always took with her to work was sitting on the floor leaning up against the low table where they ate their meals.

As Sonoka stepped up into the apartment, she realized that the sliding door leading to the space with the washing machine, toilet, and bathroom was not shut properly. The second door that led to the bathroom was wide open and the light was on inside. She could hear the murmur of running water.

"Mama?"

Sonoka's breath caught in her throat when she peered into the bathroom. Chizuko was lying sprawled out on the floor. She was still fully dressed.

"Mama," Sonoka shrieked. She shook her. No response. Chizuko's face was waxen. Her eyes were tightly shut.

Ambulance . . . Got to call an ambulance.

Sonoka rushed out of the bathroom and ripped her phone out of her handbag. In the shock of the moment, she struggled to recall the emergency number.

Chizuko passed away in the hospital about three hours later. It was a subarachnoid hemorrhage. Sonoka felt dizzy and had to sit down when the doctor who had operated on her mother gave her the bad news.

Sonoka and Chizuko had no family beyond each other. Chizuko, however, had a female friend whom she loved and trusted deeply. Back when Sonoka was a little girl, on her days off, Chizuko would take her to her friend's house to play. It was a detached house, painted white, and the woman lived alone because her husband was dead and she had no children of her own.

Sonoka always called her Nae. And she kept calling her that even after learning her full name. Nae was two years older than Chizuko. They had met at the orphanage where Chizuko worked.

Nae always gave them a warm welcome. She would have presents of clothes and toys ready for Sonoka. Nae always insisted on doing the cooking and wouldn't let Chizuko help. "You deserve a proper rest on your day off," she always used to say.

As Sonoka got older, she and her mother went around to Nae's place less and less often. Chizuko, however, still saw her regularly. When Sonoka found delicious-looking sweets laid out on the table at home, as often as not, they were a gift from Nae.

Nae was the only person Sonoka had to turn to as she reeled from the shock of Chizuko's sudden death. She called her. After a moment's stunned silence, Nae said she would be right there. Her voice was flat and devoid of emotion.

But when Nae showed up at the hospital soon after, her eyes were red from weeping. She looked shattered. She burst into tears in the ward when she came face-to-face with Chizuko's dead body. For all this spasm of grief, she proved every bit as dependable as Sonoka expected. While Sonoka had no idea what she was supposed to do, Nae briskly set about making all the arrangements for the funeral and even came to stay in Sonoka's apartment for the night, suspecting that she would feel lonely if left on her own. It was entirely thanks to her that the funeral was all over and done with inside a couple of days.

The two women brought Chizuko's ashes back with them to the apartment and ordered take-out sushi to eat together.

"I wonder what I should do now." Sonoka paused her chopsticks in midair and looked around the room vaguely.

Nae smiled tenderly.

"You don't need to worry about anything. Any problems, you just come and talk to me. That's what your mom always used to do. I want you to feel free to do the same."

Sonoka thanked her. The fact that Sonoka worked part-time while going to design college was due to Nae's advice. She thought that it was easier for a woman to get a good job if she had a specific skill set.

"Take this and spend it on whatever you want. Maybe take a trip with a friend to clear your head."

Nae held out an envelope as she said this. After a brief show of reluctance, Sonoka took it. When Nae had left, Sonoka looked inside; there was one hundred thousand yen. That was kind. Spending it on some sort of trip was the last thing she intended to do. She knew that life was about to become more difficult for her.

Thinking about the future was depressing. Chizuko had supported Sonoka financially and emotionally. She had been not just a pillar but walls and a roof protecting her from every kind of hardship. And Chizuko was not yet fifty years old! Sonoka had expected her to be fit and healthy for years to come.

It was Chizuko who found the flower shop where Sonoka was now working. And it was Chizuko who proposed moving when she got hired there. They were living in the suburbs in Chiba back then. Working at the flower shop in the day and going to the design school at night would mean a great deal of commuting. Chizuko, it turned out, was planning to get a new job herself, so moving into town would be a plus for her as well. Her new job was at an industrial kitchen that prepared school meals, she explained.

Sonoka guessed that her mother had switched jobs on purpose to help her get her life off to a good start. It made her aware of just how much her mother loved her and how determined she was to give her the best upbringing she could.

From the day Chizuko died, Sonoka's life was lonely and full of anxiety. Financially, things were a struggle, but she couldn't very well expect Nae to take care of her. At the end of the day, Nae was not family and they had no blood ties. While Nae may have had a special bond with her mother, the connection between the two of them was far less strong.

One day, the manager of the flower store, Mrs. Aoyama, called her over.

A man in a suit was standing beside her. He appeared a little over thirty.

"This gentleman is looking to buy some flowers for his work. He's told me what he's looking for and I think you're probably the best person to help him find it, Sonoka."

"What does he have in mind?"

"He wants flower arrangements that match a piece of music."

"A piece of music? What sort of music?" Sonoka asked.

The man pulled out his phone and tapped the screen a few times until music started to play. It was something classical played on electronic instruments.

"I've got seven more pieces of music on top of that one, and I need flower arrangements for all of them. Eight in all. I'd like them done in the next two or three days, if you can manage it."

"Gosh, that won't be easy," Sonoka blurted out. "It sounds like fun, though. . . ."

"Will you do it?" Mrs. Aoyama asked.

"I'll give it a go."

The man presented her with his business card and formally introduced himself. His name was Ryota Uetsuji and he was in the video production business.

The two of them listened to all the different pieces of music and discussed them. Sonoka suggested building the floral arrangements around a core of native flowers.

"Native flowers? What sort of flower is that?"

Sonoka responded with a shake of her head.

"A native flower is not any single flower. It's what we call specific flowers that come from a specific place. There are lots of them that come from Australia and South Africa. They have oodles of character."

Sonoka showed Uetsuji the leucadendrons, versailles, and silver brunias that they had in the store that day.

"These are great." Uetsuji's eyes shone with enthusiasm. "So you're going to make something by combining these, right?"

"One thing that's good about native flowers is that their petals have completely different textures. That makes it easier to produce a wide variety of different arrangements."

"Fabulous. I am in your hands."

"Very good, sir," Sonoka said. She felt a surge of energy and enthusiasm. It was the first time since Chizuko's death that had happened.

In fact, she had so much fun that she lost track of time. Uetsuji had explained that the flower arrangements would appear in some videos he was making. The idea that they would be seen by a large number of people made her a little nervous, but it also motivated her to try harder.

Three days later, when Uetsuji came in to see the eight complete arrangements, he pumped his fist in glee.

"This is *exactly* what I was looking for—something instinctive, nothing conventional or overintellectualized. These arrangements are not just about the beauty of the flowers themselves but about a sense of the power *and* the fragility of life. These are perfect."

Uetsuji's enthusiasm embarrassed Sonoka. She wasn't particularly self-confident. Nonetheless, she enjoyed Uetsuji's praise and looked at him in a new light. Her first impression of him had not been bad. He was well groomed, with regular, handsome features. On top of that, he was a good talker, with a knack for choosing just the right word or phrase. *He seems like a nice guy*, she thought to herself. When he said that he would like to invite her to dinner to thank her for helping him out, she agreed immediately, not bothering with the whole pantomime of initially declining before acquiescing.

A few days later, Uetsuji took her to a fancy French restaurant in Nihonbashi. Not having been anywhere so upscale in her life, she felt nervous. Uetsuji, by contrast, seemed confident and he ordered for both of them.

Sonoka had never eaten proper French food before and, with each dish tastier than the one before, she was in seventh heaven. Despite drinking only a tiny bit of wine, she felt as though she were floating on air.

Uetsuji's conversation was as brilliant as ever. He would embark on a difficult topic only to make a surprising link to something relatable. He would seem to be making small talk only to end up broaching a future business idea.

"I'd love to see you again," he said to her as they said their goodbyes. She saw no reason to turn him down.

That was how her relationship with Ryota Uetsuji began. Sonoka had been feeling lonely since Chizuko's death and Uetsuji helped fill the void in her heart. She turned to him for all kinds of advice: things like how best to do her job and to deal with people. Uetsuji always answered confidently and without hesitation. Sonoka saw that as a testament to his deep life experience and trusted every word he said.

She invited Uetsuji to her apartment one month after they had started going out. They had made love for the first time a week ago in a hotel room. As they lay in bed together, Uetsuji had said that he would like to see her place.

Sonoka felt ashamed at the thought of him seeing her apartment in the shabby old building but she told herself it didn't matter, as he'd have to see it at some point.

Sitting on a cheap wooden chair, Uetsuji ran an appraising eye around the room. "It's a nice place," he said in a murmur. "You keep it nice and tidy. It's bigger than I expected too."

"I used to share with my mom. Still, it is forty years old." Sonoka shrugged and pouted.

"I don't mean to pry, but what sort of rent are you paying here?"

"Fifty-eight thousand plus another two thousand for the management fee."

"Sixty thousand in all. Can you cover it?"

"For now at least."

Uetsuji said nothing. A thoughtful look crept over his face. A moment or two later, he pulled out his wallet and placed thirty thousand yen on the table. "Here's my contribution."

Startled, Sonoka shook her head. "I don't need your money."

"Come on, take it. Plus I want to come back here. . . ."

"You're welcome to come whenever you want."

"If you don't take it, you'll put me in a bind. If you do take it, then I'll be able to drop in whenever I feel like it without thinking twice."

"No need to think twice."

"You don't get it. I don't want you to treat me like some random guest."

At that point, Sonoka felt obliged to take his money. "All right, then," she said and took the thirty thousand yen.

That evening, Sonoka cooked dinner for him. It was nothing special but Uetsuji kept going on about how good it was. Afterward, they made love on the slightly chilly futon.

"Let's buy ourselves a bed," said Uetsuji as Sonoka rested her head against his arm. "Then we can skip the hassle of having to roll up the futon and stick it in the cupboard every day."

"How much does a bed cost?"

"You don't need to worry. I'll pay for it. By the way, what's the story with this doll here?"

Uetsuji had picked up a doll that was lying on the pillow. It was an old, crude handmade thing dressed in a faded blue-and-pink-striped sweater.

"It's an heirloom of my mom's," Sonoka simply said.

"You always sleep with it?"

"I like to have it near me when I'm sleeping."

"You do? Well, when I buy us a bed, I may get you to keep it on a shelf instead." Uetsuji returned the doll to its original position on the pillow.

The next morning, after they had left the apartment, Sonoka presented Uetsuji with his own key.

Uetsuji started coming over more and more, gradually, so that it wasn't unusual for Sonoka to find him lying on their bed when she got back in the evening. Whenever he came, he always stayed over. He began keeping clothes at her place, so that he could go directly into work.

"Why don't I just leave my place and move in with you here?" Uetsuji suggested one evening when they were having dinner. "I only use my place for sleeping."

Uetsuji was renting a one-room apartment. Sonoka had only been there once. It was quite nice, but not spacious enough for two.

"Really? You'll be okay in this crummy old place?"

"I'm used to it. Besides, home is where the heart is." Uetsuji grinned. "Have we got a deal?"

Sonoka grunted and nodded.

Uetsuji moved in a week later. Sonoka was surprised at how little he brought with him, but he said that he didn't believe in accumulating stuff and tried not to have any more than was strictly necessary.

And that was how they started living together. For Sonoka, waking up every morning with her lover at her side was an exciting new experience. She was also delighted that she'd found someone willing to praise her rather mediocre cooking.

2

The local precinct sent a plain white sedan rather than a marked police car. Kusanagi felt a sense of relief as he climbed into the back seat. A police car left parked for any length of time in a residential neighborhood would excite the curiosity of the locals and have them uploading images and comments onto social media.

"How long will it take to get to the apartment?" Kusanagi asked the detective sitting in the driver's seat. A senior police officer by the name of Yokoyama. Kusanagi pegged him as a little over thirty.

"A tad over ten minutes. It's three kilometers give or take."

"Not far, then. Okay, let's go."

"Yes, sir." Yokoyama nodded and switched on the engine.

In the back seat next to Kusanagi, Kaoru Utsumi was busy tapping at her phone. There was a map on the screen. Kusanagi guessed she was trying to get a handle on the local geography.

"What's the closest station to the scene?" Kusanagi asked her.

Kaoru Utsumi cocked her head a little. "Hard to say," she said. "Either Kita-ayase on the Chiyoda Line or Rokucho on the Tsukuba Express Line. They're both about half an hour's walk away."

"Not close at all, then. How do the people there get around?"

"Anyone without a car will have to take the bus," Yokoyama said. "Failing that, they can always use a bicycle."

"I see."

Inconvenient but good from a health perspective, Kusanagi thought to himself. And he meant it. He moved a lot less now compared to when he was younger. Due to the pressure of the job, he'd expected to lose weight after being promoted to section chief, but the waistband of his trousers was only getting tighter with every passing year. His superiors would often compliment him for looking more "dignified and authoritative." It was a compliment he could have done without.

The car turned onto a narrow single-lane road. There was a mixture of private houses, workshops, and home-improvement centers and other big-box stores alongside it.

They had just passed a primary school when Yokoyama braked and pulled the car onto the side of the road.

"That's the building," he said, looking to the left.

Kusanagi looked out of the window. A two-story wooden apartment block. Dolphin Heights, the name on the plaque, had faded almost to the point of invisibility. There were four apartments on each floor and a uniformed policeman was standing outside a door at this end of the second-floor external corridor. That must be the place.

Yokoyama switched off the engine and Kusanagi got out of the car.

He looked around as he walked over to the apartment building. The area seemed to be primarily residential. Just to the right of the apartments was a building with a pub sign outside. The sign promised karaoke. Was the place properly soundproofed? If the drunken singing of the customers was audible from outside, that was a sure recipe for trouble with the neighbors.

Kaoru Utsumi and Kusanagi followed Yokoyama up the exterior staircase. Yokoyama had a quick word with the uniformed officer standing guard who unlocked the door for them.

"You first, sir," said Yokoyama.

Kusanagi pulled on a pair of latex gloves and walked in.

The door opened to a cramped entranceway. Kusanagi slipped off his shoes and stepped into the apartment proper. There was a faint smell of air freshener.

Crossing his arms, he surveyed the interior. The front room was a kitchen /dining room with two more rooms beyond it. The dining table was small and square with a couple of chairs on either side of it. All that was on the table was a box of tissues. A small kitchen cabinet and a flat-screen television stood up against the wall.

Kusanagi walked to the far end and peered into the left-hand room at the back. There was a computer desk with a chair up against the window. Kusanagi got the impression that the laptop was bigger than normal.

There was also a small bookshelf. It contained more knickknacks and magazines than books, as well as a few vials of medicine.

"This room doesn't look like it's been searched," Kusanagi muttered.

"No, when we did the search, we didn't really do this room," Yokoyama said. "We were under orders to secure DNA and hair samples, and otherwise leave things untouched."

"Reasonable enough."

Kusanagi peered into the next room. It contained a double bed. A large set of shelves stood against one wall, while a clothes rack occupied the space between it and the bed. The room was jam-packed. Quite a few of the hangers on the clothes rack were empty.

Kusanagi slid open the doors of the built-in futon cupboard. It was full of plastic clothing cases and heaped-up cardboard boxes.

"Chief," Kaoru Utsumi called out. "I'm not seeing any makeup or toiletries here."

"What's that?"

"I checked the washstand and I didn't see any toiletries there. Not even any face lotion or emulsion. No cleansing oil either. I think we can assume someone's taken them away."

"Got it."

Chances were that the occupant of the apartment had gone on the run. Utsumi had a good eye for detail.

Five days earlier, on October 6, a coast guard helicopter had found a corpse floating off Minamiboso, a small town located on a peninsula on the far side of Tokyo Bay. The body was so badly degraded that they could only guess that it was male between twenty and fifty years of age, based on the clothes, the physique, and the hair. There were no clues to his identity. A closer look revealed something important: a wound resembling a bullet wound on his back. Sure enough, at the official autopsy, a bullet was discovered inside the body. The fact that he had been shot from behind made suicide unlikely, if not impossible, and the death was ruled a probable homicide.

After a nationwide inquiry, a man from Adachi Ward in Tokyo

looked to be the likeliest prospect. His name was Ryota Uetsuji and his live-in girlfriend had filed a missing person's report on September 29.

When the officer who had taken her report tried to call her, he couldn't get through. With no other means of making contact, he went around to her apartment, but she wasn't in. When he called her employer, he was informed that she was on a leave of absence. She'd applied for leave on the morning of October 2, with no advance notice, three days after filing the missing person's report.

Some additional facts had since come to light. Ryota Uetsuji had rented a vehicle in Adachi Ward on September 27, which he didn't bring back on the return date of September 28. When the car rental company tried Uetsuji's cell phone, they had failed to get through. Going to the address on his driver's license, they learned he'd moved out several months earlier. On October 5, the rental car company reported him to the local precinct.

The local police applied for an arrest warrant on suspicion of embezzlement and searched his apartment. DNA testing of samples taken from his hairbrush and razor suggested a high possibility of a match with the Minamiboso corpse.

Soon after, the missing vehicle was found in the parking lot of a shopping center in the next town over. Video footage from security cameras at the parking lot entrance showed the vehicle driving in just after 8:00 P.M. on September 27. The police suspected that the perpetrator was driving the vehicle, but they couldn't get a clear image of the driver from the video. According to the forensics team, there was evidence of the car having been cleaned with great care. They didn't find so much as a single hair.

At this stage, an investigation was launched for the murder and abandonment of a corpse. TMPD Homicide was approached to assist and the case was assigned to Kusanagi's section. Kusanagi had gone to check up on the victim's residence with the expectation that a joint task force of the Tokyo Metropolitan Police Department (TMPD) and the Chiba Prefectural Police would be set up any minute now.

"Did someone say something about the landlord living nearby?" Kusanagi asked Yokoyama.

"That's right. The detached house immediately next door. The name is Tamura," Yokoyama said.

Kusanagi nodded and turned to Kaoru Utsumi.

"Go and find the landlord. If he's in, bring him up here to me."

"Yes, sir," said Kaoru Utsumi. She left the apartment.

Kusanagi returned his gaze to Yokoyama.

"Can you go into a bit more detail about what happened when you took the missing person's report from the girl?"

"I'm here to help," Yokoyama said cheerfully.

The two men sat down on either side of the little dining table. Kusanagi extracted a folded copy of the missing person's report from his inside breast pocket. The filer was a Ms. Sonoka Shimauchi. She was the live-in girlfriend of Ryota Uetsuji.

"According to this report, the last time Ms. Shimauchi saw Uetsuji was the morning of September 27."

"That's correct. She went to Kyoto with a friend for a couple of days and found him gone when she got back home. He failed to come back the following day. She had no idea what to do or who to contact. By evening, she was desperate and came to the police station."

"What's this Uetsuji fellow's job? If he's employed somewhere, his company should be getting worried about him."

"Seems he'd quit his previous company job and was freelancing. He was doing the groundwork for setting up a business for himself. Something connected with video production. Ms. Shimauchi didn't seem to know anything very specific."

"Freelance video production . . ."

It was a world about which Kusanagi knew nothing. The fact that it struck him as a bit dodgy probably only proved that he was getting a bit long in the tooth.

"Surely Shimauchi was in touch with Uetsuji while she was in Kyoto? You know, phone calls, email, texts?"

"She sent him multiple messages, all of which remained unread. He wasn't picking up her calls either. She was worried, but this wasn't the first time this had happened. When it happened before, he'd just switched off his phone, so she thought that's what was going on this time."

"What was your impression of Ms. Shimauchi? Did you notice anything awkward or unnatural in her behavior?"

Yokoyama crossed his arms, tipped his head to one side, and emitted a pensive grunt.

"Let me see. She was in the station to file a missing person's report. She was pretty worried; she certainly didn't come across as calm or relaxed. She was pale and her hand was trembling slightly as she did the paperwork. That sort of thing's common enough with people filing missing person's reports, so, no, nothing about her struck me as unnatural or out of the ordinary."

"You mentioned that she went to Kyoto with a friend. Did you get the friend's name and contact details?"

Yokoyama looked a little uncomfortable. "I'm sorry. I didn't . . ."

"Okay. No point crying over spilled milk. Just thought I'd ask."

There was a knock on the front door. It swung open and Kaoru Utsumi stuck her face inside.

"I've got Mr. Tamura, the landlord, here with me."

"Come on in."

Kaoru Utsumi gestured with her hand and a fattish man in a cardigan followed her into the room. Mid-sixties, Kusanagi reckoned.

Yokoyama stood up and pushed his chair toward Tamura. Kusanagi also got to his feet and introduced himself.

"Thanks for coming to talk with us. We appreciate it."

Tamura sat down. There was a mixture of fear and caution in his eyes.

Kusanagi resumed his seat. "You know what we're dealing with here?"

Tamura sighed. "It's awful. You just don't expect things like this to happen."

"Did you know Mr. Uetsuji well?" Kusanagi inquired.

Tamura's brows contracted in a mistrustful frown.

"*Mr. Uetsuji?*"

"Uh . . . Chief, the situation's a bit different than we thought," Kaoru Utsumi interjected.

"Different? How?"

"It was the woman who was renting this place. Uetsuji only moved in to live with her later."

"I see."

"Sorry, I forgot to mention that." Yokoyama, who was standing off to one side, made a little bow of apology. "The apartment is in Sonoka Shimauchi's name."

Kusanagi realized that when he heard that Uetsuji was living with a woman, he'd just assumed the apartment would be in his name rather than hers.

Kusanagi turned back to Tamura, the landlord.

"I'd like to ask you about Ms. Shimauchi."

"You're welcome to do so. Let me be clear, though. I have no idea where she has gone. We haven't had much contact recently."

"Just tell me whatever you can. When did Ms. Shimauchi move in, for starters?"

"In March five years ago. She and a parent."

"A parent?"

"Yes, she and her mother. Just the two of them. The mother was the signatory to the original contract."

"Where is the mother now?"

"Dead. Around eighteen months ago."

"Some sort of accident?"

"No, natural causes. She had a hemorrhage while she was cleaning the bathroom. The daughter found her and called an ambulance. She ended up dying in the hospital. It's a sad story. I don't think she was even fifty yet."

Tamura explained that the mother had taken the opportunity of Sonoka's graduation from high school to move there from Chiba. The mother, whose name was Chizuko, worked at an industrial kitchen that produced school lunches, while Sonoka was a student at a design college who also worked at a flower store in Ueno. Although they couldn't be described as well-off, the rent had been paid on time until Chizuko's sudden death.

"It's a really sad story. The mother was so excited. With her daughter having gone from a part-time contractor to a full-time employee, she was convinced life was going to get easier for them. She told me as much just before she died. Poor Sonoka was devastated and that was the first time she was late with her rent."

"But she stayed on in the same apartment?"

"I don't think she knew what to do. Moving somewhere new involves a lump sum payment up front, plus moving itself costs a pretty penny. In the end, she came and told me she would take over the contract from her mother."

"And when did Uetsuji move in with her?"

"I am not too sure." Tamura grimaced. "It must have been about a year ago that I started seeing him around the place from time to time, but I'm not too sure about when they actually started living together. It was more like—*poof*—one day he was all settled in and completely at home. From what I could see, he didn't seem like trouble, so I kept my mouth shut. Plus the original arrangement was for two tenants anyway."

"We're told that Uetsuji had recently gone freelance. You don't happen to know anything about his previous employer, do you?"

"No, no." Tamura waved a deprecating hand in front of his face. "It's like I told you. I haven't had much to do with them recently. Just to say hello if we bumped into one another."

Tamura was starting to get restless. He was probably thinking that if he'd known how things were going to turn out, he'd have been better off terminating Sonoka's lease.

3

Standing in front of the store with flowers of every possible color on display, Kaoru Utsumi was tempted to sigh. It had been years since she'd given anyone flowers. As for the last time someone had given her flowers, that would be even longer ago!

Still, what a lovely place to work. You might think that anyone working here would be insulated from the ugly side of humanity. Perhaps that wasn't the case after all.

The flower shop was on the third floor of a building adjoining Ueno Station. Utsumi stopped a young female clerk, told her she was from the police and that she wanted to meet the person in charge.

The store manager was a rather earnest-looking woman of around forty. The tag on her chest gave her name as "Aoyama."

"Sorry to bother you, madam. I'd just like to ask you a couple of questions about Sonoka Shimauchi."

The store manager frowned.

"I thought as much. Someone else from the police was asking me about her earlier."

"Yes, I know. You told them she's taken a leave of absence."

"That's right."

"I'd like to ask you about the same thing. Do you have a moment?"

"Sure, but can you please tell me what's going on?"

Kaoru glanced around, then pushed her face closer to the store manager's.

"The fact is, we don't know where Ms. Shimauchi is. We're worried she could be involved in something unpleasant."

"No . . ." The blood drained from the store manager's face, leaving her pale.

"Shall we go somewhere where we won't be disturbed?"

Kaoru gestured at a coffee shop diagonally across the street. She'd spotted it on her way there.

"Sonoka joined us straight out of high school as a contract employee. I've known her for more than five years. I promoted her after three years. She's now regular full-time staff with all the benefits that go with that," the store manager said. There was a caffe latte in a paper cup on the table in front of her. She described Sonoka Shimauchi as someone who was committed to the job and who had never caused her any problems.

"The customers think very highly of her too. She's very friendly and empathetic when helping people choose their flowers, but she never oversteps either. They find her very easy to talk to. Sonoka always tells me how much she enjoys putting herself in the customers' shoes."

There was genuine enthusiasm in the store manager's voice. She was obviously being sincere.

"And on the morning of October 2, she suddenly requested time off?"

"She called me before we opened. Something had come up, which meant she'd be unable to come to work for a while, she said. And she asked for time off. She said she didn't mind being fired, if it was a problem."

Kaoru paused in her note-taking.

"That's quite a high-pressure approach. Makes me think something serious must have happened. Did you ask her?"

"Of course I did. She wouldn't tell me. Said it was personal."

"What was Ms. Shimauchi's manner on the phone? The way she was speaking—was it the same as usual?"

"No, she spoke much faster than normal. There was a tinge of desperation in her voice. She had been a bit strange before that as well. Very pale and moping all the time."

"'Before that' means when exactly?"

"After she came back from her trip to Kyoto. I can't be more specific than that."

"Her Kyoto trip? That was the twenty-seventh and twenty-eighth of last month?"

"That's right. She told me that she was going to Kyoto with a friend of hers on her day off. She was really looking forward to it before she went, but there was something different about her after she got back."

"Did she tell you anything about the friend she went with?"

"I think she said something about them having belonged to the same club in high school. As for the name, I'm afraid . . ."

Someone who belonged to the same school club. That should make her easy enough to track down.

"How did you deal with her request for time off?"

"I discussed it with the head office. They agreed to grant her a leave of absence. Afterward, when I wanted to get in touch with her about something, I called her and I simply couldn't get through. It was pretty inconvenient but more than that, I was worried about her."

"And you've no idea where Ms. Shimauchi could be?"

"No idea."

The store manager shook her head. Her eyes radiated sincerity. No way was she lying.

Kaoru decided on a change of tack.

"Have you heard the name 'Uetsuji'? A man. His full name is Ryota Uetsuji."

"Yes, I know him. He's Sonoka's boyfriend."

"Have you met him?"

"Only once. Mr. Uetsuji came to the store in connection with his job. That's how the two of them got to know one another."

"His job? Did Mr. Uetsuji have a job that involved flowers?"

"No, he produces videos. He came looking for flowers to use in a shoot and I got Sonoka to serve him."

"Did you happen to get his card?"

"I think he gave me one, though whether I've still got it . . . Anyway, after she finished the arrangements for him, Mr. Uetsuji never came back to the store."

"Did you know that the two of them were living together?"

"Sonoka had mentioned it to me. To be honest, I was pleased. Sonoka must have been lonely, living all alone after her mother died."

"Had Ms. Shimauchi mentioned Uetsuji to you recently?"

The store manager looked pensive.

"Recently, no. When they were first living together, I remember her telling me about them going to the movies together. Gradually, though, she stopped talking about him. I was worried things weren't going too well, but they're still young and they aren't married. I wondered if they had split up. I didn't ask, though. Unless she brought it up, it would be creepy for me to ask about it."

"Was there anything else about her that struck you as odd? Was she behaving differently? Getting unexpected phone calls during work hours?"

An earnest look on her face, the store manager pondered for a moment before speaking slowly and deliberately. "I'm not sure if this qualifies as odd or not, but . . ."

"What is it? Sometimes the insignificant things can be important."

"About a month ago, Sonoka took a day off. She wasn't feeling well. Quite by chance, someone came to the store looking for her that same day. A woman, an old woman."

"An old woman? Came to see Ms. Shimauchi?"

"That's right. She looked very worried when I told her Sonoka was sick and was taking the day off. She left right away."

"She didn't buy any flowers?"

"No. None."

So her only reason for visiting the store was to see Sonoka Shimauchi.

"Did the old woman ever come back?"

"I don't think so. Not when I was here at least."

"Did you tell Ms. Shimauchi she'd been here?"

"Yes, I did."

"What did she have to say about her?"

"That she was just an acquaintance. That was all she said. I didn't push her."

The episode piqued Kaoru's interest. She picked up her pen again.

"Describe the old woman for me. Just a rough impression is fine. It'd be really helpful."

"Describe her? That's not so easy. . . . It was a month ago now. I can't really remember what she looked like." The frowning store manager was clearly racking her memory. "I'd put her age at around seventy. If it's not rude to say so, she was very sophisticated and stylish for someone of that age—beautifully made up with very nicely done hair."

"So she seemed comfortably off?"

"Yes, she did, but she also had a certain glamor. I remember thinking, *This is a woman who's used to socializing and interacting with other people.*"

Kaoru's pen was traveling across the page at a furious pace. Her instincts as a detective were telling her that this could be important information.

4

I've discovered where Uetsuji used to work. This was found in the search of the apartment."

Kaoru took the sheet of paper Kusanagi was holding out to her. It was a photocopy of a business card for a company called UX Image Factory and next to Ryota Uetsuji's name was his job title: chief producer.

"I went to UX's website. They do anything and everything connected with video production. The impression I got is that it's not a big company. From their show reel, they seem to have made plenty of TV commercials. I'm guessing it's something they do as subcontractors for bigger outfits. Kishitani has gone to speak to them. What we do know is that Uetsuji quit his job there around eight months ago."

"Why did he quit?" Kaoru handed the photocopy back to Kusanagi.

"Search me. That's one of the things Kishitani will be asking them."

Kaoru looked around her. Investigators all around the room were busy opening up cardboard boxes. They contained the items taken from Sonoka Shimauchi's apartment.

"Have they finished searching the place?"

"For now, yes." Kusanagi made a sour face and scratched his upper lip.

"No earth-shattering discoveries?"

"Frankly, no. At the end of the day, there wasn't much there for us to bring in. Uetsuji seems to have got rid of as much of his own stuff as he could before moving in. We hardly found anything that'll lead us to people he knows. Of course, there's every chance that all his contacts are in his smartphone rather than written down. It's a problem we encounter a lot recently, but in his case it's even worse than usual. We've asked the phone company to disclose his call records but who knows what, if anything, we'll get from them."

"How much do we know about Uetsuji's background?"

Kusanagi picked up another piece of paper from his desk.

"Ryota Uetsuji. Age thirty-three. Born Takasaki, Gunma Prefecture. Parents alive and well and living at the family homestead. According to the detective who contacted them, they are estranged from the victim and they have zero knowledge of his recent activities. They'll be coming to collect the body, so I intend to speak to them myself. I'm not expecting much."

Just then, one of the younger investigators called Utsumi's name. He was holding up a book. "This is what you were looking for."

"Thanks," Utsumi said.

"What is it?" Kusanagi asked.

"Sonoka Shimauchi's high school yearbook."

Kaoru opened the volume. She flicked through several pages before pausing. The page, which had the title "Year 3, Group 2," featured rows of photos of boys and girls. In the center of the page was a girl with big eyes and a very becoming short haircut. With looks like that, it was clear that in a few years she would grow up to be a beautiful woman. Beneath the picture was the name "Sonoka Shimauchi."

The high school Sonoka Shimauchi attended was in a small town in Chiba. Kaoru had let them know why she was coming, so as soon as she arrived, she was escorted into a meeting room. A certain Mr. Noguchi, a middle-aged teacher, joined her there. He was head of the social sciences and was currently homeroom teacher for the first years.

"If you're looking for someone who was in the same club as Shimauchi and a close friend, Okatani is probably your best bet."

Kaoru had brought the yearbook with her. Noguchi opened it up to the same page and pointed at one of the female students. Her mouth was a hard, straight line and her eyes were full of determination. "Maki Okatani" was the name beneath the photo.

"They both belonged to the art club. I remember the two of them making an enormous signboard for the school festival. They worked on it until late for days on end." Noguchi had a nostalgic look in his eyes.

"Do you have contact details for Ms. Okatani? We're worried that Ms. Shimauchi might be involved in something and we're struggling to establish her whereabouts. It's likely that Okatani is the last person to have seen her, so we want to talk to her. We'll keep her cooperation confidential, of course."

Noguchi listened unsmilingly. "Could you give me a minute?" he said and left the room.

About ten minutes later, he came back. He slid a small piece of paper toward Kaoru. On it there was an address and a cell phone number.

"I called Okatani's mother and explained what was happening. I wanted to make sure that she was okay with me giving out her daughter's contact details. Under the circumstances, she said it was fine by her. Apparently, Ms. Okatani is a hairdresser in Tokyo."

"Thank you very much," Kaoru said. She picked up the memo. The address was in Koganei, a neighborhood in the west part of the city.

"This is very concerning. I hope Ms. Shimauchi is safe." Noguchi frowned.

"That's what we are worried about too." Kaoru put the address into her bag. "What was your impression of Ms. Shimauchi when you taught her?"

Noguchi thought for a moment, then began to speak.

"She was a serious girl, a quiet girl. As for her grades . . ." Noguchi tipped his head to one side. "I suppose they were in the middle of the pack, but toward the bottom end. She was low-key, not at all showy. Could have been because her family wasn't well-off."

"The family was just her and her mother, I believe."

"That's right. Her mother once told me she was a single parent."

"Did you know that she's dead?"

"What? The mother? When did it happen?"

"About a year and a half ago. Subarachnoid cerebral hemorrhage, apparently."

"I had no idea. And she was still so young! Was it from overwork? I remember Shimauchi telling me that her mother's job was mentally and physically demanding."

"What sort of work was it?"

"Her mother worked in an orphanage. Just a couple of stations along the line here."

"An orphanage . . . Do you know its name?"

"Gosh, what was it? I'm not sure."

Noguchi looked quite stumped.

"Don't worry. I'll find out for myself," Kaoru interjected.

"That's worrying news about the mother." Noguchi had a grave expression on his face.

"What do you mean?"

"I got the sense that Shimauchi depended on her mother for everything. Her mother told me the same thing: that Sonoka was quite incapable of making up her mind about anything important. At school, she never said what she was thinking and was very easily influenced by the other students. How can I put it? She was a bit too kind and gentle, a bit too considerate of other people."

"I see."

What could it mean if someone supposedly incapable of making important decisions suddenly vanished? Kaoru wondered.

She thanked him for his help, left the school, and phoned in her report to Kusanagi.

"Sounds like you've got something there. Good. Contact this Maki Okatani, explain the situation, and go see her."

"Should I contact her directly? Won't that get her guard up?"

"That's not a problem. If she has no connection to the case, it doesn't matter. If she is connected to the case somehow, then she'll be expecting to hear from the police. Don't overthink things."

"Yes, sir."

After ending the call, Kaoru punched the number she'd been given by Mr. Noguchi into her phone. A hairdresser would probably be at work right now. Where was her salon? Kaoru prayed it wasn't in Koganei, which was way over on the other side of town.

A few minutes later, having finished the call, Kaoru was relieved. Maki Okatani worked in a hair salon in central Tokyo.

As soon as she got on the train, Kaoru began looking things up on her phone. She wanted to find the orphanage Mr. Noguchi mentioned. It didn't take her long to find one that fit the bill. It was called Asakage-en.

Because Sonoka Shimauchi's mother, Chizuko, stopped working there five and a half years ago, there probably wasn't any link to the current case. *I probably won't need to visit the place*, Kaoru thought to herself.

She soon reached Omotesando, where Okatani's salon was. It was a funny part of town. Everyone was familiar with the main drag with all the high-end brand stores, but the whole ambience changed on the side streets. There were loads of idiosyncratic little stores, all with their own peculiar character and all hidden away so that anyone other than regular customers would struggle to find them.

The place Kaoru was looking for was mixed in with ordinary Japanese-style houses. You needed to get up close before you could tell it was a hairdressing salon. Once she was standing right in front of it, the brightly lit interior was visible through the window.

Kaoru Utsumi pushed open the door and stepped inside. A young woman sitting at a small counter smiled and bid her a good afternoon.

"Sorry, I'm not here to get my hair done. I need to speak to Ms. Okatani. The name is Utsumi."

"Could you wait a minute?" the young woman said and scuttled across the salon.

A woman in a white shirt and jeans came over. She looked a great deal more grown up than the picture in the yearbook. No surprise there, thought Kaoru.

"I'm Kaoru Utsumi. I apologize for bothering you at work like this." Kaoru gave a little bow.

"You said thirty minutes would be enough, right?" There was a pleading look in Maki Okatani's eyes.

"Yes. I'll be as brief as I can."

"Could we go somewhere else to do this? The staff room here is tiny."

"Of course. Again, I'm sorry for the hassle."

They left the salon, crossed to the opposite sidewalk. Kaoru pulled out one of her cards and formally introduced herself.

"As I said on the phone, I just have a few questions about Sonoka Shimauchi. I know that you two were at the same high school."

"We both belonged to the art club. My mom texted me a couple of minutes ago. Said someone from the police might be getting in touch. So something has happened to Sonoka?"

"Why are you so sure?"

"All of a sudden, I can't get through to her. I've sent her a ton of messages and my messages aren't being read. When I call, I can't get through. . . . I was getting worried."

"When were you last in contact?"

"The twenty-eighth of last month. That was the day we got back from our trip to Kyoto. Just before I went to bed, I sent a message to say how much fun I'd had. She replied instantly. 'Let's coordinate our days off and go somewhere again.'"

"Was it your idea to go to Kyoto?"

"No, it was Sonoka's. She had a voucher for the bullet train and a free night at this fancy traditional inn, so she invited me along. The salon's day off is Tuesday—that was the twenty-eighth of September—so we both took the Monday off and went to Kyoto for a night."

"Did you notice anything odd about Ms. Shimauchi while you were together? Was she preoccupied? Distracted?"

Maki Okatani cocked her head and rubbed her hands together.

"Definitely. Like, I'd say something to her and she wouldn't reply. That happened quite a few times." After making this comment, Maki Okatani waved a hand in a dismissive gesture. "On second thought, maybe that's normal for Sonoka."

"She does that a lot?"

"She's always been like that. She goes off into her own little world where no one can reach her. When she was drawing pictures in the school art club, or if she's thinking up a new flower arrangement, she just can't focus on anything else. I didn't think it was such a big deal when she was like that during our Kyoto trip." Maki Okatani paused before going on. "There was something else different that I did notice."

"What was that?"

"She wasn't fretting about her boyfriend's texts."

"Texts? And why 'fretting'?"

"When the two of us go out for a coffee or something, she gets texts from him the whole time. He's always asking stuff like, *Where are you? Who are you with? What are you doing?* He completely loses it if she doesn't reply instantly, so she is always in a tizzy about texting him back. That wasn't happening much in Kyoto. Not at all, in fact. I was curious, but in the end I didn't ask. We were having too much fun and anyway it's not really any business of mine."

"By 'boyfriend,' you mean Mr. Uetsuji, the man Ms. Shimauchi lives with, right? Mr. Ryota Uetsuji?"

"That's right."

"Have you met him?"

"No, never. I must have asked Sonoka to introduce us a thousand times, but she always fobbed me off with promises of 'soon.'"

"'Soon.' I see. Did you take any photos while you were in Kyoto?"

"Yes."

"Could you send me a couple? I won't share them with anyone outside the investigation."

Maki Okatani pulled a phone out of the back pocket of her jeans. Her lips slightly parted, she did some tapping and swiping, then turning to Kaoru. "How's this one?"

There were two women standing in front of a pond and both making the peace sign. Although Sonoka Shimauchi was much more grown up than the picture in her yearbook, her face was still small and her physique petite and delicate. *In the right clothes, she could still pass for a teenager,* Kaoru thought.

She got Okatani to send her three photos in total, including that one.

After returning her phone to her pocket, Maki Okatani directed a questioning look at Kaoru. "Personally, I think Sonoka's on the run."

"On the run? Who from?"

"You know." Maki Okatani brought her face up close to Kaoru's. "From her boyfriend."

"Why should you think that?"

"Because he was abusive."

Kaoru took a step back and looked hard into Maki Okatani's face. "Is this something she told you directly?"

"Not in so many words. But I always thought something was going on. Sonoka liked to wear one of those face masks to stave off infection. Often, though, she wouldn't take the thing off even when we were out having a coffee together. She'd stick the straw up and under her mask in order to drink! She'd always try to laugh it off, saying something about not having put her makeup on properly. I think she was hiding her bruises. And sometimes she would wear these really dark, dark glasses. One time, I asked her, 'What's going on? Someone smacked you and given you a black eye?' It was just a joke, but she got all serious and was denying it like crazy. Her reaction was weird."

Maki Okatani's tone was earnest. It was from the anxiety she felt for her friend and the sense of release that came from verbalizing something she'd been keeping to herself. She was clearly tapping into a reservoir of feeling that had been building up for quite a while.

"When did it start?"

"I can't be sure. Maybe six months ago. We'd arranged to get together and out of the blue Sonoka sent me a text canceling, saying something urgent had come up. My guess is that she'd been so badly beaten up that she knew she couldn't hide it from me."

"And you think that happened over and over until she couldn't stand it and ran away?"

"That's right," Maki Okatani said with a nod. "I think our trip to Kyoto was the first stage of her getaway. That she got rid of her phone—which is why she didn't get any messages from her boyfriend. That you can't figure out where *she* is, is because she doesn't want *him* to find out where she is. What do you think?"

It was an interesting theory and would have been quite plausible—were Ryota Uetsuji still alive. Maki Okatani didn't seem to know that he was dead and Kaoru didn't feel obliged to enlighten her. "You could be right," she said, playing along. "Assuming that is the case, wouldn't Ms. Shimauchi have discussed her plans with somebody?"

Maki Okatani tilted her head to one side.

"I feel a bit funny saying this, but I honestly can't think of anyone she was closer to than me. I suppose there could always be someone I don't know about. . . ."

"Can you think of anyone—it doesn't have to be a friend— whom Ms. Shimauchi trusted and confided in? Like a schoolteacher, say, or . . ." Kaoru gave a self-mocking laugh. "I suppose kids these days don't get so attached to their teachers."

"You're right about that. The teacher thing is a dead end." Maki Okatani grinned briefly before becoming serious again. "I suppose she could have discussed it with Nae."

"Who's Nae?"

"Sonoka always said that her late mother loved Nae as if she were her real mother, even though the two of them weren't actually related. When Sonoka was little, she was always going over to Nae's house to play. Nae also helped her big-time when her mom died."

"Do you know her full name?"

"Sorry . . . That's what Sonoka always called her. Oh, hang on. I just remembered something. Sonoka did say something about her producing picture books."

"Picture books? So she's an author?"

"That's what Sonoka said. I don't know if she does it professionally. 'Nae writes and illustrates books.' That's what she told me."

"Nae . . ."

Kaoru remembered what she'd been told at the flower shop, about that woman in her seventies who had come looking for Sonoka.

"Her name's Nae and she's a children's book author, eh?" Kusanagi leaned back in his chair, crossed his legs, and stroked his chin after hearing what Kaoru had to say.

"According to Ms. Okatani, it was Nae who got Ms. Shimauchi interested in art."

"And an old lady who *could* be this author turned up at the flower shop one month ago. Whether or not there's any link to our case, we need to follow this up regardless." Kusanagi looked up at Kaoru. There was a hint of distaste in his eyes. "There's something else we need to discuss. This business about Sonoka Shimauchi being the victim of domestic violence."

"That's just speculation on the part of Ms. Okatani."

"You should know that the last thing we can afford to do is to make light of that young woman's suspicions. And it doesn't seem out of character, based on what we know of Ryota Uetsuji's personality."

"Do you know something I don't, sir?"

"One or two things." Kusanagi's voice was loaded. "Kishitani!" he called to one of his subordinates who was compiling a report close by. "Tell Utsumi here what you told me just now."

Kishitani flipped open his notebook and walked up to them.

"I went to visit UX Image Factory. The company is four years old. It was founded by three people, one of whom was Uetsuji. All three founders went to the same film school and they started their careers at different video production companies. Whenever they got together socially, they complained to one another about not being allowed to do the things they wanted to do. That was how they got the idea to set up their own firm."

"It's a common enough story. A bunch of half-assed, self-important kids with nothing but too much confidence going for them. They never realize how green they are until the school of life gives them a couple of good hard knocks." Kusanagi had a sneer on his face.

"The chief's right. No sooner had they set up the business than they hit a wall. The CEO resorted to exploiting his connections with his former employer. They started working as subcontractors, slogging away making PR films and TV commercials and designing games. Meanwhile, bigger jobs gradually started coming in and they were hiring more people." Kusanagi raised his eyes from the document and gave a shrug. "But apparently, that was just not good enough for Uetsuji. He kept moaning that they were just doing the same boring stuff they'd been doing at their previous jobs and not what they really aspired to. His idea was for them to come up with an original project of their own and then go out and find backers for it. Uetsuji drew up a proposal for a feature film and tried to shop it around. Unsurprisingly, none of the big studios was interested in working with an unknown production company on a theatrical release. At this early stage, the company's top priority was to build a solid foundation and the pursuit of more ambitious dreams would have to wait. When the CEO explained that to Uetsuji, he simply didn't want to hear it. And that wasn't all. There was another problem."

"What?"

"Harassment. It turned out that Uetsuji was bullying the temps and the younger members of the staff. When their most promising hires started quitting, it got so bad that the CEO had to have a word with him. At that point, Uetsuji completely lost it and announced he was going to quit. There was a whole other rumpus when he went on to demand a wildly unreasonable amount of severance pay."

"He's quite the troublemaker."

"The CEO blamed himself for being a poor judge of character. While he was willing to admit that Uetsuji was a talented videographer, he went crazy if he got the slightest pushback. Basically, he was just too arrogant."

"Okay." Kaoru looked at Kusanagi. "And you think that a man like Uetsuji could well be violent and abusive toward his girl-friend?"

"I do. The perpetrators of domestic violence are often very vain and touchy people, I hear. Today, I went to see Uetsuji's parents and they said the same thing about him."

"What exactly?"

"That he's always had enormous self-confidence. He always used to brag about his grades at school. Then, when he failed to get into his top-choice university, he took it out on his parents. He was ranting and raving about how he was going to make a success of himself in Tokyo and wouldn't come home until he'd done so."

"Someone like that would never admit to having moved in with a woman in order to save money after quitting his job."

"Yes, and to top it all, he was beating the poor woman up." Kishitani shook his head in disgust. "Sounds like one screwed-up guy. I'm amazed she didn't run out on him before."

"Quite. If Uetsuji was still alive, it would make perfect sense for Sonoka Shimauchi to have run away. But Uetsuji is dead. There's no reason for her to run away anymore. So what's her reason for going into hiding *now*?"

Kaoru sensed what Kusanagi was getting at.

"You think Sonoka's involved somehow?"

"What other explanation is there? I think the missing person's report was a bluff. She filed it to put us off the scent. Later, when she started worrying that her bluff might not work, she took off before the body was found and the murder came to light."

"But Sonoka was away in Kyoto on the day we think Uetsuji was killed. We have a witness."

Kaoru was careful not to use the word "alibi."

Kusanagi clicked his tongue. "And that's a problem for us," he muttered.

5

The young man with dyed brown hair had a cup of coffee in his hand. The moment he heard the name "Uetsuji," his mouth turned down at the corners and when Kaoru asked him what sort of man Uetsuji was, he described him as the worst kind of boss and said that he didn't even want to think about him.

"At the beginning, I thought he was a good-natured guy who really cared about the people working under him. As soon as I got up to speed with the work and started making my own decisions about what to do, he suddenly became standoffish. If he'd obstructed my work openly, I could have gone to the CEO, but that's not what Uetsuji was like. He's a nasty, devious fellow. He'd deliberately withhold important information, wait for you to fall on your face, and then lay into you with endless criticisms. Stuff like, 'You're useless. You'd be better off just doing what I tell you to do.' 'You're too stupid. Don't bother trying to think for yourself.' I was worried about my mental health, so I got out of there ASAP."

Listening to the young man, Kaoru reflected that Kishitani had been right about Uetsuji's character.

"Did you have any contact with him after you quit? Email, text, phone calls?"

"Absolutely not. Why would I? I don't want anything to do with him again. Ever."

A denial that fervent was probably true.

Although she thought it unnecessary, Kaoru asked the young man if he had an alibi for September 27 and 28. Pulling out his phone, he told her he'd been at work both days.

Kaoru had started the interview by telling the young man that Uetsuji's corpse had been found. Although surprised, the young man had expressed no sorrow at the news.

When she asked if he had any thoughts about the murder, he cocked his head in a noncommittal way.

"Given the kind of person he was, he was probably butting heads with all sorts of people, but no, I don't think I have any special insights. I haven't seen the guy for months, so I've no idea what he's been getting up to recently. Honestly, my fondest wish was to have nothing to do with him." The sincerity in his tone was palpable.

"That's nice and clear. Thank you. I appreciate your help." Kaoru bowed and put her pen back into her bag. She noticed that the young man still had some coffee left in his cup. "Take all the time you need," she said as she picked up the check from the table.

She got a call from Kusanagi immediately after leaving the café. She should get back to the incident room right away. There was something he wanted her to see.

"What's this about, sir?"

"Just you wait and see." There was a swagger in his voice. They must have found something significant.

Does he really have to be so secretive about it? she thought to herself. Out loud, all she said was "Yes, sir." She ended the call.

As the investigation progressed, Uetsuji's character became clearer. The one thing that everyone agreed on was his two-facedness. He was nice enough to people who did what he wanted, but he was ruthless and aggressive toward people who dared to defy him. "There must be loads of people who really hate the guy" was a speech that Kaoru heard from multiple sources.

The domestic violence inflicted on Sonoka Shimauchi turned out not to be a figment of Maki Okatani's imagination. The investigator who did the house-to-house interviews at Dolphin Heights discovered that it was something most of the residents knew about. The woman who lived in the next-door apartment used to hear the sound of yelling on an almost daily basis, while the old man who lived in the apartment below was alarmed by all the thumps and bumps from above his head. Neither of them had complained or lodged a protest. Turning a neighbor into an enemy was the last thing they wanted.

"Everyone in the building seemed relieved at the news that those particular tenants had gone," added the investigator, lowering his voice a little.

"I came across these three books in Sonoka Shimauchi's apartment."

There were three picture books piled up on Kusanagi's desk. The cover of the topmost book had an illustration of a white bird flying across a blue sky. The title was *What Am I?*

"Can I have a look?" Kaoru picked up the book without bothering to sit down.

She flicked through the pages. It was the story of a little white bird that has just emerged from the egg and is trying to find its mother and father. It struck her as trite enough, but she kept on reading. The little white bird meets a swan, a goose, and a duck. In turn, they tell him, "You're not a swan," "You're most certainly not a goose," and "You're not a duck" and send him packing. Eventually, a bird that claims to be his mother shows up. Much to his shock, she is a crow. The little white bird is an albino and is white rather than black, due to missing genetic information. That, however, was not the end of the story. If anything, that was the point where it really gathered steam as the main character, who had always been afraid of black crows, struggled to accept who his mother was.

Kaoru replaced the book on Kusanagi's deck, a bemused look on her face.

"Isn't the story a bit difficult for children?"

"The online reviews aren't bad. Apparently, there is a section of the reading public that appreciates knottier stories."

Kaoru glanced at the cover again. The name of the author was Nana Asahi. The other two books were by her as well.

"Seems a bit strange for a woman in her twenties to have three children's picture books all by the same author," Kusanagi said. "I'm guessing that the author is probably Nae, the woman Sonoka Shimauchi's mother was so attached to."

"That sounds plausible. Have you checked her out on the internet?"

"Of course. With next to nothing to show for my efforts. I sent an investigator to her publisher. He'll speak to her editor."

"Mind if I do a little checking of my own?" Kaoru pulled out her phone.

"If it floats your boat. I think it's a waste of time."

Kaoru briskly set to work on her phone. Inputting "Nana Asahi" into the search engine instantly produced a number of articles. They were all about her books; just as Kusanagi had told her, there was no biographical information about the woman herself. Even the online encyclopedia only described her as an author of children's books and didn't list her real name.

"You're right. I can't even find a photo of her."

"See?"

Kusanagi pulled his phone out of the inside breast pocket of his jacket. He had an incoming call. He held the phone up to his ear.

"Kusanagi here . . . Really? You sent me her contact details? . . . Just a landline? . . . Okay. Are you with her editor right now? . . . Good, get her to call her right away. The editor mustn't say anything about the police being with her. Come up with some other pretext for the call. All I need you to do is check if she's at home. Thanks."

After ending the call, Kusanagi checked his email on his phone. "She writes under a pseudonym but we now know her real name. It's Nae Matsunaga." He swiveled his phone around to show the screen to Kaoru, showing her an address in Toshima Ward in northern Tokyo. Nae's date of birth was marked as "unknown" but there was a note saying her age was "probably around 70."

Kusanagi's phone started to vibrate again. He answered it.

"How'd it go? . . . Did the editor manage to get through? . . . Did she leave a message for her? . . . Is there any other way we can contact her? . . . Is there a cell phone number for her? . . . Okay, I see. Thanks anyway." Kusanagi ended the call and sighed. "Nae didn't answer her landline. The call went straight to the answering machine. The editor left a message asking her to call back. She doesn't know the number of Nae's cell. In addition to the phone call, she sent an email casually asking about her whereabouts. Let's see how it goes."

"Could Matsunaga be hiding Sonoka Shimauchi? Is that a possibility?"

"Definitely." Kusanagi consulted his watch and rose to his feet. "We're going out and you're coming with me."

"Yes, sir," Kaoru replied promptly.

Nae Matsunaga lived in a deep, narrow building that overlooked Mejiro Boulevard. It only had two or three apartments per floor and was probably designed for people living alone.

Nae Matsunaga's apartment was number 702. In the outer lobby, Kaoru pressed the buzzer on the intercom, hoping to be buzzed in. Nothing happened.

"No luck?"

Kusanagi went across to the window of the superintendent's room. A man in reading glasses, at least ten years past retirement age, was leafing through a magazine.

"We're here to see Mrs. Matsunaga in apartment 702. She doesn't appear to be in. You don't happen to know when she went out, do you?"

The superintendent contemplated Kusanagi over the top of his glasses.

"I've no idea. I don't spend my time monitoring people's comings and goings."

"What time do you start and finish here?"

"I start at nine and finish at five. . . ."

"And when do you review the security camera footage?"

"When do I . . . ? There's no fixed schedule. It depends."

"Depends on what?"

"If we've had a problem."

"So you don't check the footage at all unless there's been a problem?"

"That's not what I said, but no, I don't review it all that often. . . ." The superintendent was beginning to sound evasive. Kusanagi suspected that he was probably obliged to review the footage every day. "Anyway, who are you people?"

"Apologies. Here's my ID."

The super's face twitched when Kusanagi pulled his police badge out of his inside jacket pocket.

"We're here in connection with a case. We need to know when Mrs. Matsunaga left her apartment, the time and the date. How long do you keep your security camera footage?"

"The rule says a month. Usually, it sits on the hard drive for about three."

"In that case, I'd like you to review the footage right now. You know what Mrs. Matsunaga looks like?"

"Sure . . . What sort of dates are we talking?"

"Start from the second of this month, plus the next two or three days."

The second was when Sonoka had called her store manager to ask for leave of absence.

"Okay. Give me a minute."

The super swiveled his chair off to the side. He was doing something with his computer. Kaoru couldn't see the screen from where she was standing.

"Here we go," said the super a few minutes later. "Just after 11:00 A.M. on the second."

"Show me." Kusanagi's tone was peremptory.

The super placed his laptop on the sill and turned the screen toward Kusanagi. It displayed a high-angle still image of the entrance hall. A single old woman was making her way across it. She had on a pale coat and was pulling a suitcase with wheels behind her. The suitcase was on the large side, like something you would use for a long trip.

The time stamp read October 2, 11:12 A.M.

"This woman here is Mrs. Matsunaga. You're sure about that?" Kusanagi double-checked with the superintendent.

"Yes, it's her."

"All right, Utsumi," Kusanagi said. "Check the images before and after this."

"Yes, sir," Kaoru said. She reached for the laptop without asking permission. The superintendent said nothing.

At 11:17 A.M., roughly five minutes after Nae Matsunaga had left the building, Kaoru found footage of Sonoka Shimauchi making her way out of the lobby. She was dressed in jeans and a parka, had on a backpack, and was also carrying a large travel bag.

"So that's it. The two of them are in it together."

Kaoru kept looking through the footage. She wanted to confirm the date and time of Sonoka Shimauchi's arrival. The super watched her in silence.

"Take a look at this, Chief." Kaoru swiveled the screen to face

Kusanagi. It showed Sonoka Shimauchi entering the building. It was the same date—October 2—and the time was 9:25 A.M.

"October 2 is the day that Sonoka Shimauchi called to ask for time off work. She came here after that."

"After which, the two of them left the place and simply disappeared."

Kusanagi was sunk in thought for a moment, then he turned to the building super. "I need your help."

"Wha . . . what do you want me to do?"

"Mrs. Matsunaga of apartment 702 could be involved in a very important case. I'd like to take a look inside her apartment."

Apparently, the divine power of Kusanagi's police badge had finally reached its limit. With a startled look on his face, the superintendent shook his head.

"I'm afraid I can't let you do that. Not without her permission."

"Then please call Mrs. Matsunaga immediately."

The superintendent opened a folder and sifted through some documents. Eventually, he looked up, a hangdog expression on his face.

"It's no good. The only contact we've got is the landline here."

"But you must have an emergency contact number—someone you call when you can't get through to her."

"No, we don't." The superintendent showed the piece of paper to Kusanagi. "The number's been crossed out. I think it was a relative of hers, but they must have passed away."

"What are you supposed to do if there's a technical problem in the apartment like a leak or something?"

"I get in touch with the building proprietor and then we decide what to do."

Kusanagi pulled a sour face and clicked his tongue. His phone rang. He drew it from his inside jacket pocket.

"Yeah, it's me. . . . What? . . . You got a reply? That's perfect timing. I want to speak to Matsunaga's editor. Yeah, as soon as possible . . . No problem. I'll be bringing Utsumi with me. . . . See you in a bit."

Kusanagi ended the call. "We've got to go," he barked and headed for the door without so much as a word of thanks to the super. Kaoru knew that he wasn't being intentionally dismissive; his mind had simply moved on to the next thing.

About an hour after leaving the apartment building, they were in a meeting room at the publisher's talking to Ms. Fujisaki, Nae Matsunaga's editor.

"The detective who was here before asked me to contact Ms. Asahi to inquire about her whereabouts. This is the email I sent." As she said this, the editor held out her phone.

Kaoru peered around Kusanagi's shoulder to read it. This is what it said.

I hope you are well. It's Fujisaki here.

I just called your home. You weren't there, so I am sending this email instead.

One of your fans sent a present for you to the office. We opened it up just to make sure everything was kosher. Sure enough, it was fine. Is it okay if we forward it to your place?

If you're not at home right now, we're happy to send it to wherever you are at the moment. Let me know how you want me to proceed.

Best regards

Fujisaki

Kusanagi looked up and grinned.

"A present from a fan, eh? That's a smart pretext."

The editor sighed unhappily.

"I don't like having to lie, but what choice did I have? I was told she might be involved in a case. . . . Once things settle down, I'll apologize to her."

"I'm sorry. We really appreciate your cooperation."

Kusanagi bowed and Kaoru followed suit.

"I understand that you got a reply?"

"That's right." Fujisaki tapped the screen a couple of times and showed it again to Kusanagi.

"This is what she said."

Kaoru craned forward for a second time. The email was short.

Thanks for your note.

I'm traveling on my own. It was an impulsive thing.

I'll just be wandering as the mood takes me, so I won't be in any one specific place and I don't know how long I'll be away either.

If it's not too much trouble, could you hang on to the present
for a while?

Best regards

Nana Asahi

"Traveling on her own . . ." Kusanagi murmured. "Is that
something that Mrs. Matsunaga . . . Ms. Asahi does often?"

"Not often, but from time to time, certainly."

"Does she have a favorite place she likes to go? A traditional inn
that she likes somewhere?"

"Let me think. . . ." The editor tipped her head to one side.

"I know that she's a fan of hot spring resorts, but as far as I
know, she doesn't have one particular favorite."

Kusanagi nodded and scratched the skin between his eyebrows.

"Does the name 'Sonoka Shimauchi' mean anything to you?
She's a young woman—Utsumi, photos!"

Kaoru whipped out her phone, located the pictures she'd been
sent by Maki Okatani, and showed them to the editor. "She's the
one on the left."

"Shimauchi . . . Was that what you said her name was?" The
editor shook her head after inspecting the pictures. "No, I've never
seen her before. And I don't remember Ms. Asahi mentioning the
name either."

"Okay, thank you."

Kusanagi glanced at Kaoru and she put her phone away.

"Can you think of anyone that Ms. Asahi was close to? People she worked with? People she went out with?" Kusanagi was peppering her with questions.

"I don't think she has much to do with other writers. I can't imagine her having a group of people she goes out with. Basically, she's not a very social creature. Odd as it sounds, I'm probably closer to her than anybody else. Sometimes she invites me out shopping with her and things like that."

Disappointed at her response, Kusanagi sighed listlessly.

"Okay. Let me try another tack. What's Ms. Asahi like as a person? I know she's a little on the older side. Does that mean she's got a long career as an author behind her?"

"No. Her first book only came out around ten years ago. After her husband died, she began writing picture books as a hobby. She became a professional writer by accident when she entered a book into a competition and it won."

"Aha. So it's a sort of second act for her."

"Second act? . . . In her case, more like third or fourth."

"What do you mean?"

"She's had quite a life. She used to tell me she was unlucky with men. The husband I mentioned who died was her second; her first husband divorced her after a couple of years of marriage. He was a violent drunk. She told me that she tapped all these experiences for her books."

"All her experiences, eh? Now that you mention it, we've looked through several of her books and they are rather unusual. Like the story of the white crow, the albino crow. That was an interesting story, but can children really get their heads around something like that?"

"I edited that one. It's certainly unusual. It was surprisingly popular, though."

"So I saw. Quite a surprise."

"Ms. Asahi tackles subjects that other writers don't want to. That's what she's good at. She's produced more science books than anything else."

"Science books?"

"Like this one here."

The editor picked a book from a pile on the table beside her and slid it over to Kusanagi. On the front cover was an illustration of a cute-looking little girl in a red hat decorated with the letter *N*. Its title was *Lonely Little Monopo*.

"It's about the monopole."

"What's that when it's at home?" Kusanagi asked Fujisaki. Kaoru had a vague sense of having heard the term before, but she couldn't recall in what context.

"In the world of this book, every baby has a counterpart they are destined to pair up with from before birth. The minute the baby is born, it meets its counterpart and they start holding hands. Throughout their lives, they will keep holding hands and never let go, no matter what. The two get sick at the same time and if one of them gets hurt, both of them feel the same pain. They also die at the same time. The boy is wearing a blue hat with an *S* on it and the girl has this red hat with an *N*. You've probably worked out that *S* and *N* are personifications of a magnet."

"Oh, a magnet. Of course," Kusanagi said as if he were fully up to speed.

"A magnet always has a south and a north pole. Hypothetically, however, a magnet that only has one pole—just a south or just a north pole—could exist. Physicists call that a *monopole*. In reality, no one has ever found one, but Ms. Asahi thought it would be fun to write a book with a monopole as the protagonist. That was the genesis of this story."

"Huh. Impressive. To come up with such an unusual theme."

"She did a lot of research for the book. She even included a bibliography at the end. That's almost unheard of for a children's picture book."

Kusanagi opened the book to the last page. The minute he started reading it, his indifference evaporated and his eyes opened wide in surprise.

"Have you read this bibliography?" Kusanagi asked. There was a note of tension in his voice.

"Certainly. I remember sending a few queries to the author after going through it. Why, what about it?" The editor appeared rather puzzled.

Kaoru looked down at the book and glanced through the bibliography. It included the following entry:

Yukawa, Manabu. *If I Ever Met a Monopole.* Teito University Press.

6

He pulled off at the Yokosuka interchange and went down a meandering hill road. He then proceeded across the main local road, until he reached a block of apartments.

Kusanagi parked in the visitor parking lot and, carrying a paper bag, headed for the lobby. He checked that the name on the buzzer was Shinichiro Yukawa and pressed the intercom button for apartment 1205.

A muffled sound emerged from the speaker and the automatic door slid open. Kusanagi passed through an expansive entrance hall, got into the elevator, and pressed *12*.

Arriving at the twelfth floor, he strolled down the corridor, inspecting the apartment numbers as he did so. Apparently, 1205 was at a corner of the building.

The door swung open.

"Welcome to Yokosuka," Manabu Yukawa said, grinning benignly.

"Sorry to barge in on you."

"No problem. Like I told you on the phone, I'm bored. I've got nothing to do and no one to talk to here."

"No one to talk to?" Kusanagi glanced into the apartment. "Surely your parents are here?"

"Let me rephrase that. There's no one here I *enjoy* talking to. Anyway, come on in."

"Thanks. Oh, before I forget, this is for you." Kusanagi extracted a long, thin box from the paper bag he was holding.

Yukawa pulled a face. "I thought I told you not to bring anything."

"I can't very well turn up empty-handed at my friend's parents' house. It's not Opus One, I'm afraid, but I think it's respectable enough."

"All wines welcome here! That's very thoughtful. Thanks."

Yukawa escorted Kusanagi into the living room, where an old man was sitting on the sofa. "Dad," said Yukawa. "My old friend Kusanagi has come to visit."

The old man rose and walked over to Kusanagi. Although he was on the short side and his hair was gray, his ramrod-straight back made him look younger.

Yukawa turned to Kusanagi.

"This is my father. I think you two met once before. Do you remember?"

"Sure I do. We met at the presentation of your graduation thesis. It's been a long time, sir," Kusanagi said with a duck of the head.

"Yes, and it wasn't just any old graduation thesis presentation. As I recall, it was a presentation for an outstanding graduation thesis." Shinichiro Yukawa smiled as he said this.

"So it was. Sorry."

"You don't need to apologize. It's really not important." Yukawa scowled.

"Well, *I* think it is." The old man had thrust out his bottom lip defiantly. "Summa cum laude is quite different from your routine thesis presentation. Less than ten percent of the students get that honor. I know. I took part in the same ceremony myself. The students who are chosen need to have done some pretty darn good original research. The professors wouldn't recommend you otherwise—"

"All right, Dad. All right," Yukawa said. He sounded fed up. "You've made your point, so I think it's time to move on to something else. My guess is that Kusanagi is here to speak to me. I'm sorry, but would you mind leaving us alone for a while?"

Although he was obviously not too happy about being cut off mid-flow, Shinichiro consented.

"Oh, I see. Well, if that's what's going on, then I'd best make myself scarce. Make yourself at home, Mr. Kusanagi. It's not a lot of fun for a father and son to be shut up together all day in such a small space."

Yukawa watched Shinichiro make his way out of the living room, then sighed.

"He's like that all the time. He's getting more difficult with every passing day."

Kusanagi smiled ironically. Yukawa was a difficult enough character himself!

"Regardless, it's good to see him looking so well. He's barely changed since I met him at your graduation event."

"Don't go saying things like that in front of him, for goodness' sake! You'll only make him more conceited."

Yukawa gestured toward the sofa. Kusanagi sat down and made himself comfortable while Yukawa went to the kitchen. Kusanagi noticed the aroma of coffee earlier.

He looked around the room. A row of sliding windows gave onto a balcony, beyond which the sea was visible. Several military vessels lay at anchor in the naval base.

Enjoying the last years of your life in an apartment with a sea view— the phrase suggested a rather distinguished retirement. Apparently, the reality was not all sweetness and light.

As Shinichiro Yukawa said, the summa cum laude thesis presentation was an honor reserved for students who had produced truly outstanding work. Since anyone at the university was free to attend, Kusanagi turned up with his friends from the badminton club more as a lark than anything else. Yukawa's father had also come to see his son speak, so Kusanagi went to say hello after the presentations. While Yukawa wasn't too keen on introducing them, Kusanagi was excited. Yukawa had told him next to nothing about his family.

That was around thirty years ago now.

Yukawa came back carrying a tray with a couple of mugs on it. They were gleaming white.

"No milk or sugar for you, right?"

"No, I take mine black. From the nice aroma, I'm guessing that you're not giving me instant. Did you make it because you were expecting me? It's very thoughtful of you."

"No, you just happened to show up when I was making some."

"Oh, okay."

Kusanagi watched as Yukawa lowered himself onto the sofa where his father had been sitting. He then picked up one of the mugs, took a sip of coffee, and said, "How's your mother doing?"

Yukawa gave a little shrug.

"Getting worse, slowly but surely. She doesn't realize that the man taking care of her is her husband, so she's always thanking him politely as though he's a stranger. What's really weird, though, is that she still recognizes me, even though she only saw me at rare intervals. The human brain is an extraordinary thing."

Yukawa's tone was dry and matter-of-fact. Nonetheless, it was obvious that the situation was serious.

Kusanagi had emailed Yukawa the night before to say that they needed to talk. He'd assumed that his friend would be either at the university or at his own place, so he was surprised when he revealed that he was at his parents' place in Yokosuka. Even more so when he explained that he wasn't just visiting them but was staying there awhile.

Yukawa's parents had been happily spending their twilight years in this apartment with a sea view, until his mother, who'd already been showing early signs of dementia, broke her leg and lost the ability to walk, prompting a rapid deterioration. The father was taking care of her, but according to Yukawa, it was getting to be too much for him to deal with alone, which is why Yukawa had come to help out.

"Are you sleeping here?"

"What else can I do? I set up a camp bed in my father's study."

"That's tough. How's it going with your work at the university?"

"I'm managing. I can do my lectures and tutorials online and I hardly conduct any experiments myself since being appointed a full professor." Yukawa's face was so expressionless, he could have been talking about someone else entirely, but Kusanagi detected a hint of sadness in his friend. *Is he psychologically preparing himself for a withdrawal from active life?*

"How long do you plan to stay?"

"That's not an easy question to answer. I'm tempted to say for as long as my mother's alive—but since nobody knows how long she's got, I can't make a decision. My dad's a fighter. He's adamant that he can take care of my mom on his own. As far as I can see, though, that is simply not true. I know he used to be a doctor, but when it comes to hands-on care, he's totally out of his depth. He's useless at changing diapers."

"I'm guessing that you do some diaper-changing yourself."

"You bet. That's what I'm here for," he said nonchalantly.

Kusanagi grunted in surprise.

Unable to imagine the scene, Kusanagi felt discombobulated.

"What's wrong?"

"Nothing. . . . You're not thinking of using a home care service? Or putting her into a home?"

"We use the home care services when we need them, but my dad has zero interest in putting her in a home. He wants to handle everything himself without turning to anyone else. I just have to respect his wishes."

"I see. It's a difficult situation."

Kusanagi felt that he was seeing a new and unfamiliar side of his friend's character. He'd never thought of him as someone who'd go to so much trouble for his family.

"I feel guilty, bringing my own problems to your door at a time like this—"

Kusanagi had only gotten that far when Yukawa started waving one of his hands from side to side.

"I might have resented it before. Things are different now. I'm not busy with my own academic research and, since I have to look after my mother, I don't get to go out much either. Aside from a few times a day, I'm on standby here with nothing much to do. It's an ineffably tedious existence, so if you've got a thought-provoking puzzle for me, then bring it on."

"I'm relieved to hear you say that. How thought-provoking it will be for you, I don't know. Truth is, this is what I want to talk to you about."

Kusanagi pulled a book from his case and put it in front of Yukawa. It was *Lonely Little Monopo*.

The physicist's eyes opened wide behind his metal-rimmed glasses. He picked up the book and stared at the cover.

"I get the impression you've seen it before?"

"I have. If you dug through my lab, you'd find the complimentary copy they sent me."

"Your name appears in the back."

Yukawa opened the book at the back page, found his name and the name of his book, nodded, and put the book back on the table. "Is there a problem with the book?"

"We think the author might be connected to a case of ours. We're looking for her, but we can't find her."

"The *author* of *this*?" Yukawa returned his gaze to the book. "Is she a suspect in a murder case?"

"We don't yet know. All we know for sure is that she's acting in concert with a person of interest in the case."

"Is the person of interest on the run?"

"We can't be sure, but it seems likely."

Yukawa frowned.

"Where does this leave us? I don't understand where you're going with this."

"You have every reason to be leery. The whole case is pretty opaque."

Kusanagi talked Yukawa through the discovery and identification of the corpse and the live-in girlfriend going missing. He kept it short but he managed to cover everything important.

"We are trying to find this Sonoka Shimauchi woman. We think the quickest way to locate her is to investigate Nana Asahi, the children's book author. We believe they are together. Asahi is a complete black box. We have no solid information to help us work out where she might be. Not even her editor, who knows her better than anyone, knows the first thing about her private life. We're banging our heads against a brick wall. Our only option now is to follow up any leads connected to her as an author, no matter how flimsy."

"Hence your coming around to see me because my name appears in the bibliography. You really are pinning your hopes on the flimsiest of leads! Flimsier than the filaments of a spider's web!"

"Oh, come on. I remember you treating me to a lecture on the incredible strength of the filaments in spiders' webs! Besides, according to Ms. Fujisaki, Nana Asahi's editor, you and the author had quite an email exchange. She said that was a very unusual thing for Ms. Asahi to do. That as a general rule she had very little to do with other people."

"She emailed me some questions and I answered them. That's all there was to it. There aren't that many people out there with an interest in monopoles. When she explained that she was going to write a children's picture book about them, I felt she deserved a proper response."

"Have you kept those old emails?"

"No idea. Must be about five years ago now. They may still be on my old computer."

"Will you have a look and let us know if you find them?"

"Do you plan to treat them as investigation materials? I don't need to tell you that they're private documents."

"I'm not *ordering* you to share them with us. I just want you to tell us if you come across anything likely to assist with the investigation."

"And I get to make that call?"

"What choice have I got? Like you say, they're private documents."

"Okay. I'll call one of my students and get them to ship my PC to me here. Honestly, though, I doubt I'll find anything of much use."

"That won't be the end of the world. Sorry for the hassle. I appreciate your help."

Yukawa snorted.

"Compared to the cases you've brought to me before, it's really not much trouble."

"Have you and Nae Matsunaga ever met face-to-face?"

"Matsunaga?" The mug in Yukawa's hand came to a stop in midair.

"Nae Matsunaga is Nana Asahi's real name. You didn't know that?"

"No, I didn't. Hmm. So that's her real name: Nae Matsunaga. . . ." He took a leisurely sip of his coffee.

"So? Have you met ever her in person?"

"Never. We've only emailed."

"And you only corresponded at that one time?"

"Pretty much. Given the volume of our emails, 'correspondence' is a bit overdoing it."

"'Pretty much'? So you haven't lost touch completely."

"When she sends me her new books, I send her a thank-you email."

"Her new books? Picture books for children?"

"What else? That's what she writes. I suppose my name's on the mailing list for complimentary copies. I don't want to come out and tell them not to bother sending them—that would be rude—so I just accept them with thanks."

Kusanagi looked at Yukawa. His face was a mask. "Seriously? You actually read kids' books?"

"Since the publisher's gone to the trouble of sending them, skimming the things is the least I can do. Then I pass them on to friends of mine who have children."

"Did you read the one about the white crow?"

"The albino crow?" Yukawa nodded. "An unorthodox subject for a children's book. I enjoyed that one."

What Yukawa had said about skimming the books seemed to be true. Kusanagi was surprised by his friend's conscientiousness.

"Can you do me a favor, Yukawa? Will you email Nae Matsunaga?"

"Me? What should I say?"

"I'll leave that to you. Like I said, we're struggling to locate her. It would be very helpful if you could casually inquire what she's up to and where she is."

Sitting on the sofa, Yukawa shrugged.

"Weren't you listening to me? I only write her thank-you notes when she sends me her latest book. That's the sum of our relationship. If someone like me suddenly sends her an email asking her what she's doing, she's sure to get suspicious."

"Which is why you're going to have to get a little creative. How about this? You're part of an event designed to get kids interested in physics. You thought that illustrations would be a good way to liven it up and you want to discuss the idea with her. Can you two meet sometime soon? That sounds plausible enough to me."

Yukawa heard Kusanagi out, then fixed him with a cold stare.

"Somehow I doubt you came up with that idea on the fly. Did the staff at the incident room develop it? I'm guessing that Detective Utsumi was the one who cooked it up."

Kusanagi winced. Yukawa was right on target.

"You got me. Well? Will you do it?"

"No, I will not," Yukawa replied bluntly.

Kusanagi frowned with annoyance.

"I can't in good conscience send her a false email."

"Why so scrupulous? We need your help to crack the case."

"What was the editor's name? Fujisaki? Why don't you ask her? She could send a message about an urgent meeting."

"We considered that. The trouble is, Fujisaki couldn't come up with a valid reason for an urgent meeting. She's never proposed anything similar before and was worried that such a message would make it obvious that the police were pulling her strings offstage. There's much less chance of her suspecting you. She doesn't know about your special relationship with the police."

Yukawa scowled.

"So as far as you lot are concerned, I'm a convenient tool to exploit. I get that, but I still can't go along with it. Naturally, things would be different if Ms. Asahi was an *actual* suspect."

"She is acting in concert with a person of interest. She's about as close to a suspect as you can get. If anything, I'm inclined to think that of the two, Nae Matsunaga is the more likely perpetrator."

"And her motive?"

"Protecting Sonoka Shimauchi from Uetsuji's abuse. Nae Matsunaga loved Sonoka's mother like a daughter. That makes Sonoka herself into a quasi-granddaughter in her eyes. If her precious quasi-granddaughter is being abused, then wanting to help is the most natural thing in the world. That's why she came up with a plan to kill Uetsuji. However, since Sonoka would be the natural suspect if Uetsuji died in questionable circumstances, Nae Matsunaga made sure she had an alibi in the form of that trip to Kyoto."

Yukawa picked up his coffee mug and shook his head solemnly from side to side.

"That's quite a feat. You've really let your imagination run wild without knowing even the first thing about Ms. Asahi's personality. You're a true detective."

"It's only a hypothesis. I thought you liked a good hypothesis."

Yukawa waved his hand as if swatting away a fly.

"A good hypothesis must have a coherent, logical through line to it. Your hypothesis is self-contradictory."

"How so?"

"Sonoka Shimauchi doesn't *need* to run away because she has an alibi. And if she hadn't run away, the police would never have developed an interest in Ms. Asahi. Or am I wrong?"

"All it suggests to me is that something went wrong with her plan."

"What exactly?"

"I don't know. . . ."

"You see? Your hypothesis is so full of holes, it's not worthy of the name. It's a fantasy, not a valid theory."

Kusanagi grimaced. Scratching one of his temples, he looked probingly at his friend.

"So what you need from me is reasonable grounds for treating Nae Matsunaga as a suspect?"

"Yes, in that case I'd be willing to cooperate. Just don't expect me to swallow anything too far-fetched."

"No need to tell me that."

"And until you find those reasonable grounds, I'd be grateful if you called her *Ms.* Asahi—I mean Mrs. Matsunaga."

"Huh? Who even cares?" Kusanagi gulped down the last of his coffee and glanced at his watch. "I've got to get going. If it's okay with you, I'd like to say goodbye to your father."

"I'll go and fetch him." Yukawa rose to his feet.

"Could I go to his room—or wouldn't he like that?"

Yukawa, who was almost at the door, turned around. "You want to go to my parents' bedroom?"

"Uh-huh. I, uhm . . . I thought it would be nice to say hello to your mother as well. If it's too much trouble, then just forget about it."

Yukawa lowered his eyes, thought for a moment, and then looked back at Kusanagi. "If you're okay with it."

"Like I said, I *want* to say hello to her."

"Okay, okay. Follow me."

They left the living room and Yukawa knocked on the door of the next room. When Shinichiro said, "Come in," Yukawa pushed open the door and went inside. Kusanagi could hear a brief conversation, though he couldn't make out the words.

Soon Yukawa stuck his head around the door and nodded at him.

"Good afternoon," Kusanagi said as he stepped in.

He found himself in a bedroom bathed in natural light. There were two beds arranged side by side along one wall and the sunlight, which was pouring in through the window, illuminated the colorful quilts draped over them. By the window, there was a wheelchair in which a skinny old woman sat looking out at the sea. Shinichiro was in a chair not far from his wife. A paperback set down on the table beside him suggested that he'd been reading.

"Sorry to barge in on you when you're taking it easy," Kusanagi said to him.

"Did you get your business done?"

"For today at least."

"Glad to hear it. You're always welcome. This fellow here can't conceal just how dull he finds my company. It's soul-destroying." Shinichiro was looking at his son as he said this.

Yukawa walked over to the wheelchair and placed a hand on the old woman's shoulder. "Mother," he said. "Kusanagi has come to say hello. Kusanagi—you remember him; we were in badminton club together at university."

The old woman slowly turned her head. Her expression was benign.

"Lovely to see you again, Mrs. Yukawa. It's me, Kusanagi."

The old woman's face remained blank and her eyes unfocused. Kusanagi suspected she couldn't even see him properly.

Yukawa patted her on the shoulder a couple of times. She went back to looking out of the window.

As they left the bedroom, Yukawa announced that he would accompany Kusanagi down to the lobby.

"Seeing you with your parents like this feels a bit strange to me. I never pegged you as family-oriented," said Kusanagi as they rode the elevator.

"We all have parents. Just like the white crow."

"I know, but . . ."

They reached the first floor and were halfway across the entrance hall when Yukawa came to a sudden stop.

"Kusanagi, I'm going to think about that business you mentioned."

"What business?"

"Writing fraudulent emails is not my thing, but I may be able to assist your investigation in a different way."

This was an unexpected development. Kusanagi looked intently into the face of his old friend.

"How will you do that?"

"I'll tell you some other time. It was great to see you. Take care on your way home." Yukawa slowly turned around as he said this.

"Just a minute. Hey, Yukawa!"

Yukawa must have heard Kusanagi shouting after him but he neither stopped nor turned around before vanishing into the elevator.

7

Mrs. Aoyama, the store manager, was holding a photograph. She had a puzzled look on her face.

"No, that's not her. She was different."

"Are you sure? How about this picture? People can look different depending on the angle."

"It's nothing to do with the angle. She was a different type of person altogether. Flashier, more glamorous."

"I see . . ." Kaoru took back the two pictures. They were printouts from a video rather than conventional photographs.

She'd gone to the flower shop in Ueno to show Mrs. Aoyama the video grabs of Nae Matsunaga to see if she was the woman who'd come to the store looking for Sonoka. The answer, apparently, was no.

Kaoru thanked the manager and left the shop.

She gave a progress report to Kusanagi as soon as she got back to the incident room.

"Humph. If the old lady who went to the flower shop wasn't Nae Matsunaga, then we can forget about that whole episode, for now at least. Good job, by the way. Fancy a break? I need a coffee. And as a bonus, I can tell you an interesting little story."

"What's that?"

"I just went to visit Yukawa."

"I'd like to hear about that."

They helped themselves to some tepid coffee from the ancient coffee maker, went over to a large table in a corner of the incident room, and sat across from each other with their paper cups.

After hearing Kusanagi's account of his visit to the apartment block where Yukawa's parents lived, Kaoru put her paper cup down on the table and looked hard at Kusanagi.

"Are you quite sure that's Professor Yukawa you're talking about?"

"Indeed I am. The one and only."

"That's not my image of him at all." Kaoru waggled her head slightly. "Or maybe that's the wrong way to put it. What I mean is that I've never imagined him in any sort of family setting. Yet nonetheless, there he is, living at his parents' place to help care for his mother. Unbelievable . . ." Reaching for her cup, she took a mouthful of weak coffee.

"I get where you're coming from, Utsumi. I feel the same way. Yukawa's always been like that. He's very secretive. Or at least, reluctant to talk about anything personal. He and I were in the same sports club for all four years of university, and it was only *after* graduating that I discovered he'd had the same girlfriend for six years! By the time I found out, they'd split up. He'd thrown away any photos he had of her, so I never got to see what she looked like."

"Six years? A girlfriend?" Kaoru's eyes were wide with surprise. "Wow! That's news to me. Why didn't you tell me before, Chief?"

"Why? It wasn't the right time. More to the point, I suppose I'd forgotten all about it. I didn't think about it till just now."

"But six years! That's mind-blowing. It means they'd been together since high school."

"He said something about them being classmates in eleventh grade."

"The professor went to Towa High, one of the top-ranked schools in Tokyo. So she was his classmate there, eh?"

Kaoru made an effort to picture Yukawa as a high school boy, but her imagination was not up to the task.

"We've gotten a bit sidetracked here. Anyway, there's a lot going on in Yukawa's life right now and things aren't easy for him. Regardless, he's one of a very small number of leads we've got that connect to Nae Matsunaga. I asked him to send her an email on our behalf."

"How did that go?"

"He turned me down flat."

Kaoru sighed. "Why am I not surprised?"

"Didn't like the idea of deceiving someone who wasn't an official suspect, he said."

"Sounds like just the sort of thing he would say."

"Just as I was leaving, though, he changed his tune."

Kusanagi explained how Yukawa suggested that he might be able to assist the investigation some other way.

"I've no idea what 'some other way' is supposed to mean. Clearly, though, he's got something in mind. So I need you to be ready to swing into action when he comes up with some outlandish scheme or other."

"Ready? . . . Me?"

"Yes, you. Aside from me, you're the only person here adaptable enough to respond when he does something wacky."

"Should I take that as a compliment?"

"You certainly should."

Kusanagi was nodding gravely at his subordinate when Kishitani scuttled up to him clutching a file.

"I've managed to identify a number of the people on the outgoing call log of Uetsuji's cell phone." As he said this, Kishitani handed the file to Kusanagi. He'd gone through the records he had gotten from the phone company, he explained. "The last time Uetsuji used his phone was the twenty-seventh of last month. He placed a call to a car rental firm in Adachi Ward at a little after 1:00 P.M. I assume it was about renting a vehicle. That was the only call he made on that day, so I started looking into calls he made the day before, the twenty-sixth. There turns out to be someone I think you may know, Chief, among the people I managed to identify."

"Me? Who the heck is it?" Kusanagi frowned fiercely as he flicked open the file.

"This individual, sir," Kishitani said, reaching across to point at the page.

Kusanagi, who had been eyeing that section skeptically, blinked furiously.

"Oh, her . . . !"

"So you know her? I thought that might be the case, Chief. You are very well connected in that world."

"Hardly. I do my best, though."

"But you *do* know her?"

"Well enough to say hello, yes. Okay. Given the circumstances, I'll follow up with her."

"Thanks, Chief. Appreciate it."

"People who you know tend to be more cooperative. I'm busy, but it's the best option." Kusanagi handed the file back to Kishitani, got to his feet, and strode out of the room. Watching him go, Kaoru detected a certain eagerness in the set of his shoulders.

"Who is this person the chief knows?" Kaoru asked Kishitani.

The older detective gave her a meaningful smile and flicked open the file. He pointed at a name and address: "Hidemi Negishi, Kachidoki, Chuo Ward, proprietor and mama-san of VOWM."

"Oh, I get it. . . ."

Everybody at the Tokyo Metropolitan Police knew that Kusanagi was an aficionado of hostess clubs.

"It was when I saw the word 'VOWM.' I vaguely remembered the chief mentioning that name to me."

"Nice one, Inspector."

Kaoru was interrupted by a call on her cell. Looking at the screen, she gasped softly in surprise. The caller ID was Professor Yukawa.

She moved away from Kishitani and picked up.

"Utsumi here. It's been a while, Professor Yukawa."

"I was just thinking that I hadn't seen Kusanagi for ages, when up he pops, asking for my help on something really awkward."

"Sorry about that, Professor. We had no choice."

"I'll tell you what I already told Kusanagi: it's not right for you to ask me out of the blue to write a lying email to someone I barely know. It's just too sleazy."

"We understand, Professor. The chief told me he regretted making the request."

"He did? Not sure I believe you. Anyway, enough of that for now."

"Shall I put the chief on the line?"

"No, don't bother. Can you tell him that I tracked down the emails I exchanged with Ms. Asahi five years ago? They turned out to be my answers to some simple questions she had about magnetic monopoles. They have no relation to your current investigation."

"You're saying that you don't want to show them to us?"

"I most certainly do not. They're private documents. Still, as I was reading through them, I started feeling differently about things. If someone I helped with a book is embroiled in a murder case—perhaps even a suspect in it—then I don't want to sit idly by and let things take their course. I have decided to do a little checking up of my own."

"Okay. Let me know if there's anything I can do to help."

"I'm going to take you up on that right now. I want to know everything you can tell me about the woman who was so fond of Ms. Asahi."

"You mean Sonoka Shimauchi, the missing young woman?"

"No," Yukawa said. "It's Sonoka's mother who I'm interested in."

8

"The name 'Morning Shadows' struck me as rather dismal for an orphanage," Yukawa said. He was sitting in the front passenger seat of the car looking down at a tablet computer.

"I had a look at their web page. The place has a certain amount of history. It was founded not long after the Second World War."

"What was the mother's first name again?"

"Chizuko Shimauchi. Chi-zu-ko."

"Have you got any idea when Chizuko started working there?"

"Sorry. Not yet."

"Well, the orphanage people should know." Yukawa switched off the tablet and stuck it in his shoulder bag.

When Yukawa had phoned her about Sonoka's mother, Kaoru told him everything they'd found out so far. It didn't amount to much. All they knew was that Chizuko was close to Nana Asahi (real name, Nae Matsunaga), that she'd died from a brain hemorrhage a year and a half ago, that she'd been working in a school meal distribution center and, prior to that, at an orphanage. Yukawa promptly declared that he wanted to visit the orphanage.

He argued that discovering why Chizuko Shimauchi was so attached to Nae Matsunaga was a necessary first step to figure out why Nae Matsunaga had gone into hiding, taking Sonoka Shimauchi with her.

Kaoru raised the matter with Kusanagi.

"They must know that we are looking for Sonoka," Kusanagi said. "They decided to go on the run and that suggests a lot of resolve on their part. Honestly, I'm intrigued: how did the two women develop such a strong bond? Yes, you and Yukawa should go and see the people at the orphanage."

Kusanagi lowered his voice before he continued. "I don't know why Yukawa changed his mind and decided to help us, but it's not something we need to agonize over right now. I'm guessing that he came across something when he combed through his old email exchange with Nae Matsunaga. Either way, the man's totally pigheaded, so I'm not expecting him to share anything with us until he's cleared everything up to his own satisfaction. Probably best to steer clear of mentioning the whole email business. Nothing to be gained from upsetting him."

And that was how Kaoru had ended up driving Yukawa to the orphanage.

"That reminds me, Professor, were you okay to leave the house today? The chief told me you're having a tough time caring for your mother," Kaoru said, her eyes fixed firmly on the road ahead.

"It's not that bad. It's more that I don't feel comfortable leaving all her care in my father's hands."

"I'd no idea you were such a dutiful son."

There was the sound of a mocking laugh.

"For my part, I had no idea that you were so interested in my private life. Let me just say this: 'dutiful' is not the right word for what I'm doing. If I were a *genuinely* dutiful son, I wouldn't have held off visiting my parents for years knowing that my mother had dementia."

"But wasn't that because you were in America?"

"That's no excuse. There are loads of businessmen who spend their lives shuttling back and forth between the two countries. I could have come back anytime if I wanted to. No, I'm a bad son."

"I'm sure you're not."

"Don't feel you have to be nice to me. I'm a realist. My life now is a form of penance."

There was a note of exasperation in his voice. It was out of character for the physicist.

"Is your mother in a bad way?"

"God only knows. Since an attack of aspiration pneumonia six months ago, several of her organs are functioning at a lower level."

"Your father was a doctor, wasn't he?"

"Don't go thinking that he was the director of a major hospital. Nothing could be further from the truth. He was just a local GP."

"You were never tempted to follow in his footsteps?"

"No." Yukawa's response was instantaneous.

"How come? I mean, you were in the science faculty."

"Well, there's all kinds of science. I was always far more interested in physics than medicine. It's as simple as that."

"You belonged to the physics club at Towa High School, didn't you?"

"Surprised you remember that."

"Were you also in the school badminton club?"

"No, I wasn't."

"You weren't?" Surprised, Kaoru turned to look at him.

"As a kid, I played badminton with the local club team. I never did it as a club activity at junior high or at high school. You always have to share the school gym with the other sports clubs, so I didn't think I'd get enough practice. No, at high school, I was in the athletics club, though I did occasionally play in matches for the badminton club."

"This is all news to me."

"So I should hope. You know nothing about me."

"I do know one amazing thing. I know that you went out with one of your classmates for six years."

She heard Yukawa click his tongue.

"I suppose Kusanagi told you that. He's a great one for gossip. . . ."

"It's not silly, it's beautiful. Why did you break up with her?"

"Easy. One day, out of the blue, she told me that she'd found someone else. That was it. *She* broke up with *me*."

"So you've been through heartbreak too, Professor?"

"It was no big deal."

"Did you ever see her again?"

"A few times at class reunions. She's married with children."

"Did she look happy?"

"Search me. Why do you ask?"

"Just curious."

What she really wanted to ask was whether he thought the girl regretted breaking up with him. Not wanting to be yelled at by Yukawa, she kept her thoughts to herself.

She left the expressway, drove along a main road for a while, then turned onto a side street. There were lots of greenery and few large buildings on the roadside, so they could see quite a distance on either side. Amid all the open space, there were clusters of houses here and there. All the houses had multiple cars parked in front of them. Clearly, this was an area where life without a car was impossible.

Up ahead of them on the right-hand side of the road stood a group of solid, institutional-looking buildings. As she drove up to the entrance, Utsumi saw the words "Morning Shadows" carved onto the gatepost.

The security guard walked up to their car. Kaoru opened the window on her side and told him who she was and that the office knew she was coming. The guard had been expecting them and told her where to park and which entry to use.

Kaoru parked the car in the lot and headed for the building with Yukawa. Several little children were playing on a corner of the garden. Preschoolers, perhaps?

They entered the front door. The office was located at the end of a long row of shoe lockers. A thin man who looked about sixty approached them with a serious expression on his face.

Kaoru bowed, proffered her card, and introduced herself. She then introduced Yukawa as "one who is helping us with the case."

The man was Mr. Kanai, the orphanage's director.

"It's Chizuko Shimauchi you want to talk about, isn't it?" Kanai said after scrutinizing her card.

"That's right. Ideally, we'd like to speak to someone who knew her well."

"I've only been here for four years and I never met Ms. Shimauchi personally. There is someone here who can help you. I'll go get her now. Could you wait a moment?"

Kanai went back into the office and returned with a woman in her late forties. She looked a little nervous.

"This is Ms. Sekine, the staff member who worked most closely with Ms. Shimauchi."

"May I ask you some questions?"

"Of course. I can only tell you what I know," Ms. Sekine said in a quiet voice.

Kaoru and Yukawa removed their outdoor shoes and put on slippers instead.

Ms. Sekine led them to a sun-drenched meeting room. It contained a couple of sofas on either side of a large, low table.

She explained that she had started working at the orphanage fifteen years ago after a stint at a nursery school.

"Chizuko was my mentor. I learned so much from her. She quit five years ago this March when her daughter, Sonoka, moved to Tokyo. We worked together almost ten years."

There was a tenderness in the woman's voice.

"Were you aware that Chizuko is dead?" Kaoru asked.

"Yes," the woman replied sadly. "Her daughter called to give me the news. It was a terrible shock. She was still young, and very healthy when she worked here. . . ."

"When was the last time you saw her?"

"Her last day on the job here. We wanted to keep seeing each other but it simply never happened." Ms. Sekine looked dejectedly down at the floor.

"On the phone, I mentioned that I'd really appreciate a photograph of her from back then."

"I suppose you mean one when you can clearly see her face? I had a look around. This was the only suitable one I could find."

Ms. Sekine slid an old brochure out of a file beside her. There were several rows of portrait photos on the page profiling the orphanage staff. Beneath one of them was the name "Chizuko Shimauchi." She was a cultivated-looking woman with an oval face and shortish hair. *That's her*, thought Kaoru. *She really looks like her daughter, Sonoka.* "Childcare worker, cook, and administrator" read her job description. Clearly, the orphanage expected its staff to multitask!

"Thank you very much," Kaoru said, placing the brochure in her bag. "What about any documentation that might provide an insight into her background? A résumé, for instance?"

Ms. Sekine looked slightly embarrassed.

"I asked Mr. Kanai, the director, about this. He cleared out some old files years ago, including her résumé. I have a good idea of her history, though. She was actually an alumna of this place."

"An alumna?"

"Her earliest memories were of being here, she told me. She stayed here through her high school graduation. After that, she went and worked while attending junior college at night to get her qualification in childcare. She then worked at a number of schools and orphanages before finally returning to a job here."

"I understand that Chizuko was a single mother. Do you know anything about that?"

"Not really. All she told me was she and the father split up before their daughter was born."

"So Chizuko was never actually married?"

"Probably not. . . . That was my impression at least."

Kaoru supposed that the father already had a wife and children of his own. That was more likely than him having divorced her while she was pregnant.

"Did she ever talk about having problems with the father?"

Ms. Sekine shook her head.

"Not that I know. It was a single-parent family, but they seemed happy. I knew Sonoka, the daughter, very well. She often used to come to play here."

The two of them seemed to have had a peaceful life here.

Kaoru adjusted her position on the sofa. It was time to get on to the important question.

"Did Chizuko ever mention anything about a woman she knew who wrote children's picture books? We think that the two of them were very close."

"Picture books . . ." Sekine repeated under her breath before blinking as though a thought had come to her.

"Could that be the street theater lady? I remember Chizuko telling me that she had authored some children's picture books."

"The street theater lady?"

"It was a while ago—actually, a very long time ago now. There was this woman, a volunteer, who visited different orphanages performing traditional stories with the aid of illustrated cards. Apparently, she came here to give a performance just after Chizuko had come back to work here. The two of them became close. Chizuko had a young daughter to look after and was lonely and none too happy. The other woman listened to her problems and gave her a ton of practical help."

"Did she tell you the woman's name?"

"I'm afraid I can't . . ."

"Not to worry." As Kaoru lowered her gaze, Yukawa interjected, "Do you know why the woman was doing that traditional street theater thing?"

"*Why?*" Ms. Sekine looked thoroughly nonplussed.

"She was traveling all over the place putting on these performances without getting paid a penny. That suggests to me that it was something she really believed in. There must be a reason for that level of commitment. Didn't Chizuko ever say anything about that to you?"

Ms. Sekine thought for a moment, then spoke slightly hesitantly.

"Not in so many words. 'She loved children and wanted to put smiles on as many of their faces as possible'—I remember Chizuko saying that."

"'Smiles on their faces.' I see. Now you mentioned that she used to visit different orphanages. You don't happen to know what parts of the country they were in?"

Ms. Sekine tilted her head to one side and grunted ambivalently.

"From what Chizuko told me, I don't think it was the whole of Japan. . . . More like Greater Tokyo and its environs. Honestly, I'm not sure."

"Thank you. You've been most helpful." Yukawa nodded at Kaoru. He'd asked her everything he wanted.

Realizing that they were unlikely to get anything more out of Ms. Sekine, Kaoru decided to bring the interview to an end. She thanked her and stood up.

When the three of them were back in the entrance, Kaoru thanked the director for his assistance.

"I won't ask what kind of case you're working on, but were we of any use to your investigation?" Kanai asked.

"Very useful indeed. Thank you so much for your help."

"Glad to hear it," said Kanai with a half-sigh. "I do wish people would sometimes come to interview us about positive things and not just criminal matters. Now I come to think of it, someone else from the police was here just six months or so back."

"Someone from the police? What were they here for?"

"I'm not quite sure of the terminology. A snap inspection related to cybercrime . . . I think that was the phrase she used."

"A snap inspection?"

Kaoru was puzzled. The expression was not one she had come across before.

"To be strictly accurate, the woman wasn't actually from the police; she said she was working as a subcontractor *for* the police. It was this middle-aged woman. They had noticed we were using images of people on the orphanage's website. She wanted to confirm that we had gotten their informed consent. When I assured her that we had all the proper permissions, she told me to contact them right there in front of her."

"Right then and there? Contact the people in the images?"

"She claimed that was a crucial component of the snap inspection."

Ms. Sekine, who was standing slightly away from the other three, gasped audibly when she heard this.

"Director Kanai, the person the woman spoke to on the phone was Sonoka. Chizuko's daughter."

"Oh, was it?" Kanai put a hand to his chin.

"Definitely. I remember going to dig up Sonoka's contact details for her."

"I don't quite get this. Can you talk me through what happened?"

According to Ms. Sekine, the episode had played out like this.

When Director Kanai insisted that the orphanage had secured permission from all the people whose images appeared on
the website, the woman from the police had whipped out a tablet
computer and gone to the orphanage's website, where she picked
out several faces and demanded to see the signed image release
forms of those individuals. When the director explained to her
that they had secured oral rather than written consent, she'd then
selected a single image and demanded that they contact that particular person. The individual she had singled out was Sonoka
Shimauchi.

Ms. Sekine fetched Sonoka Shimauchi's contact details and
Mr. Kanai immediately called her. As soon as the phone started
ringing, Kanai handed it to the woman conducting the inspection.
She then checked with Sonoka if she had indeed granted permission for the use of her image. Apparently satisfied with her answer,
she then handed the phone back to Kanai.

"Can you show us the image in question?"

"Yes. Will you follow me?"

Ms. Sekine led Kaoru and Yukawa to the office. There she
called up the relevant image on her PC. It was a photograph from
a Christmas party.

"This is the picture that the inspector lady singled out."

It was a picture of a girl of around ten years old. Taking a careful look, Kaoru recognized it as Sonoka Shimauchi. *But it was a
very old photograph!*

"When we redesigned our website, we wanted to include a
Christmassy picture. When we couldn't find anything more re-

cent, we decided to go with this one; it's just kind of stayed up there since."

"So Sonoka was invited to this party?"

"She wasn't one of our orphans, but the event was open to all. She was just there to enjoy herself."

Kaoru nodded and scrutinized the image for a second time. A primary-school-age Sonoka Shimauchi was clutching a doll with a big smile on her face. The doll was long-haired and was dressed in a sweater with blue and pink stripes.

9

He glanced at his watch. It was just after 7:00 P.M. *The perfect time*, Kusanagi thought to himself as he made for the elevator lobby. He was going up to the tenth floor at the top of the building. VOWM occupied the entire floor.

The elevator hall was overflowing with grand-opening flower stands. A new bar must have opened recently in the building.

As it was still early, Kusanagi was alone in the elevator. It went straight up to the tenth floor without stopping.

The door slid open. Opposite him was a wall dotted with countless little twinkling stars. The door of the club was to his right. Before he even had the time to turn his head, an enthusiastic greeting rang out.

A man in a smart black suit stood by the door. Kusanagi had met him before but couldn't recall his name. When the man saw Kusanagi's face, surprised recognition gave way to a rather forced smile.

"Well, well, well. Mr. Kusanagi. It's been far too long." The man inclined his punctiliously combed head in a bow.

"So long that I'm amazed you remember my name."

"Of course I do. Will you be meeting a friend here this evening?"

"No, it's just me."

"Very good. I will take you right in."

"Is the mama-san in today? I mean Hidemi, not Chii, her number two."

Perplexity and suspicion flashed briefly across the suit's face. Quickly reverting to his normal blank expression, he said, "Let me check on that right now."

"Appreciate it. I'll be fine at the bar."

"Yes, sir," said the suit with a nod. He knew what Kusanagi did for a living and understood that tonight he wasn't just another ordinary customer.

Kusanagi took a seat at the bar. He was wiping his hands with a chilled towel when the barman placed a bottle of Wild Turkey in front of him. Kusanagi had bought the bottle literally years ago. It was still about one-third full.

"Do you want water with that, sir?"

"Please."

He had started drinking his bourbon and water when the suit sidled back up to him.

"Hidemi Mama isn't in tonight, so I called her. She said she'd be happy to come in and have a drink with you."

"Thanks."

"Shall I send a girl over while you're waiting?"

"I'm fine. Thanks for the offer."

After watching the suit make his way back across the room,

he surveyed the club. It was early, so there was only a handful of customers. The hostesses who had started the evening by getting their best customers to take them out to dinner would only be bringing them back to the club around eight at the earliest.

It was on September 26 that Ryota Uetsuji had phoned Hidemi Negishi. The call had lasted all of five minutes. That suggested it wasn't about anything very important. At the same time, why on earth would Uetsuji—who didn't even have a proper job—be phoning the mama of a Ginza hostess club? It made no sense. When he'd gone through Uetsuji's call log, Kusanagi found a total of three calls to Hidemi Negishi.

They badly needed a lead of some kind. Although the incident room had been up and running for several days now, the investigation had barely made any headway.

Analysis of the bullet they'd extracted from the corpse was ongoing. According to the pathologist, it was a .22-caliber. The rifling marks suggested it had probably been fired from either an illegally made or modified firearm, both almost impossible to trace. While most of the illegally made guns in Japan were imported from the Philippines, anyone familiar with machine tools with access to a blueprint could make one. And the shooter didn't have to have those skills; there were countless black market options.

Kusanagi's thoughts were interrupted by someone sliding up beside him.

"While you've been hiding from me all this time, all you've gone and done is become even handsomer than ever."

Turning to the source of the smoky voice, Kusanagi was confronted by the smiling face of Hidemi Negishi. She was dressed in a kimono. She'd always been slim, but her face now seemed even thinner than ever. Although she was around seventy, with her glowing skin, she could pass as a good twenty years younger. Maybe it was just the result of good makeup technique. The fact that she never looked over-made-up was the mark of a consummate pro, Kusanagi reflected.

"You mean that I've put on weight?"

"Not a bit of it. I'm saying that your virile good looks have gone up by yet another notch. May I?"

She sat on the stool beside Kusanagi. A whiff of expensive perfume tickled his nostrils.

"You're looking pretty good yourself."

"Only because I'm seeing you for the first time in much too long. May I order a drink?"

"Of course."

The bartender must have overheard her. He came over and mixed her a small whiskey and water.

"I believe our guest has something important he wants to discuss with me. Could you give us some space?" Hidemi Negishi said as she picked up her glass. The bartender ducked his head and disappeared wordlessly.

She thanked Kusanagi for the drink, took a sip, and gave him a sidelong glance.

"Something important must be going on if you're happy to just sit and wait for an old lady like me to show up without calling over one of the younger girls. What can I do for you tonight?"

"You always were one for getting straight to the point." Kusanagi pulled a photograph out of the inside pocket of his jacket. It was a mug shot of Ryota Uetsuji. "Ever seen this man before?"

"Let me have a proper look." Hidemi Negishi took the picture from him and examined it. Despite the smile on her lips, her eyes were grave. She shook her head and handed it back to him.

"I'm afraid to say that I've never seen him before. I thought he could be a customer of ours, but I can't locate him in my mental filing system. It's not the most reliable filing system, so I can't be completely sure."

"Except that you received a phone call from this individual. On the twenty-sixth of last month."

"He called me on the twenty-sixth of last month? Gosh, who could he be? Do you mind if I check my phone?"

"Be my guest."

Hidemi Negishi slid her phone out of her clutch bag and executed a deft series of taps and swipes. She caught her breath as if she had found something, then looked inquiringly at Kusanagi.

"Is it a Mr. Uetsuji?"

"So he is an acquaintance of yours after all."

"An acquaintance . . ." She made an ambivalent sound, twisted her head and shoulders to one side, and replaced her phone in her bag. "I'm not sure that's the term I'd use. While it's true that I have spoken to him on the phone a few times, he's not someone I particularly *wanted* to talk to."

"How do you know him?"

"It's a bit complicated. You see, six months ago, I encountered a golden goose."

"A golden goose?"

"I'm talking about a girl. She was elegant, lively, and charismatic, but she also had a hint of shadow, a touch of darkness. I knew that she'd be a big hit if I could get her to work here."

"Oh, that kind of golden goose."

So she was talking about a hostess. Kusanagi was puzzled. This was not a direction he had been anticipating.

"At my age, I need to consider the future of the business. I've been thinking that now's the right time for me to step down. That's what was on my mind when I ran into this girl. She made me want to go out with a bang. With a little polishing up, I knew that girl could become something special and make this place a ton of money. It was love at first sight."

"For you to say that, there must have been something special about her. Where was she working? Here in Ginza?"

Hidemi Negishi smiled and shook her head.

"She wasn't in the nightlife business. She works at a flower shop."

She heard a sharp intake of breath. Something she had said to Kusanagi must have made an impression.

"And what was the name of this golden goose of yours?"

"Sonoka. Sonoka Shimauchi. I think she's twenty-three. A good girl, a nice girl. This friend of mine was going to do a solo performance of French ballads. I went to a flower shop where Sonoka happened to be working. I explained that I wanted to send my friend some flowers to celebrate the occasion. She found the ballads on her phone, listened to them, and then and there picked out flowers that matched their mood. For a young girl nowadays to be able to put themselves in the customers' shoes like that is almost unheard of! She's not heart-stoppingly beautiful, but she's got a certain je ne sais quoi that makes her attractive to both sexes. That's not a quality you're going to find if you leave your talent-hunting to professional scouts. So I pulled out my card, handed it to her, and asked her if she fancied a job here at the club. As you'd expect, she was rather taken aback; she seemed to think I was teasing her. I had to make it clear that I was serious. I did my best to talk her round and she started showing some interest. I told her to take all the time she needed before giving me an answer. What happened next was a complete bolt from the blue. The man she lives with calls me up to complain: 'Enough with your sleazy proposals. I don't want my girlfriend working in a hostess club.' That man was Mr. Uetsuji."

"So that's the connection," Kusanagi said with a nod. "How did things go after that?"

"I spoke to Uetsuji a few times on the phone. My attempts to get him to change his mind went nowhere, so that was the end of it. Apparently, Sonoka didn't have the stomach to get into this world over her boyfriend's objections."

"Did you call Sonoka after that? To see if she might change her mind?"

Hidemi Negishi shook her head and smiled wryly.

"No. There's nothing so grotesque as someone who's been jilted running after the person who jilted them. That's never been my style."

"On the twenty-sixth of last month, it was Uetsuji who called you. Can you tell me what that was about?"

"I've no reason not to tell you. He asked me if the deal was still on the table."

"The deal?"

"Hiring Sonoka to work here in the club. I told him that if she wanted the job, she was welcome anytime. He said, 'I suppose that means you'll be paying her a hiring bonus.' I said that I was willing to give her something, since she would need to buy a few things for the job. What do you think he said to that?"

"Tell me."

"'If she does get into the hostess thing with you, I'll have to make her give up her current job. That means I'll need enough money to cover my living expenses for a while.' So I said to him, 'What are we talking about here?' He's like, 'I'm talking three million yen. Minimum.'"

Kusanagi burst out laughing. "That's outrageous."

"While we were on the phone, I was trying to figure out why he had picked that particular moment to contact me. It seemed odd, until he made that proposal. Then it was clear enough: it was all about the money. Something had happened and he needed money and needed it fast. I told him that I'd think about his proposal and I ended the call. In fact, I'd made up my mind to give up on Sonoka. No matter how wonderful a person she was, if she was that bad a judge of men, things were never going to work out."

"And after that? Did you call her?"

"No," Hidemi Negishi said. "I made no effort to contact her. Had she called me, I was just going to tell her that I thought that our arrangement wasn't meant to be. In the end, I never heard another peep from her. I've no idea what was going on. It certainly wasn't polite."

"So that's what it was all about. Now I get it. Sorry to pressure you." Kusanagi lifted a hand in a gesture of apology, then picked up his glass.

"What sort of job has Uetsuji got?" Hidemi Negishi asked, speaking under her breath. "He was being so pushy, he's got to be hard up."

"The way you're talking about him, I assume you don't know?"

"Don't know what?"

"Uetsuji went missing and was found floating off the coast of Chiba."

"Floating in the sea?" Hidemi Negishi gave a slightly theatrical shudder. "I don't suppose he'd been on a boat or gone swimming or anything like that?"

"Unfortunately not."

Hidemi Negishi drew herself upright with a jerk. "How awful."

"That's why I'm going around interviewing people like this."

"I see. Well, I wish you the best of luck." Hidemi Negishi looked at him earnestly and gave a brisk little bow. "So . . . uh . . . Mr. Kusanagi, what's going on with Sonoka? With Uetsuji dead, she must be on her own."

"It wouldn't be appropriate for me to discuss that. I'm sorry. It's part of an ongoing investigation. If you're worried about her, why not try reaching out to her?"

"Good idea. I'll try calling her later."

I don't think you'll get through to her, Kusanagi thought to himself.

Several couples had come into the club. Hostesses bringing their dinner companions back with them, Kusanagi assumed.

"Mama-san, I do have one final question. You may not like it, but it's something I'm obliged to ask everyone with a connection to the case."

"Don't worry about upsetting me. Fire away."

"I'll take you at your word. Do you recall what you were doing on the twenty-seventh and twenty-eighth of last month?"

"The twenty-seventh and twenty-eighth?" Hidemi Negishi took out her phone again. "I wasn't feeling well. I was at home both days."

"You didn't come to the club?"

"No. As you've probably figured out, I don't come in all that often nowadays. An old lady like me prowling about the place is hardly the best recipe for customer satisfaction! Like today, I was going to take the night off until I was told that a *very special customer* had come in and wanted to see me. I've become a complete homebody. I suppose that must mean"—Hidemi Negishi grinned at Kusanagi—"I've got no alibi."

"Your alibi will be just fine, provided you can prove you were actually at home all the time. Was there anyone there with you?"

"I'm just a lonely old lady, so sadly not. Does that make me a suspect?"

"No, it doesn't. Thank you. I think that covers it for now." Kusanagi downed his whiskey and water, which was almost entirely water now, and replaced the glass back on the counter. "How much do I owe you?"

"I'll get this."

"Not allowed. We police have rules."

"You do? All right, I'll do the usual and send you an invoice. Same address?"

"Same address. Thanks." As he said this, Kusanagi slid off the stool.

He left the club and got into the elevator. Hidemi Negishi followed him inside. She was obviously going to see him off at street level.

"Most fun I've had in a while."

"Nice to hear. Next time, you should stay longer."

"I will—and that's a promise. I'll be back soon."

"Please do. I'll put all the best girls on your table."

"I'm looking forward to it already."

They had reached the first floor. The sight of all the flower stands lined up in two rows on either side of the lobby reminded Kusanagi of something. He came to an abrupt halt.

"What is it?" Hidemi Negishi asked.

Kusanagi had pulled out his phone.

"Tonight was my first time here in ages. A special occasion deserves a nice commemorative photograph. Will you be in it with me?"

"Of course, if you want."

Hidemi Negishi called to a random suit who happened to be walking past and asked him to take the picture. He was happy to oblige, so Kusanagi handed him his phone.

Once the photograph had been safely taken, Kusanagi slipped his phone back into his pocket. "Be seeing you," he said.

"Come back soon." Clasping her hands together in front of her, Hidemi Negishi made a formal bow.

Kusanagi marched off into the Ginza night. No sooner had he turned the first corner than he pulled up the photograph he'd just taken. In the smile on Hidemi Negishi's face, he felt he could detect the bottomless resolve and cool you needed to survive in the Darwinian world of nightlife.

He might really go back to the club sooner rather than later. *And when I do, it will be a good idea to bring that friend of mine with me*, he thought.

When she saw the picture on the screen of the phone, the reaction of Mrs. Aoyama, the store manager, was quite different from the last time. Her eyes lit up and she nodded emphatically.

"That's her. No two ways about it. She wasn't quite as fancily dressed as this, but she was still extremely well turned out, especially for her age."

"Thanks," Kaoru said as she took back her phone. The picture was of two smiling people standing side by side. Kusanagi was one of them, while the other was a woman by the name of Hidemi Negishi. She was the mama-san of a high-end hostess club in Ginza.

"Can you tell me a bit more about this woman's visit? Did she ask if Ms. Sonoka Shimauchi was in that day?"

"Yes, she did, though I don't recall exactly how she phrased the question. When I said that Sonoka wasn't in, she asked me if it was her day off. I said no and that she was sick. 'Does she take a lot of days off?' she asked. And I told her absolutely not, that it was highly unusual for her."

"And was that the totality of your conversation?"

"Let me think . . ." Mrs. Aoyama frowned, then said, "Come to think of it, she also asked me about Sonoka's working hours."

"Her working hours?"

"What sort of time Sonoka had been starting and finishing her shift recently. I explained to her that it was different on different days. . . ."

"What was her response to that?"

"She asked if we'd been busy recently. I explained that our business was seasonal and that we'd not been that busy lately. 'Oh, really?' she said. Then she left. She was obviously extremely worried about Sonoka."

"And she hasn't come back since then?"

"Not as far as I know."

"Thanks. I appreciate your help."

When Kaoru got back to the incident room, Kusanagi had his phone pressed to his ear and was busy talking to someone.

"A detached house. What, in a residential area? . . . Split the men up and get them to go to every single house. . . . It would be great if someone had an idea where they've run to. Still, we'd be stupid to expect too much. Any information connected to Nae Matsunaga is welcome. Oh, and find out everything you can about her husband too—where he works, things like that. . . . And if you can discover where she does her shopping or gets her hair done, then go and talk to her hairdresser too. Get all the information you can, time permitting. . . . Yes, that's the spirit. Good luck."

Hearing Kusanagi give this rousing sign-off before hanging up, Kaoru went over to him.

"Chief, I just got back a moment ago."

"How did it go?"

"Bull's-eye. This is the woman who went to the flower shop.

No doubt about it." Kaoru held up the photo of him with Hidemi Negishi.

Kusanagi grinned broadly and smacked his right fist into his left palm.

"So I was right. I couldn't stop thinking about what you'd told me about the old woman who'd come looking for Sonoka Shimauchi. The store manager commenting on how fancily turned out she was for her age. It suddenly flashed into my head when I was saying good night to Hidemi Mama outside the club. I guess my detective's sixth sense isn't yet completely shot."

"You find it concerning that the mama-san didn't tell you that she had gone back to the flower shop to look for Sonoka?"

"'Concerning' is hardly the word for it. It's a serious issue. There's no way it slipped her mind. Frankly, it's downright weird that she didn't mention it, given the nature of our conversation. She even made a speech about how there's nothing more grotesque than someone who's been jilted going after the person who jilted them. She insisted it was something she'd never done in her life."

"And yet she actually went to the store to try to catch Sonoka there. The store manager didn't think that she'd dropped by just because she happened to be in the neighborhood either."

"What do you mean?"

Kaoru relayed everything that Mrs. Aoyama had said.

Kusanagi crossed his arms.

"From what the manager told you, it sounds as if she went there specifically to find out what was happening with Sonoka Shimauchi."

"In which case, there's every chance that she tried to track her down afterward too. Since Hidemi didn't go back to the flower shop, if they did meet, it must have been somewhere else."

"Why did Hidemi Negishi go looking for Sonoka? Was it because she didn't want to give up on Sonoka? Was she hoping to take another crack at persuading her to come and work at her club? The way she rhapsodized about her, I could tell she had taken a fancy to her. Reminded me of a baseball scout."

"What?" Kaoru said, sounding rather grumpy. "Are you saying she was scouting Sonoka for a hostess job?"

Kusanagi frowned. "I am. What's your problem? Notion doesn't appeal?"

"It's not so much I don't like it. I just can't see it. I've never actually met Sonoka Shimauchi, but I just didn't get the impression that's the kind of girl she is. Her high school homeroom teacher said she was reluctant to give her own opinions and was easily influenced by others. Is a girl like that suitable material for a hostess club? I mean, in those places it's a battle for survival, red in tooth and claw, right?"

"That's certainly true."

"Is that the way scouting even works, with someone asking a girl who's working in a flower store, 'Hey, you want to work as a hostess?'"

"Don't ask me. I've no idea."

"According to Inspector Kishitani, you know everything there is to know about fancy hostess clubs. . . ."

"He'd say anything. Don't get the wrong idea: I only go to those places a few times a year. Still, I see what you're getting at. We need to look into the links between Hidemi Mama, Ryota Uetsuji, and

Sonoka Shimauchi. If Uetsuji's outgoing call log is to be believed, those links don't seem to have been very close. The only recent call he made was that one to Hidemi Mama on the twenty-sixth. It was all of five minutes long."

"He was calling her to ask if she was still interested in hiring Sonoka, right?"

"Right. We pulled Uetsuji's bank statements. He certainly seems to have had his back against the wall financially. His five million yen of savings plunged to almost nothing over the course of the last year. The fellow can't be bothered to work, so what can you expect?"

"He can't be bothered to work, tried to turn his girlfriend into a hostess and wangle a hiring bonus for himself. If that's true, then he's a total piece of trash. I can see why Sonoka would run away from him."

"Fine, except that with Uetsuji now dead, she has no reason to remain in hiding. It's possible that she's unaware of Uetsuji's death. No, I can't believe that . . . ," Kusanagi muttered almost as an afterthought, crossing his arms on his chest.

"Have we still not found any clues as to Sonoka Shimauchi's whereabouts?"

"Unfortunately not. We've circulated her picture to hotels, inns, and short-term rentals, mainly here in Tokyo. No responses so far."

"That reminds me, on the phone just now, you were ordering a door-to-door canvass. I heard the name 'Nae Matsunaga' . . ."

Kusanagi picked up a piece of paper from his desk.

"We found Nae Matsunaga's old address. The place she lived

before she moved into her present apartment. It's over in Saitama. We don't know exactly how long she lived there. All we know is that she renewed her driver's license in Saitama for more than twenty years, starting thirty-five years ago. All that time, she was living at the same address."

Kusanagi must have gotten that information from the driver's license database.

"If she lived there over twenty years, we should be able to learn something about her."

"We'll be in trouble if we can't. They won't give us a warrant to search her apartment based only on the likelihood of her collaborating with a person of interest." Kusanagi made a sour face as he said this, then he looked hard at Kaoru, as if something had just occurred to him. "Have you heard anything more from Yukawa since your visit to the orphanage?"

"No, the professor hasn't contacted me."

"Put out some feelers. He might've changed his mind and be willing to email Nae Matsunaga for us."

"I'm on it, sir," Kaoru replied. Inside, she was skeptical about the idea.

The investigators who had been canvassing Nae Matsunaga's old neighborhood returned to the incident room in the early evening. Seeing that Kishitani, who had been leading the operation, was about to deliver his report to the chief, Kaoru, who was busy compiling her own report at her desk, stopped working and listened in.

"Nae Matsunaga moved to the area thirty-six years ago as a newlywed. Her husband had built a house there. His name was

Goro Matsunaga. He was a businessman who owned a number of bars and restaurants. Although Goro was around twenty years older than his wife, this seems to have been his first marriage. According to their old neighbors, Nae Matsunaga was a full-time homemaker; she didn't have a job. After they'd been living there for ten-some years, Goro died. According to one of the neighbors who attended the funeral, it was lung cancer and he lasted only six months after it was diagnosed. Anyway, Nae Matsunaga continued living in the house by herself until eleven years ago, when she sold the house and moved to her present apartment. We didn't find anyone who knew about her having become an author of children's picture books. That's everything, sir," Kishitani concluded.

"You got nothing that might lead us to wherever it is she's hiding?" Kusanagi said grumpily.

"At present, no direct leads, no . . . We did, however, pick up one tidbit I think you'll like, Chief. The Matsunagas loved to travel and they were often away from home for extended periods. Most of that time, they were in Japan, not abroad."

Kusanagi leaned forward slightly.

"Meaning they had a place where they could stay for long periods? A holiday home, say?"

"Nobody we spoke to today mentioned a holiday home or apartment."

"I see. Even if she did have a holiday place, I don't suppose she'd choose to lie low there. She'd expect us to find the place in quite short order."

"I think you're right, Chief. But I gather that her late husband was well connected and knew a lot of people. One of his friends could have had a holiday place he rented out to them."

"That's it." Kusanagi snapped his fingers. He liked the suggestion.

"Do a thorough check. See if anyone who was close to Goro had a holiday property."

"We're already on it, Chief," Kishitani said. His cool tone contrasted sharply with Kusanagi's overt excitement.

11

The autumn sky was a wonderful clear blue. Kaoru was looking at the little puffy clouds and thinking they resembled choux à la crème when her phone rang. She glanced at the caller ID on the screen, then picked up.

"This is Utsumi."

"I've arrived."

"Okay."

Kaoru ended the call and switched on the ignition. She had been waiting on the hard shoulder of National Route 15. Checking for oncoming traffic behind her, she slowly pulled out.

By the time Kaoru got to the taxi stand at the train station, Yukawa was already there. He jogged over and clambered into the passenger seat.

"How long will it take us to get there?" Yukawa asked as he pulled on his seat belt.

"The GPS says a little over an hour. Longer than I thought."

"I don't think so. That area is about as far from central Tokyo as you can get."

"You really know your Tokyo geography!"

"Teito University used to have a campus out there. That's

where the physics department was. We're talking twenty years ago, back when I was a research assistant."

"So this will be a trip down memory lane for you?"

"Hardly. I seldom ventured out of the university grounds. I've never even been there."

"Fair enough."

At Kusanagi's suggestion, Kaoru had contacted Yukawa the day before. When she reiterated their request for him to send an email to Nae Matsunaga, his answer was—as she had expected—negative.

"From what the orphanage staff told us, it's clear that Matsunaga is an important person in the lives of the Shimauchis, both mother and daughter. I am prepared to accept that Matsunaga is acting in concert with Sonoka. Nonetheless, it's not right to treat her as a suspect when it's still unclear what exactly her involvement in the case is."

Kaoru explained that what she was most interested in was seeing what kind of response the email would elicit. That didn't fly either. Yukawa countered that if Nae Matsunaga were actively sheltering Sonoka Shimauchi, then she would almost certainly ignore any emails from people she barely knew.

It was only when Kaoru mentioned that they had found out Nae Matsunaga's old address that Yukawa's interest suddenly perked up. He went so far as to ask Kaoru for the address so he could go and take a look for himself.

Kaoru had offered to take him there, which was why they had arranged to meet.

They got on the expressway and headed north. There was very

little traffic. Perhaps they would reach their destination faster than the satnav was predicting.

"How's the investigation going?" Yukawa asked.

"Not great, to be honest. The victim seems to have spent most of his life falling out with other people. Even if people didn't actively hate him, there seems to be a whole load of people who wanted nothing to do with him and were giving him a wide berth. On the other hand, recently he didn't have a regular job. That ought to mean less chance of friction with other people."

"Or that any trouble that did occur involved someone close to him."

"Of course, we have our suspicions about Sonoka Shimauchi. She has an alibi, though. The testimony of the friend she was with in Kyoto seems trustworthy enough."

"Which is why you think Nae Matsunaga is the killer. I would go back to what Kusanagi said. If she is, then it makes no sense for Sonoka Shimauchi to run off and hide."

"If Shimauchi had an alibi, you'd think she would have played ignorant and weathered the storm. I agree—but not everyone's like you, Professor. People don't always do the most logical thing. Some people can't help themselves; even if they know what they're doing is illogical, they can still choose the wrong path. Can you see that?"

"Are you telling me that that's what's going on in this case? Okay, so what's the 'wrong path' Sonoka Shimauchi has chosen?"

"My gut says that she's terrified at the sheer gravity of the situation she found herself in. She was okay when it came to creating an alibi, but the psychological pressure of being part of a murder was beyond anything she'd imagined. Not believing she could hold her own with the police, she decided to run away. Is that so implausible?"

"I'd be willing to accept the theory if she had gone on the run alone. But how can you explain the fact that she and Nae Matsunaga took off together? If Matsunaga was the killer, wouldn't she have tried to convince Sonoka to stay put?"

"Maybe Sonoka didn't want to be convinced. Maybe Matsunaga understood that Sonoka's fear level was so off the charts there was no way she could put on a show for the police."

"I won't dismiss either theory out of hand, but if Sonoka really was that fragile, surely she wouldn't have come up with such a plan in the first place? Murder is about as extreme as it gets. Sonoka had plenty of other options to shield herself from Uetsuji's abusive behavior."

As always, Yukawa's counterargument was on point and Kaoru couldn't come up with a rebuttal.

"Locating them is the fastest route to an answer. Where on earth can they be holed up . . . ? We couldn't find them in any hotels or inns. Now we're busy working our way through the holiday villas and apartments of all Matsunaga's friends and acquaintances."

"You're sure they're not in a hotel or inn?"

"Even if we can't be completely sure, we think it's highly unlikely. We circulated a photo of Sonoka Shimauchi to all hotels and inns, asking them to contact us if anyone like her was staying with them. That hasn't produced any leads so far."

"You circulated her photo? Are you allowed to treat Sonoka

Shimauchi and Nae Matsunaga like wanted criminals when there's no arrest warrant out for either of them?"

"We got Sonoka's employer at the flower shop to file a missing person's report. Coupled with our belief that she could be tangled up in a murder case, that allows us to designate her a priority missing person and deploy every possible means to track her down. Note, however, that we did not circulate Matsunaga's photograph. We can't classify her as missing because she informed her editor, Ms. Fujisaki, that she was planning to go on a trip by herself."

"In addition, there's no proof that Matsunaga is with Sonoka Shimauchi."

"You're right. It's like I thought: You really don't want Matsunaga to be guilty, do you, Professor?"

"What's with the 'like I thought'?"

"Look, I get it. Wanting to think the best of people you know—even if you don't know them all that well—is the most natural thing in the world. . . ."

"I really don't know Matsunaga well enough to want to take her side. The reason we're on our way to her old address is because I'm interested to learn what kind of person she is. Do me a favor. Don't make up your mind about people before you've got any evidence."

"Sorry. I'll be more careful in the future."

Yukawa's tone changed.

"What about that other thing? That business about the police supposedly using outside contractors to check that website managers have consent for any images of people they upload. Did you look into that?"

"I contacted the cybercrime division. While they do regard the uncleared use of people's images as problematic, neither the Tokyo Metropolitan Police nor the Chiba Prefectural Police are conducting any snap inspections."

Yukawa grunted. "Surprise, surprise."

"Yes, it's a funny episode. Still, since it happened more than six months ago, it's probably unrelated to the case."

Yukawa said nothing. Kaoru had stated her personal opinion. Perhaps Yukawa thought she was again making up her mind without any evidence.

They drove past several junctions and turned off the expressway. From there on, it was regular roads. As they followed the instructions of the satnav, they drove into a residential district with grid-pattern streets. When they eventually emerged, suddenly everything around them was green. Orchards of fruit trees dotted the landscape. When Kaoru commented on their sheer number, Yukawa crisply explained them away as a tax-reduction scheme.

"Lots of people around here own the land where their houses are. Turning your property into a farm is one way to bring down your annual property taxes. If the change is only superficial, the strategy doesn't work, so people do actually grow things. Chestnuts are the least hassle. There should be loads of chestnut trees around."

"You do know this area well."

"I'm talking about the economic boom time of the late '80s, the bubble-economy days. Whether it's still true or not today, I don't know."

They drove on for a while. The little orchards disappeared and were replaced by houses with well-tended gardens. Kaoru found a metered parking lot and parked the car.

"The streets are very narrow in the part we're going. On-street parking isn't an option there. We're better off walking."

"Is it close by?"

"The map says it's just over there."

They got out of the car and headed down a narrow side street. Detached houses stood at quite generous intervals. Kaoru walked ahead, consulting the map on her phone from time to time. The investigators who had canvassed the area had told her the landmarks to look out for.

When she came to a white, European-style house with the nameplate "Yamashita," she came to a halt. It matched the description from her colleagues. This had to be the place.

"Is this their house?" Yukawa asked.

"This is where they used to live. Their actual house has been demolished and replaced by this one."

"Now you mention it, it does look a little newer than the neighboring ones." Yukawa took a brisk look around and then strolled away.

He stopped in front of the next-door house. The name on the gate was "Kojima."

"According to the guys who did the canvass, Mrs. Kojima knew Nae Matsunaga better than anyone else."

"That's good news for us." As he said this, he pressed the button on the intercom.

A look of horror appeared on Kaoru's face. "What are you doing?"

Yukawa was all wide-eyed innocence. "Is something wrong?"

A woman's voice came out of the speaker. "Yes, hello?"

"I'm sorry to bother you, madam. We are from the Tokyo Metropolitan Police. We were hoping we could have a word with you. Is now a good time?" Yukawa spoke glibly into the microphone.

"Wait there," said the voice.

Kaoru sighed and glowered at Yukawa.

"If you're going to do something like that, you need to clear it with me in advance."

"Really? I find it hard to believe you thought I'd be happy to schlepp all the way out here just to take a gander at the house and go home."

"Fair point."

The front door opened, revealing a small woman wearing a cardigan. Kaoru pegged her at a little over sixty.

She made her way down to the garden gate.

"If you're here about Mrs. Matsunaga, I've already told your colleagues everything I know."

"And we're most grateful for your help." Kaoru gave a little bow. "There are just one or two more points we'd like to confirm with you." She turned to Yukawa as she said this.

"How long have you been living here, Mrs. Kojima?" Yukawa asked.

"We built the house before the collapse of the bubble economy. That's more than thirty years ago."

"Were the Matsunagas already living next door at that point?"

"Yes, they were. They completed their house a couple of years before us."

"I hear that you were very friendly with Mrs. Matsunaga."

"Yes, I was. When we moved in, I knew nothing about the area, and she gave me loads of useful tips. Good places for take-out sushi, that sort of thing."

That made sense. There were no smartphones with Web access in those days. The information Mrs. Matsunaga had provided must have been extremely useful.

"What did you make of the Matsunagas as a couple?" Yukawa proceeded to ask. "Was there anything about them—their lifestyle, their leisure activities—that made an impression on you?"

"Oh, they were such a lovely couple. The husband—he was much older—was a very easygoing character and an absolute sweetie with his wife. I never heard her say a bad word about him. Golf was all the rage back then and Nae was learning to play. It was her husband's idea. They both enjoyed traveling too. After the husband stepped back from the business, they were always off somewhere or other."

That tallied with what Kishitani had told them.

Kaoru decided to try asking a question of her own.

"We know they took a number of long trips. They didn't have a holiday home or holiday apartment, though, did they?" This was a question Kishitani and his team should have asked. Kaoru just wanted to make doubly sure.

"No, I never heard anything about a holiday home. I seem to remember her telling me they often rented a place."

"Do you know where it was?"

"I'm terribly sorry. I can't remember." Mrs. Kojima looked thoroughly embarrassed as she flapped one hand from side to side in a gesture of apology.

"The Matsunagas didn't have any children. Would you happen to know anything about that?" Yukawa set off on a new tack.

"They definitely wanted children. That was particularly true for Mr. Matsunaga. Unfortunately, they were a little too late, Nae said. She was in her mid-thirties when they got married. Nowadays, there's all sorts of fertility treatments available, but back then, the technology wasn't there. They compensated—perhaps that's not the most tactful way to put it—by being incredibly sweet with our little one."

"A girl?" Yukawa asked.

"No, a boy. I'd come home, find him gone, rush out in a panic to look for him, and find him next door having a big snack. That happened so often! It stopped after he went to junior high school, but they were still really kind to him, giving him a cake for his birthday and things like that." There was genuine warmth in Mrs. Kojima's voice. The more she spoke about the Matsunagas, the more evident it became.

"Do you remember anything about when Mr. Matsunaga died?" Yukawa changed his angle of questioning for a second time.

"I certainly do. We'd been living here about ten years then. I suddenly realized I hadn't seen him around for a while. It turned out he was in the hospital. . . . Not long before he died, Nae told me he had lung cancer. I got the impression she was resigned to the worst." Mrs. Kojima grimaced.

"And Nae Matsunaga continued living here alone after her husband's death?"

"That's right. She was always saying the place was too big for her, that it wasn't safe, and that she should move to an apartment.

Despite that, she stayed on here for another ten years. The thing is, she wasn't completely on her own. It must have been a couple of years after her husband died, a young woman with a daughter started visiting. Nae described them as friends but she treated them more like a daughter and a granddaughter."

"Was the mother's name Chizuko Shimauchi?"

Mrs. Kojima's face suddenly lit up and she clasped her hands on her chest at Yukawa's question.

"That's right. That was it. *Chizuko.* I can't recall her family name. Nae always called her Chizuko anyway. They used to visit almost every week. I was delighted; it was a real shot in the arm for Nae. Having something to live for is such a source of strength."

"Did you stay in touch with Mrs. Matsunaga after she moved away?"

Yukawa's question elicited a grimace of regret.

"She gave me her new address, but I never got around to visiting her. You still haven't found her? The detective who was here the other day said you thought she might be involved in something."

"We're currently looking into that," broke in Kaoru.

"You are?" said Mrs. Kojima, lowering her voice slightly.

"Thank you very much, Mrs. Kojima," Yukawa said. "You've been most helpful."

"We appreciate your help," Kaoru formally thanked her.

"I really hope you'll find her safe and sound very soon," said Mrs. Kojima, a solemn expression on her face.

As they walked away from the house, Kaoru asked Yukawa, "Did you get anything useful from her?"

"I got a sense of the relationship between Nae Matsunaga and the Shimauchis. The Shimauchis obviously cared for Mrs. Matsu-naga, but they seem to have meant a great deal to her too."

"Mrs. Matsunaga would definitely feel something when she found out that the little girl she loved like a granddaughter was being brutalized by her live-in boyfriend."

"Yes, I don't think she'd sit idly by."

"If you put me on the spot and asked me if I thought she'd try to murder the guy—well, that's a different matter."

"Like I said before, there were multiple paths to go down. It's not like the old days. Nowadays, there are laws to tackle domestic violence and publicly funded counseling and support centers for victims. Victims can get a medical certificate at a hospital and take that straight to the police. Murder makes no sense as a solution, no matter how you slice it."

"Then why's she on the run?"

"Search me. Perhaps she's got something to hide."

"Hide? Like what?"

"No idea. You'll need to ask her that." Yukawa was brusque.

"Hello? Wait a minute," said a voice behind them.

Kaoru stopped and turned. Mrs. Kojima scuttled up to them.

"Is there something wrong?" Kaoru asked.

"I just remembered something. It's about a holiday apartment." She was panting slightly as she spoke.

"What is it?"

"The Matsunagas often used to go to a holiday apartment in a ski resort. Sometimes they'd stay there as long as a month. They'd always come around in advance to warn us that their house would be empty for a while."

"Which resort was it?"

"Somewhere in Niigata Prefecture, I think. Honestly, I'm not too sure. I know that Mr. Matsunaga had been in his university ski club and the place belonged to one of his university buddies. As the friend got busier, he stopped going, but he let the Matsunagas use it whenever they wanted. Nae was very pleased about that. They had a set of keys for the place."

"Keys . . . ?"

This is it—Kaoru was sure of it. Her heart was racing.

"Can you remember when the Matsunagas went there for the last time? You don't have to be super precise about it."

Mrs. Kojima cupped her chin with her hand and tilted her head to one side.

"I think they kept going there until the year before Mr. Matsunaga's death."

"Okay. You did a great job remembering that."

"It had completely slipped my mind. It's so long ago and I've never been a skier myself. These things happen when you get old. I hope it's of some use."

"It's very useful indeed. Thank you."

Hearing the warmth in Kaoru's voice, Mrs. Kojima smiled contentedly.

"Give me a minute," Kaoru said to Yukawa. She pulled out her phone and called Kusanagi to relay what they had learned.

"Sounds like you've cracked it." Kusanagi's voice was hoarse with excitement.

"I think so, sir."

"Okay, I'll get Kishitani on it. We should have enough for him to find the place. Thanks. Good job."

Kaoru ended the call.

"Seems we got something."

"Something big."

"My guess would be it's in Yuzawa. From here, there's easy access to the expressway and during the heyday of the bubble economy, there were always long lines of cars waiting to get on. Lots of holiday condos were built in Yuzawa too."

"I know that. I also know that most of them didn't sell."

"By the time the apartments were completed, the economy had crashed and the ski boom petered out. Still, I imagine there were plenty of passionate skiers willing to buy. Supposedly, the facilities were fantastic. Even so, there are loads of apartments that have stood empty for over thirty years without finding a buyer. You can pick them up for a song today."

"With the recent boom in working from home, you hear stories about people from the Tokyo area moving out to places like that. No one will look twice at you, even outside the ski season. That makes it an excellent long-term hiding place."

"The signs are certainly encouraging."

"We finally seem to be making progress." Kaoru put her phone back in her pocket. "Where do you want to go next? Mrs. Kojima mentioned golf, and the range where the Matsunagas liked to practice was quite nearby. Do you want to see it?"

"Doesn't 'was nearby' mean it's no longer there?"

"Yes, I gather they built an old people's home on the site."

"So there's no point going. I think I'll take a little wander around the neighborhood. You can get going. I'll make my own way home."

Kaoru's eyes widened in surprise.

"You've had enough? We've only spoken to one household."

"There's not much point talking to a whole load of people. I think, though, there may be something to be learned from exploring Matsunaga's old neighborhood."

"Maybe. But the closest station is a very long way, if you plan to walk."

Kaoru glanced up and down the street. There was no sign of a bus stop.

"Not to worry. Say hi to Kusanagi from me."

"Oh, that reminds me, he was saying that he wants to take you out for the night. Some fancy hostess club in Ginza."

Yukawa's eyebrows shot up.

"Seriously? He seems pretty relaxed, given the case isn't yet solved."

"There's a chance the mama-san is involved. She tried to recruit Sonoka Shimauchi for her club or something."

Yukawa snorted and tipped his head skeptically to one side. "Did this Sonoka girl have the right sort of sex appeal?"

"Based on photos I've seen and what other people have told me, no, I don't think she did."

"Those mama-sans are pros. They probably see things that ordinary mortals like us can't. What's the club called?"

"It's called VOWM."

"VOWM?" murmured Yukawa, focusing his gaze on a point somewhere in the middle distance.

"Is something wrong?"

"How's it written?"

"What?"

"The name 'VOWM.' What language is it? It doesn't sound like English to me."

"Just a second." Kaoru pulled out her notebook and flicked it open. "It's spelled V-O-W-M. I've no idea what language it is."

"I see. . . . VOWM . . . ," Yukawa murmured.

"Does the name mean something to you?"

"No, nothing. You just tell Kusanagi that I'm looking forward to going there with him." As he said this, Yukawa spun on his heel and marched briskly off.

12

She heard the wind gusting. As it blew her empty paper cup across the table, she felt a chill run up her back.

Sonoka pulled together the front of the parka she'd thrown over her shoulders. She'd opened the glass door to get some fresh air, but the temperature in this part of Japan was already one season ahead, well into winter.

She slid the glass door shut and locked it. Before she shut the curtains, she took a look outside. The dark green forest was so close you could almost touch it. Another month or so, and the whole place would be blanketed in snow. This wasn't anywhere particularly remote. They were less than five minutes' walk from the bullet train station!

Sonoka went back to the sofa, where she resumed watching TV, a drama from twenty or so years ago. The young female lead was someone now best known for her mother roles. The show wasn't something she particularly wanted to watch; it was the least bad option.

She hadn't been interested in TV for years now. News, celebrity gossip, sport results—all of it was available online. She preferred the manic intensity of YouTubers ready to do anything to boost their view counts to the listless parade of celebs who cycled through the TV variety shows. It was the same story with dramas: the online ones were better and more fun to watch than their TV equivalents, which were so clogged with commercials.

Thanks to the smartphone, that engine of modern civilization, she could enjoy all this content. When Nae had told her that she shouldn't use her phone, she found it hard not being able to connect with her friends through social media. But it was only when she switched off the power and put the thing away that she realized just how much she depended on it. Now she had nothing to do—and didn't know what to do about it.

The only option was to watch TV, no matter how boring it was. It was the only source of information from the outside world and to get at least a modicum of entertainment.

Why has my life turned out like this?

It was a question she'd been asking herself ever since they had gone on the run. Although she knew that there was nothing to be gained from dwelling on it, she couldn't help picking it over from every conceivable angle.

One year ago, she'd been happy. That was when Ryota Uetsuji had moved in with her.

She'd enjoyed making breakfast for her boyfriend while he was still fast asleep. When he woke up, he would try to guess what she'd added to the miso soup that day from the smell wafting out of the kitchen. Despite usually guessing wrong, he always had nice things to say about the soup's taste.

On their days off, they'd go out shopping. Uetsuji was keen to improve the look of their apartment. "Our home is our castle," he liked to say. "This place used to be your and your mother's castle, Sonoka. Now it's *our* castle. We need to upgrade it to our level."

They bought a double bed and a new dining table. The old low table, with all its memories of Chizuko, was carted off to a secondhand shop. Sonoka felt sad to lose it, but she was willing to let it go. What else could she do? When Uetsuji told her she couldn't hang on to the past forever, she had no counter. It sounded sensible enough and she loved it when he called their apartment "our castle."

One day, Uetsuji quit his job. That was when everything changed.

"My cofounders are too apathetic. The reason we set up the company was to do what we love doing. We agreed on that. Now, the first speed bump we hit and they go groveling to their former employers, begging for scraps of work. They have no pride, no dignity. I can't work with people like that."

This wasn't the first time Uetsuji had expressed his dissatisfaction with the company. Things weren't set up right for him to put his very special talents to use, he liked to proclaim. Sonoka was surprised even so. She never thought he would quit.

He had another job lined up, Uetsuji assured her.

"There's this guy who's been on me to team up for a while now. With him, I think I can realize my full potential."

"You can? Well, that's a relief."

If you're genuinely talented, I guess switching jobs is no big deal, Sonoka thought.

Things quickly took a turn for the worse.

Despite his claims that the new job was in the bag, Uetsuji suddenly stopped mentioning it. There was no sign of him going to work. Sonoka was worried, but she kept her concerns to herself. Perhaps there were various formalities that needed taking care of first. When nearly a month had gone by with no sign of progress, she couldn't hold back anymore.

After dinner one evening, she casually asked, "How's the work thing coming along?"

Uetsuji was about to take a swig of tea. His hand stopped in midair and his shoulders seemed to twitch. "Coming along? What do you mean?"

"That company you mentioned—when are you going to start working there?"

Uetsuji grimaced. "They turned me down," he said with a snort.

Sonoka's eyes widened. "Why?" she gasped.

Uetsuji grimaced and exhaled contemptuously through his nose.

"When I took a proper look, the place turned out to be a crappy little outfit. All they do is make promotional videos for supermarkets. Shit that an amateur can cobble together. They make one or two commercials, but only for small TV stations out in the sticks. They've got zero profile. They totally misrepresented themselves to me."

"Oh, I see. So what are you going to do now?"

"I can't trust other people. I've decided to go freelance."

"Freelance? What do you mean?"

"I'm going to be independent. I'll originate my own projects and shop them around myself. When they get picked up, I'll be the producer. You know *Star Wars*? Well, that's how George Lucas made it."

The example he gave was so over the top that it came across as far-fetched and implausible.

"Do you think it'll be okay?"

The question slipped out of her before she had time to think. Uetsuji frowned and glared at her.

"*Okay?* What do you mean by *okay*?"

"I just wondered if it's going to work out. Life's tough. Most people don't have the luxury of only doing the work they want to do."

The expression on Uetsuji's face changed again. She had just noticed the beginnings of a scowl on his face when he stuck out his right hand and grabbed hold of Sonoka's chin. He was squeezing it so hard that it hurt.

"You're telling me life's tough? Don't you patronize me. Who do you think you're talking to? You have no idea about all the work I've done, do you? You know fuck all about the world I operate in. Don't ever talk down to me like that."

"You're hurting me."

"You want me to let go, you've got to say sorry. Apologize for disrespecting me."

"I'm sorry," she whimpered.

He finally let her go.

"I didn't mean to disrespect you," she muttered, rubbing her smarting chin. "I'm worried about you is all."

Uetsuji's right hand shot out for a second time. This time it was her hair that he grabbed. He yanked it and Sonoka screamed.

"And I say you disrespected me. You still don't get it?"

"Sorry, I'm sorry. I won't do it again."

Uetsuji let go of her hair and shoved her away from him.

Sonoka froze. Her mind was blank.

The silence lingered. "Sorry," Uetsuji eventually said. "If I knew you were on my side, I could stand tall and fight, even with the whole world against me. Or put it another way: you're the only person I need to believe in me. Of course I'm going to get upset when you tell me you doubt me."

His words, which he had to struggle to get out, sounded sincere. Sonoka was touched. *Maybe he's right*, she thought to herself. *If I don't believe in him, where does that leave him?*

"I guess so," she said in a whisper. "You're saying that as long as I believe in you, you're not afraid of anything. You're right. I was wrong and I'm sorry."

"I just want you to understand." There was warmth now in Uetsuji's eyes. "There's nothing more hurtful than you not believing in me."

"I *do* believe in you. I won't say anything dumb like that again. I promise."

The strange thing was that Sonoka saw herself as the guilty party in this episode and that was still how she remembered it.

It was soon after that Nae—Nae Matsunaga—came around to their apartment. Sonoka used to get the occasional email from her asking how she was doing. Sonoka invariably wrote back saying that life was good, and that Nae didn't need to worry about her. She'd concealed the fact that Uetsuji had moved in with her. She was convinced that Nae would disapprove. She still remembered something Nae had said to Chizuko: "Sonoka will need to be careful about the men she goes out with. She's so easily influenced."

Which is why Sonoka was so upset when Nae showed up with no advance warning. "Yes, hello," she'd casually sung out when the doorbell rang, only to hear Nae's voice come back at her through the door. She was so startled that she dropped the frying pan she was scrubbing.

She couldn't very well pretend to be out now. She went and opened the door. Uetsuji wasn't there.

Nae's eyes lit up when she saw Sonoka's face.

"I'm sorry, dear. Since I was in the neighborhood, I thought I'd drop in. I know you should be at work, but my sixth sense told me I might find you in. Seems my instincts were right." She laughed. She was wearing spectacles and no makeup.

"You should have let me know you were coming."

"I was all ready for you to be out. It's not like I'm here for any special reason." As she said this, Nae shot a quick glance around the apartment. Just for a second, her face clouded over, Sonoka noticed. "Look, if now's a bad time, I can go."

"No, don't do that."

"Can I come in for a minute?"

Sonoka couldn't very well say no. She nodded and gestured for Nae to come in.

They sat on opposite sides of the dining table. It was a new acquisition.

Nae turned and looked at the rooms at the back of the apartment. The sliding door of one of them was pulled shut. It was the room Uetsuji used.

"So what's he like?" Nae asked brightly. "He seems to have moved in with you."

She'd guessed that it was a man she was sharing with.

"He was a customer at the flower shop. I helped him with some flowers he needed for his work. . . ."

Sonoka explained how their relationship had developed. She wanted to keep things as vague as possible, but, since brevity was not her forte, she ended up revealing all sorts of interesting details. She even let slip that Uetsuji had quit his job and was working as a freelancer.

Nae listened patiently, a smile hovering on her lips. It was only when Sonoka looked at her eyes that she could see the disapproval.

"Do you really love him?" Nae asked after Sonoka had finished. Sonoka was taken aback. She blinked furiously.

"Yes, I really love him. Why do you ask?"

Nae cocked her head and made an ambivalent sound.

"Why? Because listening to you, I get the impression that things aren't quite as you make them out to be. Let me try another question, Sonoka. Are you truly happy with your life right now?"

Sonoka recoiled at the directness of the question. Was she panicking because Nae had put her finger on the nub of the problem? The question was one she'd never tried to think through for herself.

Nonetheless, Sonoka did her best to look calm and unruffled. "Am I happy? Of course I am," she said.

"Are you sure? Then let me ask you another question, Sonoka. What does happiness mean for you? Are you one of those people who, provided they're happy in the moment, regard themselves as happy and never worry about the future?"

"I'm not like that. I am thinking about the future, I really am."

"What about your boyfriend? Is he thinking about the future? Can you put your hand on your heart and tell me that?"

"Yes, I can. He is thinking . . ." Sonoka's voice lacked conviction. She could feel herself flushing.

"What exactly is he thinking? How long do you plan to stay in this apartment? Have you got a plan to move somewhere else? Forgive me, but this is hardly the right kind of place for a couple to live long term. And what are his plans for you? I don't regard marriage as the be-all and end-all, but he still needs to take a clear stand on the future. Am I wrong?"

"He's promised to sort himself out," Sonoka said, her eyes fixed firmly on the floor.

"Oh, and how's he planning to do that? Come on, is the guy even doing any work at all? I'm no expert, but I bet you that free-lance video production is no walk in the park. It's not something you can do in a sloppy, slapdash way. What has he been working on recently? Has he said anything to you? I'm prepared to bet he hasn't."

Nae's words struck Sonoka like hailstones. Unable to counter any of the criticisms, she could only keep staring at the floor.

That didn't mean she was willing to be honest with Nae either. Doing so would be to negate her own life up till then. As far as she was concerned, she'd made a good go of living alone since Chizuko's death.

Feeling cornered, she burst out, "Leave me alone!"

"What did you say?"

Sonoka raised her head.

"I told you to leave me alone. I have my own view of things. It's not like I'm not thinking about the future. I trust my boyfriend and I believe that things will work out fine for him eventually. Stop criticizing me. Give me some space. I am not Chizuko. Maybe you were a mother figure for Chizuko, but that's not what you are for me. For me, you're just another person, nobody special, a stranger."

Sonoka had never spoken so aggressively to anyone in her life. She was well aware that her final remark would cause Nae genuine pain. Sure enough, the old woman sank into a dejected silence.

The atmosphere was intensely uncomfortable.

Sonoka quickly realized that she had been much too brutal, especially given all that Nae had done for her. She started casting about for something conciliatory to say.

Just at that moment, the front door opened.

No random person would come barging into the apartment like that. Sure enough, it was Uetsuji. Startled at the sight of an old lady he had never seen before in his life, he just stood there and didn't utter a word. Then he turned and gazed piercingly at Sonoka, as if to say, "Who the hell is this person?"

"This . . . this is Nae Matsunaga." Sonoka made the introductions. "I've told you about her. She did a lot for my late mother."

That was true. She really had told Uetsuji about her.

Uetsuji grunted. His face suggested he remembered.

"She just dropped in out of the blue."

"She did, eh?" The tension went out of Uetsuji's face and he slipped off his shoes. "Sonoka has told me all about you. You have been incredibly helpful to her. She even said that most of the reason she's happy now is because of you. That's quite a compliment! Right?"

Sonoka couldn't recall ever having said anything like that, but she felt obliged to play along. "Right," she said, nodding.

"You really said that?" Nae directed a meaningful look at Sonoka.

"I'm guessing that you popped by today to see if Sonoka was living a proper and respectable life. Am I right?" said Uetsuji. His tone was jocular and there was a smile on his lips.

"Oh no, it was nothing like that. I was nearby, so I thought I'd drop by." Nae forced a smile and rose to her feet. "I really had no business coming. All right, Sonoka. See you soon, I hope."

Sonoka nodded and said nothing.

Nae left. The door banged shut behind her. They could just about make out the sound of her footsteps as she made her way down the exterior staircase. The moment the sound died away, Uetsuji kicked over the chair Nae had been sitting on. "You shouldn't have nodded along like that."

"Wha . . . What do you mean?"

"You shouldn't have nodded like an idiot when she said, 'See you soon.' Why didn't you tell the old bat to never show her stupid face here again?"

"Aa . . . ," gurgled Sonoka.

She was mystified. She had no idea why Uetsuji was so angry.

"More importantly, what do you think you're doing inviting people round here without getting the okay from me first? You think that's normal?"

"What can I do? She just turned up at the door. . . ."

"You tell her to piss off. Tell her you're in the middle of something, that you're busy. There's any number of excuses. Why didn't you send the old bag packing?"

"Sorry. It never occurred to me. She's an old friend and she's always been kind to us. . . ."

"Kind to your mother, you mean. She's never done damn all for you, has she? And is she doing anything for you now? Has she given you any money? What's she doing for you? Well?"

"No, you're right. . . . She's not helping me right at this moment."

"See what I mean? So cut the bitch loose. I don't want you to let her in again. And don't go meeting her outside the house either. Block her calls. You got that?"

"You really hate Nae . . . you really hate her that much?"

"I hate her frickin' guts. And I bet she hates me back. I know she wants you to leave me. Well? Am I right?"

Sonoka was taken aback at Uetsuji's remark. He was quite right. His ability to sense Nae's opinion of him within seconds of meeting her for the first time showed that making snap judgments as to whether people were for or against him was second nature to him.

"She was asking about our future," Sonoka mumbled. "'Is your boyfriend thinking seriously about the future?' sort of thing."

"And what did you say?"

"I said that you definitely were."

"You did, huh? What did the old bat have to say to that?"

"She started asking about your work."

"My work?"

"She wanted to know if I'd asked you if you really were working and what sort of projects you'd been working on recently."

"What did you say?"

Sonoka said nothing. Since she hadn't given Nae an answer, she had no way of giving one to Uetsuji either.

She felt a blow. Next thing she knew, she was sprawled on the floor. Her right cheek was taut and burning. He had hit her. It took a moment or two for the pain to come.

"Why couldn't you give her a proper answer? Why didn't you come out and tell her that I'm working on all sorts of things? You know I am. Like now, today, I just got back from a meeting. So why couldn't you give her a proper answer? Come on, tell me. Why? Why?"

Uetsuji grabbed Sonoka by the shoulders and started shaking her furiously. As he shoved her from side to side, she began feeling nauseous.

"I don't know . . . ," she just about managed to say.

"You don't know? What don't you know?"

"Why I didn't give a proper answer. I honestly don't know. I should have answered her question properly. I'm sorry."

Tears welled up and dripped down her cheeks. In one part of her brain, she was wondering why she was crying. She put that thought to one side.

Uetsuji stared into Sonoka's face, then hugged her hard.

"I need you to remember something: for me, keeping what we've got together is the most important thing in the world. It's all I think about. No one else even cares. No one. So you shouldn't trust anyone except me."

"I know. You're right. I'm grateful."

She was oblivious to the abnormality of thanking someone who had punched her in the face just a minute earlier.

After that day, everything changed.

Uetsuji had always been critical of Sonoka's behavior, but the volume of criticism rose dramatically. He forbade her to leave the apartment for anything other than work. When she did get permission from him to go out, she wasn't allowed to do anything she hadn't cleared with him in advance.

Uetsuji hated Sonoka seeing other people. Even when she was with her high school girlfriend Maki Okatani, he used to bombard her with texts asking her when she was coming home. When she got back, he would bombard her with questions about what the two of them had done and what they had talked about. To top it all, he would ask her why she even enjoyed meeting her old friends. If she made the mistake of saying that it made for a nice change, he would accuse her of suggesting she felt trapped with him and start beating her up. The more restrictions he imposed on her, the more violent he became.

There was no way that the situation was normal or healthy. Sonoka, however, interpreted everything as an indication of just how much Uetsuji loved her. Even now, she was uncertain if she'd bought into the fantasy, or if she'd just forced herself to believe it.

Hearing a thump behind her, Sonoka snapped out of her daydream and turned around. Nae was coming out of the next-door room, pulling a large suitcase behind her.

"Are you going somewhere?" Sonoka asked.

"We're moving," Nae said.

"Moving?"

"We're getting out of here, Sonoka. Hurry up and pack. I want us to be out of here within the hour."

Although Nae's voice was calm, Sonoka knew she was only trying to keep her from panicking.

Sonoka reached for the remote and switched off the TV. What was going to happen to them? She had no idea, but she'd made her mind up. She wasn't going to think. She was just going to do exactly what Nae told her, which meant shutting up and going along.

13

The monitor flickered on. A light brown building appeared on the screen. With a long frontage and more than ten stories tall, it was much larger than Kusanagi had been expecting.

"The place looks new. When was it built?" It was Director Mamiya asking the question. He was sitting diagonally behind Kusanagi.

Kusanagi glanced to his right. "Utsumi?" he said.

"The building is thirty-one years old," Kaoru Utsumi said, checking on her smartphone. "Sixteen years ago, it underwent a major refit and the exterior was renovated."

"Interesting. Well, it's a grand-looking place for its age," Mamiya said with a note of surprise in his voice.

"It dates from the bubble economy of the late 1980s. I suppose it's got all sorts of fancy facilities?" Kusanagi was addressing Utsumi again.

"It's got a hot spring, a gym, and a swimming pool. There used to be a restaurant as well."

"It's almost like a hotel. What's the monthly maintenance fee?" It was a trivial detail, but Mamiya seemed to think it important.

"Fifty thousand yen," Utsumi said.

Kusanagi caught Mamiya's eye and shrugged his shoulders.

No big surprise for a building that went up in the go-go years. Even if the capital value goes through the floor, the maintenance costs don't go down with them.

He glanced at his watch. It was just before 3:00 P.M.

"Can I give the order, Director?"

"Your call."

Kusanagi moved his face closer to the PC's microphone. "Kishitani, can you hear me?"

"Loud and clear," came a voice from the built-in speaker.

"The video feed is working fine. Go on in. Keep the camera on."

"Roger that. We're going in."

Kusanagi looked at the monitor. He could see a back view of Kishitani as he approached the building. One of the two junior detectives he had sent with him must be handling the camera. Normally, he would have dispatched a larger group. On this occasion, however, they were dealing with a couple of women, one of whom was an old lady. They were unlikely to put up much of a fight.

Kishitani was in Yuzawa in Niigata Prefecture. He and his team were about to go into a luxury resort apartment block a few minutes' walk from the rail station. The police believed Sonoka Shimauchi and Nae Matsunaga were inside.

After hearing from Kaoru Utsumi that the Matsunagas were frequent visitors to a resort apartment, Kusanagi had ordered his team to start looking for the place. The apartment's owner was thought to be a university ski club buddy of Nae Matsunaga's late husband, Goro. The team found out which university he'd attended, got hold of the old ski club membership rolls, and called all his contemporaries. The questions they put to them were simple enough: Do you own a holiday apartment? What sort of use do you make of it? Do you let other people use it? They were careful not to reveal that their inquiries had any link to a criminal case and had a plausible cover story ready to fend off any awkward questions.

This morning, they had located someone who seemed to fit the bill. The director of a company based in Tokyo, he owned a holiday apartment in Yuzawa, which he allowed the Matsunagas to use. Since it was a chore to physically hand them the keys every time they went, he'd given them a spare set and told them they were welcome to use the place whenever they wanted. According to the investigator who had spoken to him, the friend was an elderly man with bad legs who could no longer ski. Since he had no intention of living in the apartment, he'd put it for sale but was unable to find a buyer. The place was just sitting there, he explained.

Kusanagi ordered the investigator to get hold of the key along with permission to search the apartment. When the investigator explained that they thought that Nae Matsunaga, who was suspected of involvement in a criminal case, could be making use of the place, the owner handed over the key. Kishitani and his two subordinates set out from the incident room a couple of hours ago.

Is this the light at the end of the tunnel? Kusanagi's heart was racing as he looked at the monitor. Finding and securing both women would enable them to bring the investigation to a conclusion. He was confident of that. That was why he'd suggested to Director Mamiya that he come and watch the live stream with him.

Kishitani was now in the outer lobby of the apartment block.

An image of the metal panel with the buzzers for the different apartments filled the screen.

"I don't need to ring the bell, do I, Chief?"

"Of course not. You've got keys. Go straight on in."

"There's a superintendent. Should I say anything to him?"

"No need. Just act normally."

"Yes, sir."

Kishitani, who had on earphones with a built-in microphone, was communicating with them by phone. It was much less conspicuous than a two-way radio.

Kishitani unlocked the door and went into the lobby. Kusanagi swallowed. *This was it.*

Kaoru Utsumi reached out and placed a paper cup in front of him. An aroma of coffee wafted up his nostrils. "Chief, you've got to stop jiggling your leg. . . ."

"Oh, sorry, was I?" Kusanagi slapped his right leg. It was a bad habit of his when he was nervous. He'd told his subordinates to call him out if they ever caught him doing it.

He picked up the cup and took a sip of coffee, keeping his eyes on the screen.

Kishitani and the two junior detectives were making their way through the entrance hall. It had a huge, framed painting on one wall and a little fountain in the middle. The fountain was not working.

They were now in the elevator lobby. The apartment they wanted was on the ninth floor. They all piled into the elevator, and Kishitani pressed *9*.

The screen went black. There was no mobile signal in the elevator.

"We've not seen a single resident," Utsumi murmured.

"That's true," Kusanagi replied. No one else had shown up in the camera footage. Given that it was neither high summer nor the ski season, that was no great surprise.

The stream resumed. Kishitani was now out of the elevator and on his way down the interior corridor. The dark carpet looked expensive despite the slightly degraded video image.

Kishitani stopped in front of a dark wooden door. There was a number on the door but no nameplate.

"We are outside the apartment," Kishitani whispered.

"I can see that. Try ringing the bell."

"I am now ringing the bell."

Kusanagi watched as Kishitani pressed the button on the intercom. He caught the faint sound of a chime.

Kusanagi leaned forward in his chair. Would anyone answer? Would anyone open the door? Even if they saw Kishitani through the peephole, it would make no difference. The apartment was on the ninth floor. They couldn't very well escape through a window!

"No reply, sir," Kishitani said. "I'll try again."

"Go ahead."

Kishitani's finger pressed the button for a second time.

It was the same again. No sound from the speaker. No sign of anyone opening the door.

Kishitani pulled off his earphones and pressed his ear to the door for a few seconds, then he stepped back from the door and put the earphones back in.

"Hear anything?" Kusanagi asked.

"Nothing. I don't think there's anyone inside."

Had they gone out? If they had popped out somewhere, then at some point they would have to come back. Kishitani and his team would need to find a discreet place where they could lie in wait. For now, though, checking the inside of the apartment was their top priority.

"Kishitani, I want you to unlock the door and go in."

"You're sure, Chief?"

"It's okay. We've got the owner's permission."

He could see Kishitani turning the key in the lock. Kusanagi took a swig of coffee to keep his impatience at bay.

The door was open. Kishitani and his subordinates removed their shoes and went in. They didn't want to leave any footprints.

The interior of the apartment was dark. Someone must have found the switch, as the lights suddenly came on. Given that it was daylight outside, the place must be fitted with blackout curtains, Kusanagi reflected.

The monitor showed a living room with sofas and armchairs and a dining table behind them.

Kusanagi glanced rapidly around the room. He was looking for evidence of someone being there. From what he could see on the screen, there was none.

"What about the other rooms?"

"We'll take a look, Chief." Kusanagi slid open the door that led to the next room as he said this.

The room contained two large beds. Both neatly made up and covered with bedspreads.

Kusanagi heard Mamiya groan behind him. "What is this farce, Kusanagi?"

Kusanagi moved his face closer to the built-in microphone. "Give the place a thorough going-over. Try and find something, anything—shoes, items of clothing, whatever." He could hear the hoarseness in his own voice.

Kishitani opened the closet. There was a small set of shelves and some drawers. He pulled them open.

"Nothing here, sir."

"How about the trash?"

Kishitani reached for the trash can beside the bed and wordlessly presented the inside of it to the camera. It was empty.

"Try the bathroom."

"Yes, sir," Kishitani said. He went out into the passage, then switched on the light in the area with the washbasin, which led to the bathroom. Kishitani pushed open the bathroom door.

"What about the floor? Is it wet?" Kusanagi asked.

"It's dry, sir. The room's got a ventilator, so it would only need a couple of hours to dry." Kishitani squatted down as he said this. He appeared to be checking the plughole in the floor. "No residue. Not even a single hair."

Kusanagi clicked his tongue and stamped his foot on the floor. Had they been completely wrong about Sonoka Shimauchi and Nae Matsunaga hiding out there?

From the speaker, he could hear someone calling to Kishitani. "Boss!" One of the junior detectives came in from the passageway and handed something to Kishitani.

"What's going on?" Kusanagi asked.

Kishitani held the thing up to the camera lens. It was a piece of transparent cellophane. "It looks like a sandwich wrapper. And there's a label with a best-before date."

Kusanagi leaned forward. "What does it say?"

"2:00 A.M. this morning."

The screen showed an image of the building's outer lobby. Two women appeared at the back end of the lobby and then made their way outside. With both of them wearing hats and surgical masks, their faces were impossible to make out. There was, however, one thing they couldn't hide: their luggage. One of the women was pulling a large rolling suitcase and the other had a duffel bag.

"Pause it there," Kusanagi said.

Kaoru Utsumi paused the image.

They were examining the security camera footage from the Yuzawa apartment. Kusanagi had instructed Kishitani to look through all the footage for the time when Nae Matsunaga and Sonoka Shimauchi were likely to have left the building. He had found them and emailed them the data. The time stamp was 5:10 P.M. from the day before.

Kaoru Utsumi slid two printouts in front of Kusanagi. Still frames from the security cameras at Nae Matsunaga's Tokyo apartment, they showed the older lady and Sonoka Shimauchi on their way out.

"The suitcase and duffel look the same to me," said Kaoru Utsumi quietly.

Kusanagi nodded, then called Kishitani on his cell phone.

"It's me. Listen, the security camera footage you sent us. It's definitely them."

"I thought so. We spoke to the superintendent. He said he saw them from time to time over the last few days. He doesn't know when they arrived, so we're busy trawling through the security camera footage looking for that."

They'd almost certainly gotten there the same day they'd left Tokyo. Having access to a good hideout might have been a factor in their decision to go on the run.

"Did you check the building's trash bins?"

"We did. Unfortunately, the trash was taken away this morning."

"I see. . . ."

The important questions were why they had left and where they had gone.

"I want you to go to the nearest train station and take a good look at any CCTV footage they've got there. I've already called and cleared it with the local police."

"Yes, sir."

After ending the call, Kusanagi sighed and glanced sideways. His eyes met those of a glum-faced Kaoru Utsumi.

"Something on your mind?"

The woman detective looked back at him meaningfully.

"I think you're the one with something on your mind, Chief."

"What d'you mean?"

"Exactly what I said. You should come out and say what's on your mind. It's much healthier."

"I'm going to throw that right back at you. Utsumi, this is an order from a superior officer. If there's something you want to say, then say it."

Kaoru Utsumi creased her brow slightly, then nodded as if to encourage herself. She started to speak.

"I gave you my report about the Matsunagas having made frequent use of a resort apartment yesterday morning. Correct me if I'm wrong, but I think it was about 11:00 A.M."

"That's right."

"Nae Matsunaga and Sonoka Shimauchi vacated their holiday apartment roughly six hours later. There's something about the timing that strikes me as a little too good to be true. What do you think, Chief?"

Kusanagi crossed his arms and looked around. No one else seemed to be listening.

"You mean you think someone tipped them off? Told them the cops had figured out the holiday apartment angle?"

"It seems a reasonable assumption to make. A lot more likely than one of them just deciding it was a good time to move on right before the police were about to swoop down on them."

"Assuming you're right about that, there's only a limited number of people who could have tipped them off."

Kaoru Utsumi shook her head very deliberately from side to side.

"It's not a limited number of people. There's only *one* person. You know that as well as I do, Chief."

The sharp gleam in Utsumi's eyes left Kusanagi at a loss for words. Instinctively, he looked away. Just at that moment, his phone started to vibrate. It was one of his subordinates whom he had sent out into the field.

"Kusanagi here. How'd it go?"

"I've been showing the photograph of Hidemi Negishi to the residents of Dolphin Heights, Sonoka Shimauchi's apartment building. I found a woman who claims to have spoken to her about one month ago. She's a married woman and lives on the floor beneath Sonoka Shimauchi at the opposite end of the building."

Kusanagi's grip on his phone tightened. "How solid is this?"

"Pretty solid. Among other things, the woman recalled being impressed at how nicely made-up Negishi was for her age."

That sounded convincing. Kusanagi nodded.

"So what was Negishi doing there? What did the two of them talk about?"

"The neighbor was heading out to the shops, when a strange woman called out to her and stopped her. She asked her if she knew the couple who lived in the apartment at the far end of the floor above. She said that she knew them by sight but had not actually spoken to them. She was keeping her distance because the man looked like a nasty piece of work. When the other woman asked her why she had that impression, she said that she didn't know much about it herself, but the lady in the apartment right beside theirs had told her that he often beat the girl up."

"Anything else?"

"That's their conversation in a nutshell. The other woman tried to ask the neighbor more questions, but she was eager not to get involved. She just kept saying that she didn't know anything, then beat a retreat."

"Have you a precise date and time for their meeting?"

"The neighbor wasn't too sure. She reckoned about a month ago."

"I see. . . . Did you speak to everyone in the building?"

"There are a couple more apartments to cover. No one is at home right now. We'll just have to wait."

"Okay. Keep up the good work."

Kusanagi ended the call and relayed what he had just learned to Kaoru Utsumi.

"It fits with what I heard at the flower shop in Ueno. About Hidemi Negishi coming to the shop looking for Sonoka Shimauchi on her day off. About her asking the manager all sorts of questions about how Sonoka had been doing lately. That also happened about a month ago."

"Hidemi, the mama-san, eh . . . It does seem that we'll need to factor her into the equation. But what's the connection between her and Nae Matsunaga going on the run with Sonoka Shimauchi?"

"Chief, what are you going to do about that other thing?" Kaoru Utsumi asked. "About the person who gave Nae Matsunaga the tip-off?"

Kusanagi started to massage his left shoulder with his right hand, while rotating his head. There was the sound of bones cracking. Since his promotion to chief, Kusanagi had a terrible problem with pain in his neck and shoulders.

"This is nice timing. We can kill two birds with one stone." As he said this, Kusanagi pulled out his cell phone. Before tapping the screen, he glanced at Kaoru Utsumi. "I want you to go to the flower shop in Ueno. There's something I need you to check."

14

Kusanagi pressed the button to summon the elevator and turned around. Yukawa was inspecting the row of plaques on the wall with great interest.

"Getting nostalgic?" Kusanagi said.

"I was just thinking that I've not been to a place like this for years. Probably not since you took me with you to that weird place, the club with the clairvoyant hostess. That's got to be my last time."

"The clairvoyant hostess. I remember her."

That was many years ago. Kusanagi couldn't remember how Yukawa had seen through the trick the hostess was using to fake clairvoyance. He'd even forgotten what the trick was. What he did remember was that the hostess had been murdered and that Yukawa's puzzle-solving skills had helped them solve the crime. And that was far from the only occasion. His physicist friend had helped him out more times than he could count.

As soon as they reached the tenth floor and emerged from the elevator, the same energetic greeting rang out: "Good evening, gentlemen." A suit marched over to them.

"Mr. Kusanagi, what a nice surprise to see you back so soon," he said obsequiously, before glancing over Kusanagi's shoulder.

"There are two of us today. We'd like to be seated in or near a corner of the club. And we need to see Hidemi, the mama-san. Don't send any girls over while we're waiting."

"Very good, sir. Recently, Hidemi Mama has been coming in almost every day. She should arrive any minute now."

"Great."

He escorted them to a table at the back that overlooked the whole club. It was the reserved seating for VIPs. It was empty but it was still early. The suit must have intuited that Kusanagi's business wouldn't take long and that they would be leaving before the real VIPs arrived.

A younger man, also in the regulation black suit, brought out Kusanagi's personal bourbon bottle.

"No, give me an oolong tea."

The suit nodded.

"You're off the booze?" Yukawa asked.

"I'm not going to drink today. I may have to go to HQ after this. But that's no reason for you not to indulge."

"That's precisely what I intend to do."

Yukawa ordered himself a whiskey and soda.

"How's the investigation coming along?" Yukawa asked after the suit who had delivered his drink was a certain distance away from the table.

"'Well' would be an exaggeration, but we're starting to see light at the end of the tunnel. A bit of a hazy light, I admit."

"Do you still regard Nae Matsunaga as a serious suspect?"

"Our position on her hasn't changed. She's disappeared, taking Sonoka Shimauchi with her, and is deliberately staying off the grid. It's hard to think she's not involved."

"I don't disagree."

"Glad to hear it."

"Aren't you forgetting one important thing, though? If those two women are the perpetrators, then their running off and hiding is an utterly meaningless thing to do. At some point, they're going to run out of money. Do you think they intend to keep running until they literally starve to death?"

"I doubt it. They've got to have a plan."

"What kind of plan exactly?"

"That I don't know. But let me tell you what I think is likely going on. The two women may not be acting entirely on their own initiative. There could be another person in the background, pulling the strings." Kusanagi looked directly into Yukawa's eyes as he said this.

The eyes behind the wire-framed spectacles didn't even flicker.

"Ha. That's interesting. What gave you that idea?"

"It's confidential information pertaining to the investigation. I'm not at liberty to say."

"Okay. Well, that's that, then."

Yukawa's gaze was now directed somewhere over Kusanagi's shoulder. He swiveled around. Hidemi Negishi was gliding toward them, dressed in a kimono.

"Ah, Mr. Kusanagi. You kept your promise! I'm delighted to see you here again."

Hidemi sat down opposite them.

"With work affording me an excuse to visit a fancy club like this, I'd be a fool to pass up the opportunity. Let me do the introductions: this is Manabu Yukawa, a friend of mine from university."

"Is that right? Mr. Kusanagi is a dear old friend of mine." Hidemi was already proffering her card to Yukawa.

"Appearances can be deceptive. This fellow's actually a professor at Teito University."

"It's an honor to meet so distinguished a gentleman." Rising halfway to her feet, Hidemi moved her face closer in toward Kusanagi. "And what kind of girls does Professor Yukawa like?"

"That's easy. Good-looking ones. Get him something young and gorgeous."

"Coming up."

Hidemi summoned one of the suits and whispered a word into his ear. Kusanagi turned toward Yukawa and noticed that he was looking away. Was he pretending not to hear what they were saying?

A few moments later, a tall girl in a cream dress came over, introduced herself, and sat down on the banquette next to Yukawa. She was a stunner. Yukawa had to be feeling pleased.

"What about you, Mr. Kusanagi? Shall I get a girl for you too? Though if I'm not mistaken, you did say something a moment ago about using work as a pretext."

"Thanks, I'm good for now. I need to ask you a question. It's about our old friend Sonoka Shimauchi. I know this must be getting annoying, but please bear with me."

"It's fine by me. What do you want to know?"

"Last time we spoke, you told me that you hadn't had any direct contact with her. Was that actually true? Think carefully before you answer. Are you quite sure you didn't call her or go around to the flower store?"

Hidemi tilted her head thoughtfully to one side.

"Ah," she said. "It must have slipped my mind. Now you mention it, I *did* go to the flower shop in Ueno. Either last month or the month before. I was just curious to see how Sonoka was doing, you know. She turned out to be off work that day—she had a cold or something—so in the end I didn't get to see her."

"Last time I was here, didn't you say something about how going after someone who's jilted you was the height of inelegance?"

"It wasn't like that. It was a whim, nothing more."

"Are you sure? From what I heard, you asked the store manager a ton of questions about Sonoka—what hours she worked, if she'd been busy recently, stuff like that."

"I was just making conversation. It didn't mean anything. I should have mentioned my visit last time you were here, but it completely slipped my mind. Is that what you've come to check up on? Naturally, I'm delighted to see you, but I do think you're on a bit of a wild-goose chase."

"I don't think I am. You remember what I said about using work as a pretext?"

"I don't have a problem with that."

"Well, then, I have another question for you. It's about your first meeting with Sonoka Shimauchi. If I remember right, you said that you got Sonoka to pick out some flowers for a friend of yours who was giving a solo performance of French ballads?"

"Yes, right. What about it?"

"Where did your friend perform?"

"You want the name of the place? Let me see. . . ." Hidemi Negishi cast her eyes up to the ceiling. "No, I'm sorry. The name escapes me."

"What part of town was it? Around here in Ginza?"

"No," said Hidemi Negishi, frowning thoughtfully. "I don't think it was Ginza. Where on earth was it now . . . ?"

"Please! Are you telling me you went to the concert and can't even remember where it was?" Kusanagi said incredulously.

"I must be going gaga. But no, you're wrong. I didn't actually go."

"You didn't go? What do you mean?"

"My friend invited me. I was unable to go, so I sent flowers instead."

"Okay. Well, can you tell me your friend's name?"

"Her name? Uhm . . . Uchida. . . . No, Uchiyama. . . . No, no, it was Uchida. And her first name? Well, I described her to you as a friend, but the truth is, I don't really know her very well at all. I met her at a party hosted by a member of parliament. She just happened to be seated at the same table as me."

"You don't have her card?"

"Not on me, no. I could probably dig it up, if I had a look at home."

"Will you do that? And when you find it, give me a call." Kusanagi jotted down his personal cell phone number on his card and gave it to her.

"Will do," said Hidemi Negishi, putting his card into her handbag. "But what's this all about? Is there a problem with the concert?"

"No, nothing like that. As the police, we're part of the whole government bureaucracy. We have to be scrupulous about keeping full written records of every little detail, no matter how insignificant. Those are the rules."

"That's what this is all about? Goodness, how hardworking you policemen are." Hidemi Negishi placed her hands on her knees and bowed formally at Kusanagi.

"Have you two finished?" broke in Yukawa.

"For now, yes."

"Could I ask you a question, Mama-san?"

"Be my guest," Hidemi said. "What do you want to know?"

"It's about the name of this club. What does 'VOWM' mean? I tried to find the word in the English dictionary, and it wasn't there."

"Ah." Hidemi Negishi nodded. There was a smile on her face as she extracted a business card and a ballpoint pen from her handbag. "My customers often ask me the same thing. When I first launched this club, I swore to myself that I'd make a big success of it. When I looked up the equivalent expression in English, this is what I found."

She wrote the words "Make a vow" on the blank part of her card.

"So all I did was add an *m* to the word 'vow.' That's the origin of the club's name."

Craning forward to look at the card, Yukawa shook his head appreciatively from side to side.

"So that's where the name comes from. I must confess I'm a little surprised."

"How so?"

"I thought it had a Japanese root. I tried matching the name with different kanji characters."

"You did? But no, it's not Japanese. Sorry to disappoint you."

"Why did you think it was Japanese?" Kusanagi asked offhandedly.

"Like I said, it was just a feeling I had. No special reason. For-get about it."

Yukawa waved a hand dismissively and picked up his glass. Looking at his profile as he drank his whiskey and soda, Kusanagi was thinking that his physicist friend was unlikely to have brought up the subject for no reason.

"Well, if that business is out of the way, let me call over a girl for you, Mr. Kusanagi. You just relax and have yourselves a very pleasant evening."

"Good idea. We'll do that."

No sooner were the words out of Kusanagi's mouth than he felt a hand on his shoulder. It was Yukawa.

"Sorry to be a party pooper, but I've got to get going. I had fun. Thanks."

"What do you think you're doing? The fun's only just getting started. If you're doing this on my account, then don't bother. It's nothing to be proud of, but I can have a grand old time drinking nothing more than oolong tea."

"I had fun and I am *not* doing this out of consideration for you. I just remembered something important I need to do—Mama-san, I hope we will meet again in the not-too-distant future." Yukawa extracted his card from the inside pocket of his jacket as he said this.

Hidemi Negishi took it with both hands.

"I'm sorry to see you go. Please come back soon."

"There's not much point in me sticking around, if you're going to leave." Kusanagi swallowed the last of the oolong tea in his glass. "Mama-san, I'll pay the usual way."

"Oh, you're deserting us too, Mr. Kusanagi? Early again like last time."

"Next time I come, I promise it'll be for the long haul." Seeing Yukawa get to his feet, Kusanagi also stood up.

Like the time before, Hidemi Negishi escorted them down to street level to see them off. As they walked away from the building, Kusanagi shot a glance at the opposite sidewalk. A man in a suit stood in the mouth of an alleyway. He was the detective tasked with keeping an eye on Hidemi Negishi.

Kusanagi came to a stop as soon as they had gone around the first corner.

"Yukawa, bear with me, just for an hour. What you said in there about having something important to do—it wasn't true, was it?"

Yukawa gave Kusanagi a meek look.

"I wasn't making it up. I do have something important to do. I've got to get back and help care for my mother."

Kusanagi sighed.

"Oh, I see. Look, give me thirty minutes, then. I know a good coffee shop nearby. I'm buying."

"I can't have that. Let's go dutch."

"You don't want to be obliged to me even for that? Okay, your choice."

The café was on Gaien Boulevard. It was famous for its retro atmosphere and its iced coffee.

"This really is good," said Yukawa after taking a sip of the coffee. He was drinking it black without using a straw. "Amazing for an iced coffee to have this level of body and aroma."

"See? I knew you'd like it."

Yukawa put down his copper tankard and straightened his back.

"So what did you want to discuss? Let me be clear: in thirty minutes, I'm leaving whether you're done or not."

"Fine. I'll just come right out and ask you straight. How long have you been working with them? Right from the start? No, I doubt that."

Yukawa raised his right eyebrow. "What are you talking about?"

"Don't play the innocent. We've only got half an hour. Let's not waste time playing silly games. You contacted Nae Matsunaga and you warned her to get out of the Yuzawa apartment, didn't you?"

Yukawa used the tip of one finger to push his glasses higher on his nose. "Why should you think that?"

"Oh, it's straightforward enough. When the investigators I sent got into the holiday apartment this afternoon, the place was already empty. We located security camera footage of Nae Matsunaga and Sonoka Shimauchi leaving the place yesterday evening. We found out that the Matsunagas made frequent use of the holiday apartment of a friend of her late husband around midday yesterday. Utsumi called me to give me the news. It was only a few hours after that that Matsunaga and Sonoka made their move. It's just too much of a coincidence. I think we have grounds to assume that someone tipped them off, don't you?"

"What grounds have you got for accusing me?"

"Because you're the only person it can be. You were with Utsumi when she was told about the existence of the apartment. Plus, you're one of only a handful of people able to contact Mrs. Matsunaga."

Yukawa reached for his tankard and took a swig of iced coffee. Kusanagi decided to interpret his silence as assent.

"I've been feeling unsure about you ever since visiting you at your parents' place in Yokosuka. The way you became so cooperative all of a sudden. You may have a personal connection to Nae Matsunaga, but it shouldn't count for much, given that it's based on no more than a brief email exchange. Despite that, you made the trek out to the orphanage where Sonoka Shimauchi's mother used to work and then to Nae Matsunaga's old neighborhood. What is it you're looking for? What are you hiding from me?"

Yukawa put his tankard back down on the table and looked Kusanagi straight in the eye.

"I haven't double-crossed you. Nor have I impeded the investigation."

"Just stop it!" Kusanagi smacked the table.

The other customers were now all staring at them.

Kusanagi cleared his throat. "I'm shocked to hear you say that after helping Sonoka Shimauchi and Nae Matsunaga elude us," he said, lowering his voice.

"Sonoka Shimauchi is not a murderer. She has an alibi. And I hardly need to say that Nae Matsunaga didn't commit the murder either. Going after people like them is simply absurd."

"Then why are they on the run?"

"Because they don't want to be arrested."

"What? Just listen to yourself; you're talking nonsense."

"Okay, let me ask you a question. Do you genuinely believe that Sonoka Shimauchi and Nae Matsunaga are guilty of the murder?

You don't, do you? Your prime suspect is Hidemi, the mama-san of VOWM. Well? Am I wrong?"

Kusanagi scowled and scratched one of his temples. "Let's just say that she's a key suspect."

"And why do you suspect her?"

"Because I've caught her in a number of lies. Her relationship with Sonoka Shimauchi is much less straightforward as she's tried to make out. She told me that she had Sonoka pick out flowers for a friend of hers who was doing a concert. I got Utsumi to go over the shop's records. They haven't sent flowers to a single live-music venue over the last year."

"Just now she told you that she didn't actually go to the concert. That means she didn't deliver the flowers herself either."

Apparently, Yukawa had been eavesdropping on Kusanagi and Hidemi Mama's conversation at the club after all.

"Exactly. And she's concealing something else too. She went to Sonoka Shimauchi's apartment and quizzed her neighbors about her and her circumstances. Likely as not, that's when she learned that Uetsuji was a violent abuser. Still, none of that's grounds enough to say outright that she's the killer."

"What about motive?"

"Well, that's what I don't know. As you remarked to Utsumi, there's any number of other ways to save Sonoka from his abuse without resorting to murder. Right, I've answered all your questions. Now it's your turn to answer mine. I need to know what you're plotting."

Yukawa looked down at the floor, then lifted his eyes and looked at Kusanagi head-on.

"I promise that I'll tell you. I just need you to wait a little while longer."

"I can't do that. Not this late in the game. You remember the time I arrested you for obstructing a public servant in the discharge of his duties?"

Yukawa grinned. "Are you planning an encore?"

"I'm not joking, Yukawa."

"Nor am I." Yukawa unexpectedly placed both hands flat on the table with the palms downward. "I won't keep you waiting long. Just give me a little time. That's all I'm asking." As he said this, he made a deep bow.

Kusanagi was wrong-footed. He had never seen his friend do anything like this before.

"Yukawa. What are . . . ?"

He wanted to ask him what it was he wasn't telling him, but he pulled himself up short. Yukawa would never tell him. Instead, he just said, "There's no need to hold that pose forever. Listen, were you telling the truth just now, what you said about not having obstructed the investigation?"

"I swear it. And I swear I won't double-cross you."

"Okay." Kusanagi nodded. "I'm going to trust you on this one."

Yukawa smiled, then glanced at his watch.

"Turns out we didn't need the full half hour." He produced his wallet from his inside breast pocket and placed a thousand-yen note on the table. "It's been a fun evening," he said, getting to his feet.

Kusanagi watched Yukawa make his way out of the café, then pulled out his phone and called one of the preregistered numbers in his contacts lists. It was a junior detective who was nearby. The phone was answered immediately.

"Yes, sir?" said a voice.

"Where are you right now?"

"On the far side of the street outside the coffee shop you're in, sir."

"Yukawa should have come out."

"Yes, I can see him. He's walking away."

"Tail him and don't lose him."

"Copy that."

Kusanagi ended the call and picked up his tankard. Regardless of whether or not he trusted his friend, as a policeman, he still had a duty to perform.

15

Hidemi watched the elevator doors close on the last customer before she consulted her watch. It was almost 1:00 A.M. Officially, the club closed at midnight, but running late like this was nothing unusual.

Hidemi asked the floor manager to take care of closing the place, quickly got herself ready in the staff cloakroom, and then left the club. She took several deep breaths as she rode the elevator down. She had no way of knowing what was about to happen tonight but she wasn't expecting anything good. No, if anything happened, it was sure to be something bad. She prayed she would be able to deal with whatever was coming.

Hidemi exited the building and started making her way down the street. Because it was after one, she could easily pick up a cab without lining up at a taxi stand, but her destination was so close, she felt too embarrassed to take one.

The bar was down a side street off Chuo Boulevard. She had checked the location while at work, so she had no trouble finding the place. It was in the basement of a small building.

She went down the narrow staircase and opened the door. The interior was dimly lit. There was a counter with a barman standing behind it. "Good evening," he said, speaking softly.

Hidemi ran her eyes around the room. The person she had arranged to meet was sitting at a small table in one corner. No, "arranged to meet" wasn't the right expression.

"Sorry I'm late," Hidemi said.

"I thought you weren't coming." It was Yukawa, the university professor Kusanagi had introduced her to a few hours earlier. He had a grin on his face.

"I would never do that. Not when someone has handed me something as intriguing as this." Hidemi sat down opposite Yukawa, extracted a card from her bag, and laid it on the table. It was one of Yukawa's ordinary cards, but on a blank part of it he had scribbled the words: "I'll be in Bar Crossbow in Ginza after closing time."

A waiter came over and asked Hidemi what she wanted.

Hidemi looked at Yukawa's drink. He had a long, thin glass containing an amber liquid in which fine bubbles danced.

"What have you got there?"

"This? It's a highball—whiskey and soda. Ardbeg."

"I'll have the same, please."

"Very good, madam," the waiter said and went away.

Hidemi picked up the card from the table.

"When did you write this? I know you didn't do it when you were in my club. You didn't have the time for that there."

"That's very observant of you. I prepared it in advance. I didn't know if I was going to have to give it to you. It all depended on your answer."

"My answer? What do you mean?"

"I mean the explanation you gave me about the origin of the

name of your club. Had your explanation been a little more convincing, we could have postponed this meeting."

"You found it unconvincing?"

"What you said about it coming from the English expression
'to make a vow'—that was plausible enough. You never got around
to explaining why you had stuck an *m* on the end of the word. I
couldn't help feeling the whole thing was a bit far-fetched."

"What can I say? It was just a whim." Hidemi put Yukawa's card
back in her handbag.

The waiter came over and placed Hidemi's glass on the table.
She thanked him and took a sip. The smoky fragrance traveled
from her throat up to the back of her nose.

"There's an orphanage in Chiba. It's called Morning Shadows.
Have you heard of it?"

"Morning Shadows . . ." Hidemi haltingly repeated the name,
then tilted her head quizzically to one side. "No. No, I've not."

"Around six months ago, something funny happened there.
This woman claiming to be doing research on behalf of the police
showed up and started asking if the orphanage had gotten the proper
permissions from the people whose images it was using on its website. When the head of the orphanage insisted that they were doing
everything by the book, the woman conducting the research pointed
to one image in particular. 'I want to run a check on this individual
here. I need you to get in touch with her right away.' The orphanage
guy duly made the call and then handed the phone to the woman.
That's as far as things went—but what *is* strange is that the police
aren't actually conducting any such inspections. In other words, the
woman researcher was a fake. I wonder what that was all about."

"What does that have to do with me . . . ?" Hidemi gave a small shrug. Although confident that she could keep her anxiety out of her face, she still felt uncomfortable inside. "I have no idea what this is all about. What are you trying to say?"

"I think this next detail will probably pique your interest. The photograph the researcher picked out was a picture of Sonoka Shimauchi. In fact, it was a picture of Sonoka at primary-school age."

"Sonoka?" Hidemi frowned in puzzlement. "I wonder why."

Yukawa picked up his cell phone from the table, made a few taps and swipes, then showed the screen to Hidemi. "This is the picture in question."

Hidemi leaned toward him. It was a picture she had seen countless times, but she forced a look of surprise onto her face as if she were seeing it for the first time.

"That really is Sonoka. She was a pretty child. No surprise there."

"Sonoka's mother was working at the orphanage and Sonoka went to the orphanage's Christmas party. That's where this picture was taken." Yukawa put his cell phone back down on the table. "What do you think the woman posing as a police researcher was really after? If we look at things in purely practical terms, she got her hands on two solid pieces of information. First, that the name of the girl in the picture was Sonoka Shimauchi and, second, her contact details. It's logical to assume that the researcher's primary goal was to confirm the identity of the girl in the Christmas party photograph. The trick she used to elicit that information was pretty ingenious. The proof's very much in the pudding: no one at the orphanage was in the least suspicious of her. She had excellent acting skills and plenty of chutzpah. Could your normal, everyday person do what she did? No, her performance was one that no casual amateur could ever pull off. So here's my hypothesis: The woman was a professional. A professional whose specialty is checking on the identities of specific individuals at the request of clients. In other words, she was a private investigator."

"An investigator? Wow, this whole thing has taken a sudden turn for the dramatic! It's like a TV drama." Hidemi forced her mouth into a smile and raised her eyebrows in fake surprise. "University professors—I suppose telling stories is part of your job."

"Assuming that the woman was indeed a private investigator, then that begs the question of who her client was," Yukawa calmly proceeded, ignoring Hidemi's mockery. "I'm guessing it was someone who had come across the photograph of the party on the orphanage's website and wanted to discover the identity of the little girl. The girl in question is a pretty little thing about ten years of age. All right, so what sort of person does that make our someone?"

"Not anyone normal," Hidemi said. "Only a pervert would come up with a plan like that. Sadly, there's nothing uncommon about men with a thing for little girls falling for a girl they find online and then trying to track down their real identity."

"That's a perfectly reasonable suggestion. In this instance, though, it doesn't cut the mustard. Take a closer look in the picture and you'll see that one of the decorations on the Christmas tree is a set of four foil numbers indicating the year. From that, it's clear that the party took place more than a decade ago. While a pedophile might take a fancy to the girl in the picture, that girl is now a grown woman. The person who hired the private investigator was fully aware that it was an old photograph and *still* wanted to know the girl's identity. A pervert couldn't care less. Okay, so what was that person after?"

"Search me! I have no idea. I really can't understand why you're even bothering to tell me all this, Professor. To be quite honest, I'm a little—no, I'm totally baffled."

Yukawa tapped his phone a few times and then turned the screen toward Hidemi. The image showed Sonoka in close-up, or, more specifically, the doll she was clutching to her chest. Hidemi felt her pulse starting to race.

"Whether the photo had been taken ten or even twenty years ago made no difference to the person in question. And I will tell you why. People change with the passage of time, but dolls do not. What interested that person was not the girl, it was the doll she's holding."

"Why? What's so special about the doll?" The skin of Hidemi's face tightened and she was unable to keep the tremor out of her voice.

"I went to Morning Shadows myself and I asked a few questions about the doll. I discovered that it was Sonoka's prized possession and that she always brought it with her when she went to the orphanage to play with the children there. I also learned that the doll didn't originally belong to Sonoka; it was something that her mother had passed on to her. Sonoka's mother was a woman by the name of Chizuko. Chizuko had herself been brought up in Morning Shadows because she was an orphan with no extended family. What Sonoka is holding in the photo is a handmade doll that had once been her mother's most prized possession. That in turn begs the question, why was the investigator's client so interested in that doll? I have a theory that I'd like to share with you. I think her client was the person who made the doll long ago!"

Hidemi said nothing. She gazed blankly into the middle distance.

For a moment, everything seemed to have gone silent. The whole world seemed to have ground to a stop. She wished that it really had. She wanted everything to freeze and stay still forever.

It didn't look as if the stern professor opposite would let that happen.

"Very soon after the investigator's visit to the orphanage, something happened in Sonoka's life. This woman who approached her. I understand she told Inspector Kusanagi that she did so because she wanted to offer Sonoka a job at the club she ran. Is that the truth, though? I suspect her real motivation was something quite different."

"What do *you* think it was?" Hidemi asked. Things had reached the stage where she was desperate to see how much this man knew about her.

"She wanted answers to some questions she had. Where had Sonoka gotten the doll from? Where was the doll's original owner now? Ms. Negishi—" Yukawa addressed her softly by name as he pointed at the screen of his phone. "Be honest with me. This doll in the picture—you made it, didn't you?"

Hidemi stared into Yukawa's handsome face. Rather to her surprise, she felt herself growing calmer with every passing second.

"Why should you think that?"

"Because of the name."

"What name?"

"This doll has a name. One of the staffers at the orphanage told me about it. Sonoka had told her what it was. The doll has a secret name. If you undress it, you'll find its name written on its back. It's written with these characters."

Yukawa took a small piece of notepaper out of his inside breast pocket and placed it in front of Hidemi. On it were written the two kanji characters: 望夢.

"I don't know what sex the doll is meant to be. If it was a boy, this name would be pronounced 'Nozo*mu*'; 'Nozomi' if it was a girl. I suspect that this was the name the parents planned to give their child before it was born. Ultimately, the child was a girl, but 'Nozomi' wasn't the name she ended up with. The name, however, got a second lease on life a very long time later when a certain nightclub opened in Ginza. The club wasn't called 'Nozomu' or 'Nozomi'; instead it was called *VOW-MU*, based on the Chinese, rather than the Japanese readings of the characters."

Hidemi burst out laughing. She found what Yukawa was saying genuinely comical. It wasn't because she thought his theory was silly. Far from it. The fact that a smart man could so easily unravel the secret she'd kept for decades made her look ridiculous.

"What an imagination you have! Truly impressive." Hidemi clapped her hands ironically. "But have you got any proof?"

"If anyone wants proof, a simple DNA test is the quickest solution. We test the person who made the doll and the person who owns the doll. Either they're completely unrelated, or, should they be grandmother and granddaughter, the test is pretty definitive when it comes to second-degree relatives."

Hidemi took a deep breath.

"Why are you so keen to clear this up, Professor? What's in it for you?"

"I have my own reasons for wanting the case to be wrapped up as fast as possible. And as amicably as possible too. With the perpetrator turning themselves in, for example."

Hidemi stared intently into Yukawa's eyes.

"Are you saying I'm the perpetrator?"

"I have no proof of that. And I don't think the police have conclusive proof yet either. Kusanagi, however, suspects you. Starting tomorrow, though, he'll start taking aggressive measures like arresting you on some pretext or other and then searching your house. If he goes down that road, the police will probably force you to disclose the location data on your cell phone."

A search of my apartment won't turn up anything, Hidemi thought. Three days ago, she had also bought herself a new smartphone, though she wasn't sure whether the phone company would have retained the location history data from her old one. She vaguely remembered someone telling her that it depended on the make.

"To complicate things further, the police have got their eye on me."

"On you, Professor?"

Yukawa took a swig of his highball, put the glass back on the table, and moved his face in closer to hers.

"There's a man sitting at the far end of the bar. He came in a couple of minutes after me. Most likely he's a detective and he's tailing me. You're also being watched. There's probably a second detective outside."

Hidemi picked up her glass. Her throat was dry with anxiety.

"Forget about me for a moment. Why are the police interested in you, Professor?"

Yukawa adjusted his spectacles on his nose and grinned broadly.

"Because they think I hold the trump card they need to solve the case."

"What card is that?"

"*I know how to contact Sonoka Shimauchi.*"

Hidemi was so startled that she almost knocked over her glass.

"Sonoka? You? How come?"

Yukawa shook his head.

"I don't know, Ms. Shimauchi. I've never even met her. The person I know is the woman who has gone on the run with Ms. Shimauchi."

So there was someone else with her after all! Suddenly it all made sense to Hidemi. She had never believed that Sonoka had taken off on her own. Still . . .

"Who is this person, for God's sake?"

"You really have no idea?"

"None at all."

"If you don't know her, then there's no reason for me to tell you who she is. Let me just say this: it's a person I trust. The problem is, I can't hide this information from Kusanagi indefinitely. At some point, I will have to show him my trump card. As far as I am concerned, I'd prefer for the murder to be solved *before* that happens. And in the most amicable way possible."

That was the second time Yukawa had use that "amicable way" phrase. Hidemi guessed that was the particular message he wanted to get across to her.

"I suspect that Sonoka Shimauchi feels the same way," Yukawa went on. "She dropped out of sight to keep herself out of the hands of the police. My hunch is that she doesn't want to be the one to reveal the truth of what happened. I'm sure she's hoping that the real culprit will hand themselves in to the police."

Hidemi sighed. The urge to admit defeat was overwhelming. From the start, she'd known she wouldn't be able to fool everyone forever.

"Even if you admit under questioning to having committed a crime *after* they've launched a criminal investigation into you, you won't be seen as having turned yourself in voluntarily. There's a much better chance of your case being treated as a voluntary surrender if you turn yourself in *before* the police take any specific actions against you. Basically, what I am saying is this: if you plan to turn yourself in, then the sooner, the better."

Hidemi smiled and looked into Yukawa's face. "I appreciate the advice. Thank you."

"I'd appreciate it if you would make up your mind."

Hidemi looked serious again.

"I need time to think. Oh, and I have a favor to ask of you."

"What?"

"I want to speak to Sonoka—that is, if what you said about being able to get in touch with her was true, Professor."

Yukawa turned his gaze upon her. After moment or two, he solemnly nodded his agreement.

"I'll contact the woman who's with Ms. Shimauchi and get her to ask Ms. Shimauchi to call you. Please understand that I can't guarantee she will actually do so."

"That's fine. My phone number is on the card I gave you earlier."

Yukawa extracted her card from his inside jacket pocket.

"I said that I thought your explanation of the origin of the name 'VOWM' was rather far-fetched. To be honest, I was quite impressed with your creativity: that whole 'make a vow' thing."

"That's because my explanation wasn't far-fetched or contrived at all. When I set up my club, I did vow to make a success of it. That much is true."

"I'm sure you did. In that world of yours, only the paranoid survive."

"You're right about that."

Yukawa swallowed down the last of his highball, put his card away, and then pulled out his wallet.

"Let me pay," Hidemi said. "I would like to stay a little longer. Who knows when I'll next be able to come to a place like this?"

Yukawa's hand stopped mid-movement. He looked down, appeared to think for a moment, then nodded. "All right. That is very kind of you."

"This has been a very—what's the mot juste?—a very meaningful evening. Good night."

"Good night." Yukawa got to his feet.

Hidemi watched him leave the bar out of the corner of her eye. A moment later, the man at the bar slid off his stool and left. Yukawa was right about having a tail on him.

As Hidemi picked up her glass, the coaster beneath it caught her eye. It was decorated with some sort of bow and arrow. She quickly realized it had to be the crossbow in the bar's name.

The first time Hidemi had ever seen a cardboard coaster was at the bar where Hiroshi worked. They never used them, because they always met in the daytime before the bar was open and drinks were being served.

Hiroshi—Hiroshi Yano. With his broad back and his long limbs.

He was the father of the baby girl Hidemi had abandoned at the front gate of Morning Shadows. The girl whom she had intended to call Nozomi, written with the characters 望夢.

16

Despite having sacrificed her own daughter, Hidemi had no grounds for hope. Back in Tokyo, her future looked bleak. She quickly ran out of money and was evicted by the super when she couldn't pay the rent. If he was suspicious about the sudden disappearance of her baby, he kept his thoughts to himself. He didn't want to get involved.

It was at this point that the mama-san of the last bar where Hiroshi had been working came around to see her. The two women had barely spoken despite having run into each other a few times. They'd just exchanged a few words at the simple funeral service.

The mama-san said that she was worried about the baby.

"Last time we met, you were heavily pregnant. I was wondering how you were getting on. You had the baby, didn't you?"

Hidemi lied. She claimed that she had taken her infant daughter back to her parents, knowing that she would never be able to bring it up on her own. "Oh, really?" the mama-san said. From her tone, Hidemi couldn't tell if she believed her or not.

"Have you got a job?"

"No . . ."

"No?"

The mama-san looked intently at Hidemi, as if appraising her, then pulled a card out of her handbag.

"Do you fancy working here?"

Hidemi took the card. On it was printed the name of a famous establishment in Shinjuku. A nightclub.

"A friend of mine runs this place. She's always asking me if I know any suitable girls. What do you think?"

The question was unexpected and Hidemi was unsure how to respond. She'd never considered working in a nightclub. As someone who worked in that nightlife world, Hiroshi had done his best to keep her away from it. He set strict rules and forbade her to visit his bars during regular hours. He was worried about tipsy male customers forcing her to pour drinks for them.

But Hiroshi wasn't around anymore. She couldn't afford to be fussy. "I'll give it a go," she said after only a moment's hesitation.

Three days later, she made her debut in the Shinjuku club. The nighttime world was more glamorous and intriguing than she'd expected. There was plenty of heat and drama; at the same time, it was a cruel arena where a brutal fight for survival was always being waged. The ritual was always the same: the women and their male customers would size each other up and then join battle to catch their desired prey. In her first week on the job, Hidemi was slapped in the face by two of her fellow hostesses. She apologized profusely, despite having no idea what she was supposed to have done wrong. She was touched and groped by customers more times than she could count. Men routinely forced kisses on her in the elevator.

It wasn't easy, but she couldn't run away. She had no choice; she had to grin and bear it and push on with her life.

Over time, she slowly learned how to take care of herself and survive in this strange alternate universe. She learned how to drink in moderation and how to handle men. She was prepared to give herself physically, if it would advance her career. She was unsentimental about that. Several mama-sans she worked for told her she was a born hostess.

Time passed quickly. She was twenty-seven when she secured her first patron. The chief priest of a Buddhist temple, he was more than sixty years old. Wily and good-natured, he was a fun and stimulating person to be around. He was generous too, setting her up in a smart apartment and giving her tens of thousands of yen in pocket money every month. They even traveled abroad together.

The priest told her that, if she got pregnant, he was happy for her to have the baby. That never happened, though. Since he had a childless marriage, Hidemi reckoned that the problem was probably on his end.

Thinking about that always reminded her of her own baby daughter. If she was honest with herself, her baby was always somewhere in the back of her mind. *What is she doing now? Is she safe? Is she happy?* Though she often thought of going to the orphanage to check up on her progress, she never followed through. How could she possibly look her daughter in the eye after sticking her in such a place? She had no right.

Her relationship with the chief priest lasted until he died from a stroke at the age of seventy-two. A man claiming to be his executor came around and instructed her to pack up her things and be out of the apartment by the end of the month. When he left, he handed her an envelope containing ten million yen as a parting gift from the priest. This was at the very height of the economic boom of the '80s, so Hidemi wasn't all that surprised.

Not long before he passed, with the priest's financial backing, she'd opened a small club in Ginza called VOWM. It was a modest enough place, with just five or six hostesses, and Hidemi ran it well. When the priest asked her how she had come up with its name, she explained that it came from the English phrase "to make a vow." The priest approved. No one had any idea of the name's real origin.

Hidemi went on to have relationships with several other men. All of them had families of their own and none of them asked her to marry them. The last one had underworld connections. She'd never asked him what he did for a living, though at some point, he had let slip something about "handling exotic animals," so she guessed he was a smuggler of some kind.

This last boyfriend was the man with the illegal handmade gun. He claimed he carried it for his own protection. It was a completely different shape from a normal pistol and held only one cartridge, needing to be reloaded after every shot.

The boyfriend had invited her along when he tested it. Deep in the mountains of Okutama to the west of Tokyo, Hidemi had fired it at a tree. Her boyfriend laughed when the recoil flung her backward.

He stored the illegal gun at Hidemi's apartment. He took good care of it and kept it safely wrapped in oil paper. He taught Hidemi how to take it apart and clean it.

"I need it to be ready for use at all times," was what he always used to say. As far as Hidemi was aware, he'd never actually fired the thing in anger.

Then that particular boyfriend had disappeared. One day, he just disappeared from her life. The gun and the cartridges, however, remained safe in their secret storage space.

In this way, several decades passed in what felt like the twinkling of an eye.

Hidemi had just celebrated her sixtieth birthday when the breast cancer was detected. She opted for a mastectomy, thinking that she was unlikely to meet another man who would want to see or touch her body. The nasty scarring she was left with never failed to upset her. No matter how many years passed, she never got used to the sight of herself in the mirror. The ever-present fear of the cancer recurring depressed her. Every time she was tested, she would go into a funk, expecting the worst.

When she reached her mid-sixties, she handed over the running of the club to her staff and more or less stopped dealing directly with customers. Thanks to the support of her patrons, VOWM had expanded, while several other side ventures had also prospered, meaning that she had plenty of money squirreled away. She could retire whenever she wanted to. The thought of death occurred to her on a daily basis, but when it did, she always told herself that she'd lived a full life and had nothing to regret.

Nonetheless, there was something lurking at the back of her mind. It was the thought of the baby daughter she'd abandoned almost fifty years ago.

Hidemi knew how to search the internet. There was one particular website she liked to visit from time to time. It was the home page of Morning Shadows, the orphanage where she'd left her little girl. Although the site was not updated often, new pictures would be uploaded after special events. She enjoyed looking at the smiling faces of the children and letting her mind wander: *What sort of childhood did my little girl have? What kind of woman has she grown up into?* These conjectures were always accompanied with a generous helping of self-reproach.

On one occasion, one particular photograph caught her attention. It showed a girl in the upper years of primary school, but it was what the girl was holding that made Hidemi catch her breath sharply.

It was the doll. The doll with the long hair dressed in a blue-and-pink-striped sweater. She would have recognized it anywhere!

The photograph was from an old Christmas party. The date they gave in the caption was from more than ten years ago. That meant the girl in the picture would now be over twenty years old.

Hidemi shivered violently. *Who was the girl? Why did she have that doll?* Asking the orphanage was a dead end. They would only be suspicious and would never tell her.

Now she felt restless, unsettled. After much soul-searching, she decided to hire a professional. She located a detective agency and went to talk to them.

"So you want us to establish the identity of this girl here? Apart from her name and address, what else do you want to find out about her?" asked the head of the agency as he scrolled through the orphanage website on his computer.

"If you can, I'd like you to find out what her life is like . . . and anything about her personal background—her family, that sort of thing."

"This photograph was taken a long time ago, but you say it was only uploaded recently. Are you quite sure about that?"

"I'm sure. It certainly wasn't on the site last month."

"Good. That may give us a way in."

"What do you mean?"

"With an official website like this that belongs to an institution, they need to get permission from the people whose images they use. The fact that this picture was uploaded recently would suggest that permission for it was secured recently. They should have a record of some kind. We just need to get them to show it to us."

"Will they do that?"

"Normally, no, but figuring that sort of thing out is what this job's all about. It won't be a problem. We have all sorts of people on the payroll." The head of the agency seemed very confident.

Two weeks later, Hidemi had her result. The first page of the report they handed her gave the subject's name as Sonoka Shimauchi. Her current address was in Adachi Ward in eastern Tokyo. She was twenty-three and worked at a flower shop. She had lived out in Chiba until five years earlier. Sonoka hadn't actually been raised in the orphanage herself; she had just happened to have her photograph taken when she attended a Christmas party there.

Sonoka's mother had gotten sick and died a year ago. (The specifics of her condition remained unknown.) The key thing about the mother was her personal background. She had been raised at the Asakage-en orphanage. Since they hadn't managed to find a marriage record for her, she must be a single mother.

The mother's name was Chizuko Shimauchi. If she were still alive, she would now be forty-eight years old.

Hidemi began to tremble uncontrollably. Going from when

she had dropped her baby daughter off, the dates were a perfect match!

Sonoka was currently living with a man by the name of Ryota Uetsuji in an apartment in Adachi Ward. No details were given about him.

From that day on, Hidemi could only think of one thing. Chizuko Shimauchi had to be *that* baby, had to be *her daughter*. If that were the case, that would make Sonoka her granddaughter.

The investigator had taken some photographs of Sonoka at work at the flower shop. As Hidemi looked at the pictures, she felt that she could see something of herself and Hiroshi in the girl.

I want to meet this Sonoka. I want to meet her and clear things up, one way or the other. The feeling got stronger with every passing day. Her cancer might recur at any time. If it did come back, she might well not have long to live. She couldn't die leaving this half-done.

But if she made herself known to Sonoka and if Chizuko Shimauchi really was her daughter, then what would Sonoka think of her? Chizuko might well have said hateful things about the mother who had abandoned her.

It made no difference. One day, Hidemi just made up her mind to go and see her. She was ready: if the girl was aggressive, she would apologize.

She found the place. It was a decrepit old apartment building. As she walked along the main road, she could see the rows of doors. The apartment was number 201, so it was probably at the near end of the second floor. She pressed her hand to her chest, took a couple of deep breaths to calm herself, and began to climb the external staircase. But just at that moment, one of the doors on the second floor opened. It was the room at this end! A young woman emerged, turned around to say a few words to someone inside, closed the door behind her, and started walking toward her. Hidemi stopped in her tracks and looked away.

The young woman came down the stairs, walking right by Hidemi as she did so. Hidemi stole a glance at her profile. *There was no doubt about it. She was the woman in the photograph the detective had given her. She was Sonoka Shimauchi.*

Hidemi wanted to run after her, but her legs refused to obey her. Besides, she had no idea what to say to her. As she dithered, Sonoka disappeared.

Now she was angry with herself. *What the heck was she even doing?* She thought she was confident and ready; in fact, she was psychologically unprepared. She felt ashamed of herself. She wanted to burst into tears.

Just then, she heard a sound from the second floor. Glancing up, she saw a man coming out of Sonoka's apartment. *This must be Ryota Uetsuji, the live-in boyfriend.* He locked the door and descended the stairs.

Hidemi hurriedly got her breathing under control. *God was giving her a second chance!*

She looked hard at the face of the man who was now at the foot of the stairs. Conscious of her scrutiny, he was eyeing her suspiciously.

"Excuse me," she said. The man came to a halt.

"You are the gentleman who lives with Sonoka Shimauchi, aren't you? A Mr. Uetsuji, if I'm not mistaken."

The man looked at her warily. "That's right. Who're you?"

"I'm sorry to intrude like this. My name is Hidemi Negishi. This is who I am." Hidemi took one of her cards out of her handbag and handed it to him.

Uetsuji's face darkened.

"A nightclub? What's this all about? Are you trying to recruit Sonoka?"

"No, it's nothing like that. It's nothing to do with my work. I just have some personal questions for Sonoka. About her mother, in particular . . ."

"Sonoka's mother? Far as I know, she's dead."

"Yes, I know that. I'm hoping she can tell me something about her mother when she was alive."

The expression on Uetsuji's face was as wary as ever.

"What's your connection to her mother, then?"

"It's a long story. . . . Of course, if you happen to have the time?"

"What? Now?" Uetsuji's voice rose in surprise. "I know next to nothing about Sonoka's mother. Never even met her."

"Well, then, you can tell me about Sonoka instead. I have so many questions. Can't you help me? Naturally, I'd be prepared to make it worth your while. Please." She ducked her head in a series of little bows and nods.

Although Uetsuji was doing his best to appear reluctant, she could see that he was wavering. Perhaps she had piqued his curiosity. He checked his watch. "Okay, just a few minutes, though," he said.

They went into a nearby café and sat down across from each other.

"I'd like you to take a look at this," Hidemi said as she pulled up a picture on her phone. It was Sonoka at the Christmas party.

"This little girl here. This is Sonoka."

"It certainly looks like her. So that's what she was like as a kid."

"Have you ever seen the doll she's holding in the picture?"

Uetsuji took a closer look and then nodded.

"Sure. Sonoka has it in the apartment. The thing's ancient. I told her to throw it away. She said she couldn't possibly do that because it had belonged to her mother."

"Belonged to her mother . . ." Hidemi couldn't prevent her voice rising.

All the other customers turned to look at her.

"I'm sorry," Hidemi apologized to Uetsuji. "Is that true?"

"I can't really say. That's what Sonoka told me, though."

Hidemi felt a bit dizzy. It was too much excitement too fast. *She was right. Sonoka's mother was the baby she had abandoned way back when.*

She suddenly realized that she was crying. Uetsuji was clearly starting to feel uncomfortable.

"What's wrong with you? This is a bit . . . It's embarrassing."

Hidemi hastily dabbed her eyes with a handkerchief. "I'm sorry," she said. "That's the last thing anybody would want: an old lady bursting into tears."

"What's this all about?"

Under the circumstances, Hidemi felt that she had to tell Uetsuji the truth. Besides, if she wanted to take the next step, she would need his help.

"The truth is . . ." Hidemi began. She told him what she had done fifty years ago. She didn't hold anything back.

At the start, Uetsuji looked skeptical, but that changed when Hidemi explained how she had hired a detective agency to verify Sonoka's identity. His expression became serious and thoughtful. He now realized that the old lady sitting in front of him was not some raving lunatic. He nodded sympathetically as she explained that it was the fear of her cancer recurring that had made her want to track her baby daughter down.

"For her to have died a year ago—that was the last thing I could have expected. Still, if my baby daughter had a baby daughter of her own, then of course I want to meet her. That's why I'm here. I'm terribly sorry. I know I'm just being selfish."

Uetsuji sighed heavily. "This is quite a surprise," he said. "Like I said just now, I know nothing about Sonoka's mother. I did know that she had no family. So she was abandoned as a baby."

"I know what I did was stupid. At the time, I simply had no other options. . . ." Noticing the embarrassed expression on Uetsuji's face, Hidemi grimaced. "Sorry. You really don't want to hear me spout excuses."

"What do you want me to do?"

Hidemi drew herself upright on her chair, leaned forward a little, and looked into Uetsuji's eyes.

"It is a big ask, I know, but could you tell Sonoka about me? Tell her that you met the old woman who abandoned her mother at the orphanage?"

Uetsuji crossed his arms across his chest and grunted.

"Sure. I can do that. I know for sure she'll be surprised. She may have trouble believing it."

"Maybe she will . . ."

"And what's the next step after that . . . ?"

"I'd like you to tell me how Sonoka reacted when you gave her the news. If she gets really angry, don't be afraid to say so. There's no need to hide anything."

"Okay. I'll have a word with her. She may want nothing to do with you."

"Back then . . . you know . . ." Hidemi forced a smile. "What can I say? It's all my fault. Sonoka has every reason in the world to hate me. I will just walk away."

"I see," said Uetsuji. He was looking thoroughly miserable. She was probably forcing him to do something he didn't want to do.

Hidemi asked Uetsuji for his contact details. He gave her his cell phone number.

"Are you taking the day off today?" Hidemi asked.

"No, I work from home. I just popped out for a bit of air."

"Interesting. What line of work are you in?"

"Video production. I'm a freelance producer."

"Hence your working from home."

Although she found it hard to reconcile her image of video production with the shabby old wooden apartment building, Hidemi decided not to delve too deeply. Uetsuji was a key ally for her.

"Do forgive me. I've interrupted you at work and asked you to perform a difficult task." Hidemi took her purse out of her handbag and extracted a couple of ten-thousand-yen notes from it. "Properly, I should give these to you in a nice, clean envelope. I apologize. Treat yourself to a nice meal or something."

"Really, there's no need. . . ."

"It's the least I can do. Please, take it."

After a brief show of reluctance, Uetsuji took the money. "Well, if you insist."

From then on, Hidemi's emotions were in turmoil. How would Sonoka react when Uetsuji gave her the news? Would she be shocked and confused to learn that a woman claiming to be her grandmother had shown up at this late stage? For her not to want to meet with the person who had dumped her own child in front of an orphanage—that would be the most natural thing in the world.

Exactly one week later, Uetsuji called. He started by apologizing for being slow to get back in touch.

"Sonoka was very shaken, very confused, when I spoke to her. That's only to be expected. She really seemed to have no idea what to do. It took her a long time to settle down and get her feelings under control."

That's hardly a surprise, thought Hidemi. "How is she doing now?"

"She's much calmer. In fact, she says she wants to meet you."

At Uetsuji's words, Hidemi's heart missed a beat. "She does?"

"Yes, she does. 'If I have someone else who's family, then of course I want to hear what they have to say,' she said. So, what do you want to do?"

Hidemi did not hesitate. "I want to meet her. More than anything," Hidemi replied.

"Okay. Where shall we do it?"

Hidemi racked her brains. She couldn't think of a suitable place. She was uncertain how emotional she might become at the meeting. She didn't want to break down in tears in front of strangers.

Timidly, she suggested that the two of them should come to her place. "We can have a nice quiet chat here," she said.

"Fine," said Uetsuji. "That will work for us too."

Hidemi felt a wave of relief when he signaled his agreement.

The next day, Sonoka Shimauchi came to Hidemi's apartment with Uetsuji. Her face was tight, revealing her nervousness. Hidemi was pretty sure she looked just as tense herself.

She had Uetsuji and Sonoka sit on the sofa, while she sat with her knees tucked under her on the floor.

"Did you bring it with you?" Hidemi asked.

Uetsuji shot an encouraging glance at Sonoka beside him. She opened up her tote bag and extracted the handmade doll. She placed it gently on the table.

Hidemi reached out and picked it up. Her hands were trembling. *It was fifty years since she'd last touched it!* The thought was enough to move her to tears.

Although the colors were very faded, the blue-and-pink-striped sweater was still in one piece. She lifted it a little to inspect the doll's back. There they were, the characters 望夢 written in marker.

"This is the doll. I should know. I made it. Thank you for taking such good care of it." Hidemi looked intently at Sonoka.

"My mother often said that this doll was the one and only clue she had if she ever wanted to find her mother," Sonoka said. "That if they'd had the internet when she was young, she'd have uploaded a picture of the doll to see if anyone recognized it."

Hidemi clapped a hand in front of her mouth. She wasn't fast enough to suppress the sound of a sob. "I'm sorry, I'm so sorry," she kept saying.

"You don't need to say sorry," Sonoka said. "My mom didn't hate you or resent you. 'I'm sure my mother had her own very good reasons for doing what she did,' she always said. She always hoped to be reunited with you. Right up until the end."

"The end . . ."

Sonoka explained that Chizuko had died from a subarachnoid cerebral hemorrhage. Since Hiroshi had died from the same thing, Hidemi wondered if it was a hereditary condition.

"Listen, Sonoka, I don't want to force you to do anything you don't want to, but can we see one another in the future? I'd love to hear more about your mother."

"I'd like that too."

"Isn't this great, Sonoka?" Uetsuji chimed in. "You thought you were all alone in the world and now you've got a real grandma of your own. This is your chance. Let her spoil you."

"Uetsuji's right. Let me spoil you. I want to do everything for you that I couldn't do for my own daughter. Come around and see me whenever you want to. You're always welcome."

Fluttering her long eyelashes, Sonoka nodded her agreement.

After that first meeting, Sonoka started visiting Hidemi's apartment frequently. Hidemi found much of what Sonoka told her about Chizuko painful, but there were also a few heartwarming stories. As a child, Chizuko had never found life at the orphanage disagreeable, which is why she resolved to work there herself someday. In her case, "someday" meant after trying different jobs and then having Sonoka as the result of a relationship with a married man with a family of his own.

The precise circumstances may have been different, but Hidemi couldn't help feeling the hand of karma when she learned that Chizuko also had her daughter out of wedlock.

The time Hidemi spent with Sonoka was now the most precious part of her life. She put it ahead of everything else and was ready to sacrifice anything to hang on to it. She got the impression that Sonoka was starting to feel attached to her in return.

On one occasion, when Uetsuji had accompanied Sonoka to Hidemi's place, he came out with something unexpected. Just to be certain, he wanted to do a DNA test. That meant he would need a sample from Hidemi. He had found a company that did the whole thing by post.

Hidemi couldn't very well refuse. She felt anxious when he was taking the sample from her. She was terrified that the test might prove there was no blood tie between her and Sonoka.

Her fears proved groundless. The results, which arrived two weeks later, confirmed that the two of them were related.

Emboldened, Hidemi made a proposal to Sonoka. "I'd really like it if you called me Grandma."

Sonoka's eyes shone. "Can I really call you that?" she asked.

"Of course you can. After all, I *am* your grandma."

"So you are! So that is what I'll call you from now on."

"Yes, please do. And let's stop being quite so formal and polite with one another. We don't need to treat each other like strangers anymore."

"Okay, Grandma," Sonoka said. She sounded a little embarrassed.

What followed was a period of dreamlike happiness for Hidemi. Every day was a delight.

At a certain point, however, the intervals between Sonoka's visits started getting longer. She had begun by visiting Hidemi every two or three days; that then became once a week, then once every two weeks, and finally even longer than that. When Hidemi asked her why, Sonoka would simply say that "there was a lot going on in her life."

When Sonoka didn't visit for almost an entire month, Hidemi reached a breaking point. Still, calling her up and urging her to come visit didn't seem the right thing to do. Sonoka had a busy life of her own and calling her would be too intrusive. It occurred to Hidemi to go and have a peek at the flower shop where Sonoka worked. At a pinch, she could even buy herself some nice fresh flowers. That way, she wouldn't be interfering with her work.

Sonoka was nowhere to be seen at the flower shop. The older woman Hidemi approached explained that Sonoka was feeling poorly and was at home for the day. Had she been particularly busy recently? Hidemi asked. No, said the older woman, that was not the case.

Hidemi suddenly felt anxious. What did "feeling poorly" even mean? If all Sonoka had was a common cold, then that was fine. If she had something more serious, then it was another matter altogether. Perhaps that was the reason she hadn't come to see Hidemi recently.

Hidemi felt ill at ease as she made her way to Sonoka's apartment. A feeble voice responded when she pressed the buzzer of the intercom and the door opened.

Hidemi gave a start at the sight of Sonoka. She was wearing a disposable face mask. Plenty of people had started wearing them as a matter of routine since the pandemic. Even so, this was the first time Hidemi had seen Sonoka in one. *So she did have a cold after all, then.*

"Grandma . . . what are you doing here?"

"I went to the flower store. I needed so badly to see your face. They told me you were off work, so I got worried. Have you caught cold?"

She was about to ask if Sonoka had a temperature, when she broke off mid-flow. She had noticed a blue bruise emerging from one side of Sonoka's mask. Looking more closely, she noticed that her right eyelid was also swollen.

"What's going on, Sonoka? You're a mass of bruises."

Sonoka covered her face with her hand. "It's nothing. I'm fine."

"No, you are not. Here, show me. Come on, take off the mask."

"I told you I'm fine. Now leave me alone. I'm sorry, but I've got stuff I've got to do." Sonoka pushed Hidemi backward and slammed the door on her. Hidemi heard the lock turning.

She just stood there in shock. *What was going on?*

She went down the stairs, but she couldn't bring herself to leave. She was debating what to do, when one of the doors near her opened and a middle-aged housewife came out. Her apartment was diagonally below Sonoka's room. She walked past Hidemi and made for the main road.

On a hunch, Hidemi dashed after her. "Excuse me a moment," she said.

A few minutes later, Hidemi was back, standing outside Sonoka's apartment for a second time. Using the intercom was probably a waste of time. Instead, she used her phone to call.

Had Sonoka blocked her? No. Someone picked up and she heard Sonoka's feeble voice saying hello.

"Sonoka. I'm right here outside your front door. There's something I've absolutely got to check up on."

"I told you to leave me alone. Please, go. Just go."

"It's something the woman from downstairs told me. She thinks your boyfriend is beating you up."

An abrupt silence.

"Please, let me in. Tell me what's happening."

A moment later, she heard the sound of the lock turning and the door opened.

Now they were facing each other inside the apartment. With an air of utter defeat, Sonoka slowly peeled off her mask.

Hidemi breathed in sharply. One side of Sonoka's face was a huge blue-black bruise and she had a painful-looking scab at the corner of her mouth.

"Uetsuji did that?"

Sonoka nodded and grunted.

"When did this start?"

"Not long after we started living together."

"Why does he do it?"

"Various reasons. It's mostly if I contradict him or answer back. If I talk back to him even a little, he completely loses it."

Hidemi felt crushed. She knew that there were plenty of men who look nice from the outside but are quite happy to beat their wives and children in secret. Although Hidemi had never been an abuse victim herself, she'd come across her fair share of such bullies. How could she have been so obtuse? How could she have failed to see Uetsuji for what he was?

"Do you still love him? Do you want to stay with him?"

"I used to. He was very sweet to me when he wasn't being violent and he'd always say sorry straight after hitting me. 'I'll never do it again,' stuff like that. I always ended up thinking that I deserved it and I was the one to blame. . . ."

"But he keeps doing it, right? Men like him never change. It's like a disease. He'll be the same till his dying day."

"I know that now. Honestly, now I just want to get away from him."

"Then do it. You should break up with him. What's stopping you?"

"I know that something terrible will happen if I even mention it. He might even kill me."

"Oh, come on . . ."

"I'm serious. Once, when I just hinted at it, what do you think he did? He went and got a big knife from the kitchen and said, 'You ditch me and I'll kill you and then I'll kill myself.' He really said that."

"That's just talk."

"No, it isn't. He really meant it. He was all nice and sweet to me afterward, but I never want to feel that afraid again."

Hidemi felt a sense of hopelessness. Sonoka was unlikely to be exaggerating. Men like that existed. She knew they did.

From that day on, she was never free from worry. For such a calamity to befall the granddaughter whom she had finally met after so many years—that was the last thing she had expected. *I've got to do something. I've got to help her.* That single thought ran through her mind all day every day.

The decision she eventually reached had been lurking somewhere in the back of her mind the whole time. *She was going to have to rid the earth of Ryota Uetsuji, even if it cost her her life.* She didn't have very long to live herself anyway. If that was what it took to secure Sonoka's happiness, then it was a small price to pay.

The problem was how. What was the best method for an old woman of more than seventy to kill a young, strong man outright?

I'm going to have to use that gun. It's the only feasible way, she thought.

17

The different-size naval ships merged into the gray background. Was it because of the clouds in the sky that the sea itself appeared to have turned dark gray? Either way, it seemed a thoroughly appropriate color scheme for a navy base, Kaoru Utsumi thought.

The people strolling along the shoreline would probably have preferred a blue sky and a blue sea and the people busy taking photos of the colorful flower beds would also have been happier with a background that set off the flowers to better advantage.

This color of sky and sea is good enough for me, thought Kaoru as she unscrewed the top from a plastic bottle. She couldn't remember the last time she had sat on a bench on a wooden deck and enjoyed contemplating the sea.

She'd just put the bottle back in her bag after a quick drink when a voice said, "Sorry to keep you waiting." She looked up. It was Yukawa.

"Sorry to intrude like this. . . ."

"It's fine by me. I imagine it's what Kusanagi told you to do? 'Go and see the guy. And don't bother to give him any advance warning.'"

"'If you want to get a useful statement out of someone, the less time you give them to prepare, the better,' is what he actually said. 'It's a principle that applies across the board, even with physicists you've known for a long time. . . .'"

Yukawa snorted disdainfully. "Just the sort of thing I'd expect Kusanagi to come out with. But you gave me some time anyway. A good twenty minutes must have passed since you buzzed me from the downstairs lobby."

"I wasn't expecting you to be able to come out right away."

"Yes, my mother had had a bit of an accident. I was helping my father change her. She isn't very cooperative, which makes it all rather difficult. She is old, but when she fights back, she's as strong as a horse."

"That sounds grim."

"Not really. It won't last forever, after all. So, what did you want to talk to me about?"

Kaoru straightened her back and turned to face Yukawa.

"Hidemi Negishi called Chief Kusanagi this morning. She said she had something important to tell him and asked him to go to her place. When he got there, she confessed to the murder of Ryota Uetsuji."

"Really?" was Yukawa's understated reaction.

"You're not surprised?"

Yukawa looked at her incredulously.

"What would you do if I pretended to be surprised at this stage of the game?"

"I'd tell you to stop playacting."

"Precisely. Which is why I'm not bothering to put on a show."

Kaoru sighed and looked at the bland expression on Yukawa's face.

"'When are you going to get rid of that bad habit of yours?' That's what the chief told me to ask you."

"My bad habit?"

"Yes, your bad habit of figuring out the solution to a case and, instead of sharing it with the police, confronting the suspect directly yourself. You appear to have gone and done it again."

"What could Kusanagi possibly mean?" Yukawa said. Then he cracked a lopsided smile. "I get the feeling I should skip the whole 'playing ignorant' stage."

"We know that last night, after you and Chief Kusanagi went your separate ways, you met with Hidemi Negishi at a bar in Ginza District II."

"I'll admit to having enjoyed an Ardbeg and soda with her."

"What did you two discuss? No, let me rephrase the question. What did *you* say to her? That's what we want to know. The chief would like to ask you directly, but he's up to his neck in the paperwork for Hidemi Negishi. 'I've got my hands full getting the case ready for the public prosecutor. I can't leave the incident room right now. You go and talk to him in my place.' That's what he said to me. So think of me as Kusanagi's rep. I'll repeat the question: What did you say to Hidemi Negishi last night?"

"Why don't you put your cards on the table before you make demands of other people? What did Hidemi Negishi say in her statement?"

"I'd prefer it if you went first, Professor."

"No, you've got to show your hand first. Turn me down and this conversation as a whole is over. I'll go back home. What does it matter anyway? Her statement will be made public somewhere down the line."

Frustrating though it was for Kaoru to acknowledge, Yukawa was right. With him, hard bargaining never worked.

"She said she committed the murder to protect someone close to her. The person close to her was, of course, Sonoka Shimauchi."

"Close in what way?"

"She described Sonoka as her idol."

"Her idol?" Yukawa frowned in perplexity.

"Six months ago, Hidemi Negishi caught a glimpse of Sonoka at the flower shop in Ueno. It was like being struck by lightning, she says. She was infatuated. She bought some flowers in an attempt to form a connection. Wanting to stretch out her interaction with Sonoka for as long as possible, she cooked up some story about needing her to choose some flowers as a gift for a concert performer friend. In fact, there was no such concert and she simply took the flowers home with her."

"The scouting her for a hostess job? What about that part?"

"Apparently, that stuff was true. In her statement, Hidemi Negishi said she tried scouting her because she wanted Sonoka nearby, not because she thought she had any particular talents in that direction. Whether she agreed to take the hostess job was irrelevant; Hidemi Negishi just wanted an opportunity to talk to her. It's not a lesbian thing. Sonoka was special, she said; just looking at her was enough to make her happy and she never wanted anything in return."

"I see. That explains why you used the word 'idol.'"

"Uetsuji's abuse of her precious idol was not something Hidemi Negishi could ignore. With Sonoka too terrified to leave the man, Hidemi Negishi concluded that killing him was the only viable course of action. So she told Sonoka to take a trip somewhere while she 'dealt with' Uetsuji. Of course, she never said anything explicit about killing him; she presented it as 'ne-gotiating a solution.'"

"And the whole thing culminated in murder. How did that play out?"

"Negishi covered it all in her statement. It's quite complicated."

Sonoka Shimauchi had arranged to go to Kyoto with Maki Oka-tani on September 27 as instructed by Hidemi Negishi. Negishi, however, got Sonoka to tell Uetsuji that she was going to Tateyama with her. While she thought he might take exception to Sonoka taking a trip with a friend, he guessed he would be better disposed to one involving herself, because he was interested in getting So-noka a job at VOWM to earn money for him. Sonoka had no idea what Hidemi Negishi had in mind. After Sonoka told Uetsuji about the planned Tateyama trip, Uetsuji called Hidemi Negishi to con-firm that the two of them were indeed intending to go. Hidemi Negishi assured him they were. Knowing that the phone company would have a record of the call, Hidemi was expecting the police to track her down after the murder.

On the afternoon after Sonoka and her friend Maki actually went to Kyoto, Hidemi called Uetsuji and told him that Sonoka had had an anemic attack in Tateyama and collapsed. Luckily, one of the locals was letting her rest in his house. She then asked Uet-suji to come and pick Sonoka up.

He agreed to rent a car and set off immediately.

Uetsuji showed up a few hours later. In the interim, Hidemi Negishi had switched off her phone.

Uetsuji looked rather unsure of himself as he got out of the car. The place Hidemi Negishi got him to come was right by the sea, far from the tourist spots and with almost no houses around.

Hidemi Negishi led Uetsuji down a narrow lane, a dead end leading to a ten-meter-high cliff with the sea below.

Hidemi had spent the previous few days scouring the area before finding this place.

That was when Hidemi pulled out her weapon. It was an illegal handmade pistol that she'd been given by a man she'd been in a relationship with. She pointed it at Uetsuji, who was still completely bewildered.

He stood rooted to the spot with the cliff top behind him. He didn't say a word.

Hidemi commanded him to turn around and face the sea. He did as he was told. Unbidden, he raised both hands above his head, then asked her what she was doing.

Hidemi did not reply. She just pulled the trigger. She knew the gun had a powerful recoil, so she had adopted the right stance, with her legs well apart. She barely moved when she fired.

It was a different story for Uetsuji. Quite unprepared for what was about to happen to him, he was flung over the cliff as if scooped up by a mighty hand.

"Hidemi then got into Uetsuji's rental car and drove it to the parking lot of a shopping mall in the central Tateyama. She used a handheld vacuum cleaner to carefully clean the car's interior, before returning to Tokyo by train. She claims to have thrown the gun into the Sumida River. She lured Uetsuji out to Chiba because she knew the area and had found a place no one would see them or hear the sound of gunshots. Him being thrown into the sea was not part of the plan, but she hoped it would make the body unidentifiable."

Kaoru shut her notebook. "That's everything."

"When did Hidemi Negishi tell Sonoka Shimauchi what she had done?"

"She never said it in so many words. Sonoka must have known, though."

"What do you mean?"

"Because when Uetsuji failed to come home, Hidemi Negishi told Sonoka not to worry, that everything had been sorted out, and that she should file a missing person's report with the police."

"Meaning Sonoka couldn't help but know what had happened."

"But Hidemi Negishi never imagined that Sonoka would go into hiding. That was a miscalculation. She was expecting the police to be suspicious of Sonoka, but she had a solid alibi. They would never guess that a complete stranger—someone Sonoka had nothing whatsoever to do with—would commit the murder to protect her from her abuser. If Sonoka hadn't run away, no one would ever have connected Hidemi Negishi with the murder. The problem, according to Negishi, was Sonoka's lack of mental toughness."

"'A complete stranger, someone she had nothing to do with' . . . ? Were those Hidemi Negishi's exact words?"

"Apparently. Why? Do they suggest anything?"

"Not really. If that's how things played out, then she certainly miscalculated."

"Good." Kaoru put her notebook away and looked at Yukawa.

"I've put all my cards on the table so now it's your turn, Professor. Can you tell me what you discussed with Hidemi Negishi yesterday?"

Yukawa nodded and launched into an explanation.

"What I told her is this. I am capable of finding out where So-noka Shimauchi is. At some point, I intend to share that information with the police. If, however, the murderer is prepared to hand themselves in, then I can hold off for a little while. That I thought that was what Sonoka was hoping would happen and the reason she went on the run in the first place."

Kaoru's eyes widened in surprise.

"The chief was right! You *are* personally involved in this case. Or rather, you have a personal connection to someone directly involved in it. And that someone is Nae Matsunaga. Am I right?"

"She has nothing to do with the murder. Although she is hiding Sonoka Shimauchi."

"Then tell me this. What is your relationship with Nae Matsunaga? There's got to be more to it than the two of you collaborating on a kids' picture book."

Yukawa knit his brows and turned his face toward the sea. Eventually, he said, "How long have you and I known one another? Ten years . . . No, it's longer than that."

"I was only in my twenties."

"So you were." Yukawa nodded. "I was planning to come clean to Kusanagi. I don't think he'll mind if I tell you first. After all, like you said, you're here as his representative."

"That I am." Kaoru looked at Yukawa's profile.

"Nae Matsunaga"—Yukawa exhaled loudly before he went on—"is my birth mother."

18

I'm just going out a minute."

Hearing Nae say that, Sonoka, who'd been looking through the window at the night sky, turned around to see the older woman pulling on her coat.

"Where are you going?"

"To the bar in the basement. I need a change."

"Why now . . . ?"

It seemed out of character for Nae.

"Sonoka, you stay here," Nae said, her eyes grave. "Someone will come to the room in a minute. Let them in. Okay? It's a man, but he is someone you can trust."

"Who is he? What does he want?"

"You'll find out when he gets here. Don't worry. I'm sure he will tell you the right path to take."

Sonoka had no idea what Nae was talking about. Perplexed, she just stood there. "See you later," Nae said and left the room.

Sonoka felt confused as she sat down on the sofa. It was a magnificent leather thing worthy of the suite it was in. After they had left the holiday apartment in Yuzawa, Nae had informed Sonoka that they were going to Tokyo. They had ended up at this hotel.

She started when the door chime sounded. *He was here.*

Sonoka rose, walked to the door, and opened it. A tall man wearing glasses was standing there. "Good evening," he said, a smile on his intelligent face.

"Good evening," Sonoka answered quietly.

"May I come in?"

"Oh . . . uh . . . sure."

The man entered the room. After surveying the room, he strode over to the window, looked outside, and nodded complacently.

"This is a pretty good room. I'm pleased. When I booked it online, I only had a thumbnail to go on, so I couldn't be sure."

"*You* booked it?"

"I assumed the police would never imagine that you had come back to Tokyo. Do you mind if I sit down?" The man pointed at an armchair.

"Oh . . . uh . . . be my guest."

Once he was seated, he gestured at a small two-seater sofa. "Why don't you take a seat yourself?"

"Okay," said Sonoka and sat down.

"I haven't introduced myself properly," the man said. He extracted a card from his inside breast pocket.

Sonoka took it. She blinked in surprise as she read it.

"Mr. Yukawa . . . A university professor . . . Why . . . ?"

"Who I am is irrelevant. You don't need to think about it. Much more importantly, were you aware that Hidemi Negishi has turned herself in to the police?"

Sonoka nodded weakly. "Yes, I was."

"Did you speak to her the night before she did so?"

"Yes, I did."

"I believe she issued you some instructions."

Sonoka's eyebrows jumped. *How does this man know so much?*

"If I am not mistaken, one of her instructions was for you *under no circumstances* to reveal to the police you are her granddaughter and she is your grandmother?"

Sonoka responded with a wordless nod. Yukawa was right.

"I'll keep things short and sweet. I figured out that you and Ms. Negishi were probably related. I guessed that she'd worked out that you were her granddaughter based on the doll, and I asked her about it." As he said this, Yukawa pointed at the writing desk across the room. The doll was sitting on top of it. "I told her that I could share that information with the police, but would hold off if she turned herself in first. She agreed on the condition that she could speak with you. That's why I got Nae Matsunaga to have you call Ms. Negishi."

So that's what had been going on. It had been bewildering at the time. Now it all made sense.

"Based on what I've heard from the police, Ms. Negishi hasn't told them that you two are related; she's just described you as a young girl she took a strong liking to. She must have decided that it would be to your advantage if she kept your true relationship a secret. I then realized she could have another reason. That second reason is more powerful and helps explain why she was convinced that killing Uetsuji was the only viable course of action open to her. To put it in a nutshell, Negishi *wants* to believe you. Even if you've tricked her, she simply doesn't want to know."

Sonoka was stunned. Yukawa hadn't just seen through her and Uetsuji's scheme, he had also grasped Hidemi's true motivation for killing Uetsuji.

"At some point, the police will interrogate you. You may be tempted to come clean about everything. That'll be the least uncomfortable option for you. However, you need to be aware of something. Telling the whole truth will only make things worse for everybody. You will be accused of fraud and poor Ms. Negishi will be made even more unhappy than she is already. If you want to show her that you're sorry, then keeping your mouth shut is the best thing to do. That's what I've come here tonight to tell you."

Although his tone was cool and matter-of-fact, every word he uttered was like a dagger deep in Sonoka's heart. She was paralyzed, dumbstruck.

Yukawa glanced at his watch and got to his feet.

"I've done what I came for, so I'll be off. The rest is up to you."

In her frozen state, Sonoka couldn't even follow Yukawa with her eyes as he left the room. The thump of the shutting door lingered in her ears.

It was only when the last reverberations had died out that she regained the ability to move. She got to her feet and slowly walked over to the writing desk. As she picked up the doll, she thought back over the last few months.

It had all started that day. Ryota, who was quite excited, had come out with a funny story about an old lady who had come up and talked to him around lunchtime.

He showed Sonoka a card. On it was printed the name "Hidemi Negishi." Ryota explained that the woman ran a club in Ginza.

"She wanted to know all about your mother."

"My mother?"

Who was this woman? Sonoka had no idea. Perhaps she was a friend of Nae Matsunaga's? They'd been out of touch for a while now.

"The first thing she did was show me a photo. You as a kid at a Christmas party at some school or something."

"Oh . . ."

Sonoka guessed what he was referring to. *The orphanage.* Come to think of it, someone had called her not long ago to check if she'd given permission for her image to be used on the website.

"She asked me if I had ever seen the doll you were holding in the photo."

Ryota gestured at the top of the shelf, where an old doll in a blue-and-pink-striped sweater was sitting.

"When I told her I had seen it and that you had inherited it from your mother, the woman suddenly burst into tears. Sure gave me a shock. We were in a café and there were loads of other people there. 'What's going on?' I asked her. That was the real shock: she told me she was your mother's mother."

The whole thing was so unexpected that Sonoka felt quite nonplussed.

"She's my mother's mother—meaning she's my grandmother?"

"That's the long and short of it. She made the doll. And she put the doll in the basket with her baby when she dumped her baby at the orphanage."

"Dumped? Baby? What are you talking about?"

"Just listen." The excitement in Ryota's voice was tangible. "Your mother was abandoned, wasn't she? She had no family of her own. That's why she was raised at an orphanage. You told me that. The old lady on this card is your mother's mother."

Sonoka shook her head and waved her hands deprecatingly.

"This must be a mistake."

"Why?"

"Because it's not what my mom told me. She told me she was found wandering alone in a park when she was three. She was taken into protective care when her parents failed to come forward to claim her and then was sent to an orphanage. She always believed that she had negligent parents who'd abandoned her on purpose."

"But what about the doll?" Uetsuji jerked his chin toward the shelf.

"Mom said it was the orphanage's and they gave it to her."

"Are you sure? Your mom could have been lying."

"Why would she do that?"

"I have no fricking idea. I'm just saying it's a possibility."

Ryota's tone was becoming increasingly harsh. He was clearly starting to get agitated. Contradicting him was the worst possible thing to do at a time like this. "You're probably right," Sonoka said in a murmur.

Ryota went quiet. He was thinking.

Sonoka gazed up at the doll. She was remembering when Chizuko gave it to her.

"The staff at the orphanage told me that this doll used to belong to an orphan girl who died when she was very little. I've always tried to look after it for her. Now I'd like you to take good care of it."

Sonoka refused to believe that her mother had not been telling her the truth. *The old lady Ryota had met must be the mother of the orphan girl who had died young.* She knew that Ryota would only get angry if she pressed the point, so she kept her opinion to herself.

Ryota didn't bring up the subject for the next three days. Sonoka was curious to know what he was planning, but she said nothing for fear of stirring up trouble.

"That business we discussed—I've decided to follow it up," Ryota announced out of the blue.

Unsure what he was referring to, she echoed his words back at him. "Business we discussed?"

"That business of your grandmother. I think you should meet the woman."

It was the last thing she had expected Ryota to say. She felt disconcerted.

"Meet her and then what? Do you want me to tell her the truth?"

"What do you mean, 'the truth'?"

"That what she told you doesn't tally with what my mom told me. . . ."

There was a loud bang. Ryota had smacked the table with his open palm.

"Have you got any proof that what your mom told you was true? She could easily have been lying, couldn't she? God, why must you make me say the same thing over and over and over again?"

Although she was unaware of having done anything of the kind, Sonoka shook her head and mumbled an apology. It was purely reflexive now.

"For starters, you're going to meet the woman face-to-face. You're going to sit down with her and avoid saying anything stupid. She'll ask you a shitload of questions, but I'll tell you exactly how to answer them. You got that? Well? Have you?"

"Yes, I get it. . . ."

"Good. Well, let's get to work. Here's what I want you to say."

Then there began a walk-through for the meeting proper. Despite having very little grasp of what Ryota was planning, Sonoka did as she was told. The crucial thing was not to make Ryota angry.

It was several days later that, escorted by Ryota, she met with Hidemi Negishi. Hidemi Negishi radiated sophisticated style and charm. She was, as the saying goes, a woman who had aged well.

"Have you got it with you?"

Sonoka opened her bag and pulled out the doll in response to Hidemi's question.

Hidemi's eyes started reddening the moment the doll was in her hands. She turned it over and lifted its sweater up its back. "I made this doll. There's no doubt about it."

Ryota was elbowing Sonoka in the ribs. She began speaking.

"My mother often used to tell me that this doll was the only clue she had to help her track down her birth parents; that if the internet had been around when she was young, she'd have uploaded a picture of it to try to find people who recognized it."

Ryota had made her memorize that speech. It sounded phony and unconvincing to her, but judging by its effect on Hidemi, she couldn't have been more wrong. Struggling to hold back the tears, Hidemi kept repeating, "I'm sorry. I'm sorry." Sonoka guessed she was apologizing for having abandoned her daughter.

Despite feeling guilty, Sonoka knew she had to push on with the script.

"There's no need for you to say you're sorry. My mother never hated you or resented you. 'She had her reasons for what she did,' she used to say. She was hoping to find you. Right up to the end."

"The end . . ."

The tears were now streaming down Hidemi's cheeks. Sonoka felt a pang of remorse at the sight of her dabbing at her eyes.

Hidemi went on to ask Sonoka all sorts of questions about her mother. Her desire to know everything about the daughter she had abandoned was the most natural thing in the world, so Sonoka dutifully told her all about Chizuko. When she got to the part about her having died from a subarachnoid hemorrhage, Hidemi muttered something about it probably being a hereditary problem.

That brought their first encounter to a successful conclusion. Hidemi announced that she wanted to see Sonoka again. Sonoka, in no position to say no, agreed.

"Sonoka, isn't that wonderful? Hidemi has been alone for so long, and now she's finally found you, her one and only grand-daughter. Now that she has the chance, you should let her spoil you rotten."

Though Ryota's words rang false in Sonoka's ears, they again provoked a positive response from Hidemi.

"Yes, Ryota is right. Let me take care of you. I want to do all the things for you that I couldn't do for my own little daughter. You can come around and see me whenever you want. You're welcome anytime."

Sonoka looked down at the floor. "Thank you," she said. She had no choice in the matter.

After they had said goodbye to Hidemi, she couldn't keep the gloom out of her face. "What's wrong?" Ryota asked.

"I'm wondering if it's really okay. . . ."

"What?"

"She lapped up everything I said."

Ryota darted a sharp glance at her. "You got a problem with that?"

"Yes, I mean . . ."

That was as far as it went for now, but he shoved her hard as soon as they got back home.

"Now, you listen to me, and you listen to me good. I've investigated the old lady. She's not just a hired manager. She owns that Ginza club outright, plus a few other places. She may have been hard up once upon a time; now she's absolutely rolling in money. You getting to be the granddaughter of a woman like that—what's not to like?"

"She'll find out."

"Find out? How? I can't believe you're still saying that."

He grabbed her hair. It was painful but she was too frightened to make a sound.

"No one really knows the truth of this business. You *could* be the old lady's granddaughter. Can anyone prove you're not? No, I didn't think so. You're fine. Or is there something else you want to give me grief over?"

Sonoka shook her head. The idea of DNA testing had flashed into her head, but she couldn't bring herself to say anything.

Ryota let go of her hair and shoved his face right up to hers. "Sonoka," he said softly. "This is the chance of a lifetime. This is your chance to be happy. I don't want us to lose it. You can under-stand that, can't you?"

"Uh-huh." Sonoka nodded in agreement.

"You're a good girl," Ryota said, stroking her head.

From then on, Sonoka became a frequent visitor to Hidemi's apartment. Under duress, she was doing what Ryota had ordered her to do.

Sonoka had to admit that the time she spent with Hidemi was by no means unpleasant. They mostly talked about Sonoka's mother. When Hidemi asked her what sort of person she was, Sonoka would describe Chizuko. She spoke openly about her up-bringing at the orphanage, about what she had done after leaving it, and how she had ended up as a single mother. Since there was no need to lie, it was easy enough to do. As she watched Hidemi, her eyes moist with tears, drinking it all in, Sonoka sometimes thought how nice it would be if Chizuko really had been her daughter.

On one occasion, Ryota announced that he would come with her. When she asked him why, his explanation startled her. He wanted to take a sample from Hidemi for a DNA test.

"Are you really going to do that?" Sonoka asked.

Ryota glared at her. "Why not? You got a problem with it?"

She hastily apologized, while backing away from the expected blow.

Ryota just grinned cheerfully at her. "Don't you worry. Just leave it all to me," he said.

When Ryota broached the idea of a DNA test with Hidemi, Sonoka could see the anxiety in the old woman's face. She realized that Hidemi wasn't completely confident that the two of them were related after all.

What exactly was Ryota planning? He certainly didn't believe that she and Hidemi were blood relatives.

Sonoka couldn't believe her eyes when the test results arrived a couple of weeks later. There was a "99.5 percent or over" probability of she and Hidemi being related.

"What does this mean?" Sonoka asked Ryota.

"No more ifs or buts. The result is what it is. I told you it would be okay."

Seeing the smirk on Ryota's face, Sonoka realized what he'd done. He'd taken samples from some completely different woman and her grandmother and sent them to the testing company instead!

That's not okay. That's a crime, pure and simple. Still, Sonoka couldn't bring herself to protest. Defying Ryota was something she simply couldn't do.

Hidemi was over the moon at the test result. She admitted to having been nervous about the outcome, despite being confident that they were related.

This was the moment when Hidemi said she wanted Sonoka to call her Grandma and that they should stop using stiff and polite forms of language when talking to each other.

Sonoka couldn't very well say no, so she did as she was asked. Simply being addressed as Grandma was enough to make Hidemi tear up. In spite of feeling guilty, Sonoka managed to persuade herself that since it made the old lady happy, there couldn't be any harm in it. She resorted to twisted logic: if she was using the word "grandma" as a generic term for "old lady," then she wasn't really lying, she reassured herself.

It was at this point that Hidemi started providing Sonoka with financial support. Previously, she had handed her twenty thousand yen, while suggesting that she and Ryota go and get themselves something nice to eat. Now she was giving her more than one hundred thousand yen at a time. This was much more than pocket money. "Use this for your day-to-day expenses," she would say. She had obviously twigged that Sonoka and Ryota's life was far from easy.

"See. It's just like I said." Ryota beamed with pleasure every time Sonoka reappeared with a wad of money. "The old lady's loaded with no family and no one to inherit. That's all changed now. She's got someone to leave it to. Okay, Sonoka, it's time to move on to the next stage."

"What do you mean?" Sonoka had a bad feeling about what was coming.

"We want to formalize the relationship. Get the old lady to legally adopt you. Let's suggest it. She's sure to go for it."

"Isn't that a step too far?"

"It's a step we've got to take. Look, I'll let you in on a secret. The old lady's sick—sick with cancer. A few years back, she had an operation. The consensus is that she won't last long. She could pop her clogs at any time. See where I'm going with this? If she dies on us with things the way they are now, we wouldn't get a penny. We need to hustle. Once she's adopted you, then she's welcome to croak whenever she likes. All her money will go to you. Frankly, the sooner she dies, then, the better."

"But . . . that's downright nasty, no matter how you slice it."

"Why? And what's with this 'slicing' crap?"

"It's criminal. It's fraud. It's got to be. Tricking her into adopting—"

Sonoka was sent flying before she could reach the end of her sentence. Ryota had fetched her a mighty smack on the side of the head.

Following his usual playbook, Ryota now grabbed her by the hair.

"*Trick her?* You need to mind your language. When did I trick her? Come on, think. Was it me who initiated contact? Well? No, she just rolled up here and announced that you were her granddaughter. Maybe I strung her along a bit, but that's about as far as it goes. Why are you giving me that look? Something you want to get off your chest?"

She wanted to mention the DNA test Ryota had used to trick Hidemi. Instead, she just shook her head. She was afraid he would beat her again.

"You listen to me. I'm all in on this. It's too late to go back now—and frankly, I don't want to. If what I'm doing is a crime, Sonoka, then you're my accomplice. You can't bail out now. You've been happy enough to eat the food you bought with her money. You've been drinking fancy drinks and buying yourself nice clothes. Am I wrong?"

I'll repay the money—was what she wanted to say, but her lips refused to move.

Ryota grinned merrily.

"Don't worry about it. Everything'll go fine, I promise. I've said this a thousand times already: I'm doing this for you. If it all goes smoothly, then all you have to do is sit and wait. The minute she keels over, happiness will drop into our laps."

No, you can't call that happiness—was what she wanted to say. Instead, she just closed her eyes. Misinterpreting her reaction, Ryota began stroking her head and called her his good girl.

Her attitude changed. *I just want out of this*, she started to think. *Ryota's hairsplitting is nonsense. This is a crime. There's no other word for it.*

Sonoka would tell Ryota that Hidemi was busy as an excuse for not going around to see her place even on her days off work. She knew that if she did see Hidemi, Ryota would expect her to broach the subject of adoption—and that he would be furious if she came back having failed to do so.

Things went on like this for a month. One day, Sonoka got home to find Ryota drinking whiskey. She had a bad feeling. It wasn't like him to drink before dinner.

Her instincts were right. Ryota sprang to his feet, threw himself at her, knocked her to the floor, and started pounding her face and body.

"You've been lying to me. I called Hidemi just now and she told me that you're the one who's been too busy to see her recently. What are you up to? Tell me."

"Please . . . I can't . . ."

"What? What did you say?"

"I can't do this anymore. I want it to stop."

"Want it to stop? Why do you need to make a big deal of it?

You just go to the old lady's place and play along with her. Is that so hard?"

"That's not what I'm talking about. . . . It's this life, I can't take it anymore."

"This life? What are you saying? You don't want to live here with me anymore?"

Sonoka did not say anything or even nod. Ryota, however, must have sensed her feelings, as he suddenly leaped up, dashed over to the kitchen area, and then came back. Sonoka shuddered when she saw what he had in his hand. A large kitchen knife.

He stood over Sonoka and held the knife to her face.

"Don't think you can betray me. There's no turning back now. You can't run away from me. I will find you and kill you, and then I'll kill myself. This is no empty threat. I'm deadly serious."

Seeing the glint of madness in Ryota's eyes, Sonoka was frozen to the spot.

He will *murder me*, she thought. *If things keep on like this, he really will murder me.*

Hidemi's surprise visit to their apartment was not long after that. With Ryota out, Sonoka opened the door. Even though she had a mask on, Hidemi managed to spot the bruise on her cheek.

Hidemi wasn't prepared to give up even when Sonoka slammed the door on her. She approached another of the residents, who told her Ryota was physically abusing Sonoka.

There was no point in trying to hide it anymore. Sonoka opened up about the abuse she was suffering, while taking care to keep the reason for it vague. She couldn't bring herself to tell Hidemi that she was deceiving her.

"I see what's going on. Grandma will sort this out. Don't you worry," Hidemi said. Then she left. Sonoka had no idea what the older woman had in mind.

When Hidemi called her one week later, Sonoka went around to see her. The timing was fortuitous. Ryota had been pressing her to go and see the old woman now that the bruises on her face had cleared up.

What Hidemi proposed took Sonoka by surprise. She told her that she wanted her to take a trip with a friend in the coming days.

"It's got to be for a minimum of two days with an overnight stay. The farther, the better. I'll pay for it. Is there any particular place you want to go?"

Sonoka felt confused. The whole thing had come out of left field.

"Why are you suddenly suggesting a trip like this?"

"You need a change from time to time. We all do. I bet you haven't taken a trip for years."

"No, I haven't but . . ."

With Sonoka still sitting on the fence, Hidemi abruptly broke into a grin.

"The truth is, I'm planning to deal with that problem of yours. Your abusive boyfriend, I mean. I've thought things through carefully. I think I can talk to him and we can work out a solution."

"You really think so?"

"It certainly won't be easy. We'll need a third person to help us sort things out and that will cost money. Still, I'm sure we'll be able to work something out. I'll make sure that by the time you get back, you need never have anything to do with him again. I won't let him anywhere near you."

We'll need a third person to help us sort things out and that will cost money—

Did she mean some sort of gangster? Sonoka knew nothing about that world, but Hidemi probably had all the right connections.

"You think it will work out?"

"I'll make sure that it does, though there's always a small chance of things going awry. If that does happen, I'll protect you from the fallout. Trust me."

"Ryota may not let me go anywhere."

"Just tell him that I've invited you. He's unlikely to say no then."

"Yes, that'll probably do the trick."

If anything, Ryota would get angry if Sonoka refused an invitation from Hidemi.

The next problem was who Sonoka should get to go with her. Hidemi recommended she take a close friend she could trust completely. Only one person sprang to mind.

She texted Maki Okatani. Everything was agreed on at high speed: they would go to Kyoto on September 27.

When Sonoka informed Ryota that she and Hidemi were planning to take a trip together, he called Hidemi on the spot, suspecting that Sonoka might not be telling him the truth. "This is your golden opportunity," he said to her with a smile after finishing the call. "I want you to use this trip to get the adoption business sorted. Got that?"

"Yes, I get it," she replied. If Hidemi could deliver on her promises, she was free to lie as much as she wanted without fear.

She enjoyed the trip to Kyoto with her friend Maki. The unfamiliar sense of freedom was a joy. Of course, the thought of Ryota weighed upon her. Would Hidemi really be able to work things out with him? She didn't get so much as a single text from Ryota, although he would normally have bombarded her with them. She chose to interpret that as a sign that negotiations were progressing well. In the evening, she got a text from Hidemi. "Everything is going fine. You just relax and have a good time," it said.

Nonetheless, she felt anxious on the day of her return to Tokyo. She kept picturing Ryota, waiting in the apartment, his anger at the boiling point, ready to take a swing at her the moment she walked through the door.

The reality was an anticlimax. Ryota was not there. Sonoka called Hidemi, who assured her that everything was fine.

"Don't worry. Just enjoy a good night's sleep. Tomorrow you've got to go to work, haven't you? Give me a call when you have a moment. There are a couple of things I need you to do for me."

"What kind of things?"

"I'll tell you tomorrow."

Hidemi wished her good night and rang off. She sounded a little colder and more distant than usual.

Ryota still wasn't back by the next morning. Sonoka went to the flower shop and did her job as normal, but couldn't help feeling unsettled.

"What's with the long face? Is something wrong?" Mrs. Ao-yama, the manager, asked.

"No, nothing," Sonoka said.

During her lunch break, she called Hidemi. Over the phone, the old woman instructed her to do something mystifying.

Hidemi told her to call every person and organization connected to Ryota she could think of and ask them if they knew where he was.

"What's this about? You make it sound like Ryota's gone missing or—"

A shiver ran up her spine and she broke off. Suddenly, she realized what had happened. She couldn't quite believe it. At the same time, it was the only way to make sense of things.

"Uhm . . . Ryota . . . Did you . . . ?" She was too frightened to complete the question.

"Sonoka." Hidemi said her name with enormous tenderness. "Yes, I did. Ryota is missing. He disappeared while you were away in Kyoto so today you need to start phoning around and making inquiries about him. Then, this evening, I need you to go down to your local police station. Tell them that your live-in boyfriend has disappeared."

"But what's happened to him?"

"The less you know or even think about that, the better. Just do as I say and you'll be fine. You don't need to worry about anything."

"Grandma . . ."

There was no room for doubt. Although she had no idea what had really happened, Sonoka knew for a fact that Ryota was never going to reappear. That he was dead—

"You mean everything to me, Sonoka. All I want is for you to be happy. My own life means nothing to me. Please, just do what I tell you."

The intensity of feeling in the voice on the phone was overpowering. Sonoka had to fall in line.

"You told me to call people to ask if they know where Ryota is. The trouble is, I don't know anyone to call. His contacts . . . they're all in his phone."

"I hadn't thought of that. No one has an address book anymore these days. Okay, not to worry. Try contacting Ryota—calling him or whatever—from time to time yourself. It would be weird if his live-in girlfriend did nothing when he'd gone missing. After that, go to your local police station and file a missing person's report this evening, like I said before. Is that clear?"

Sonoka detected an undercurrent of urgency behind Hidemi's flat, unemotional delivery. "Yes, got it," Sonoka said.

"Good. Thanks, Sonoka. Hang in there. Give me a call if anything comes up." The relief in Hidemi's voice was palpable.

Sonoka was in a daze after ending the call. Something truly terrible had happened.

She had already decided on a different course of action while she was away. She was planning to tell Hidemi the truth, if she managed to get away from Ryota. And she also intended to return all the money Hidemi had given her, even if it took her years.

None of that mattered anymore. Hidemi had obliterated Ryota's existence precisely *because* she believed that Sonoka was her granddaughter. Now was hardly the moment for Sonoka to come out and tell her that it had all been a lie.

In her confusion, to follow Hidemi's instructions was the least she could do. She called Ryota's phone and followed this with a text asking where he was. She repeated the process several times. Naturally, she never got a response.

In the evening, she made her way to the local police station and spoke to someone in the Community Safety Division. It was an Officer Yokoyama who dealt with her. He asked her if she had noticed anything unusual about Ryota the last few days. She couldn't think of anything, she said.

She left the police station after filing a missing person's report. She couldn't tell if her manner had come across as natural or not.

Hidemi praised her for a job well done when she called her.

"Good. We can relax now. You've done your bit and now you're free. Don't start celebrating, though. You never know who might be watching."

"What should I do now?"

Sonoka's question elicited a moment of silence, then Hidemi said, "This isn't the easiest thing for me to tell you, but you need to know, so listen up. The police will contact you quite soon. They'll say that they've found someone they think is Ryota and that they need you to identify him."

Sonoka gulped. What was "someone *they think* is Ryota" supposed to mean?

"Sonoka, are you still there?"

"Yes."

"You should do exactly what the police ask. It won't be very nice, but you need to identify the body."

"What then?"

"If it is Ryota, then the police will tell you what the next steps are. You can always contact me if you are unsure what to do."

"I understand."

"Stay strong. You only need to tough it out a little longer. We can get together as soon as things have settled down. Take care."

"You too, Grandma."

"Thanks."

That night, Sonoka couldn't sleep. Whenever she thought about the future, she felt crushing despair. Was her only option to keep lying to Hidemi? The old woman truly believed that for her granddaughter's sake she'd murdered a vile man.

Morning came. Sonoka had barely slept. At work, Mrs. Aoyama, her manager, commented on her pallor.

"You weren't looking well yesterday either. You're welcome to take the day off, if you aren't feeling well."

"No, no. I'm fine."

In fact, she was in no mood to focus on her job. She was intensely anxious about getting a call from the police.

That was the moment that Nae Matsunaga called. "So lovely to hear your voice. It's been ages," Matsunaga said brightly.

Sonoka couldn't respond in kind. From her listlessness, Matsunaga sensed that something was wrong.

"What's happened? Come on, Sonoka, you can tell me."

Sonoka's resolve crumbled in the face of so direct a question.

"Something really awful's happened, Nae," she admitted.

"What? What is it?" Nae asked, shocked.

Sonoka didn't know where to begin. She was struggling to formulate a reply when Nae broke in. "So it's not something you can explain over the phone?"

"No . . ."

"Well, in that case, why don't you come to my place? Meeting face-to-face would work better for me too."

"Okay," said Sonoka. They arranged to meet that evening. After the call, Sonoka was lost in her own thoughts.

She couldn't be open and honest about what she had done. She had tricked an old woman—even if she had been forced to do so by someone else. And that woman had committed a murder as a result.

What should I say to Nae? As she mulled the question, she made any number of blunders in her work.

She still hadn't figured out the answer by the time she got to Nae's place. Nae, meanwhile, seemed to have sensed that there was something wrong. "Just tell me as much as you can. I'm guessing that it won't be easy for you," she said.

Sonoka nodded. "I think my boyfriend's been killed," she began. The best thing was probably to start with what Nae knew already.

Nae showed no surprise. "Killed? Who by?"

"I . . . don't want to say. But they did it for me."

Nae stared at Sonoka. "I see," she murmured. "What do you want to do, Sonoka?"

"I have no idea. I have no idea what to do." Sonoka shook her head. "I'd like to disappear, if I could. . . ."

"Sonoka," said Nae in a whisper. Then she went quiet.

Sonoka, who was hunched over, looking down at the floor, had no idea what sort of look was on her face.

"Okay," Nae eventually said. "Let's do that."

Sonoka raised her head and looked at her. "What do you mean?"

"We'll do exactly what you said. Disappear. It's okay—I'll go with you."

"Disappear? Where?"

"Trust me. I've got an idea."

Things became frantic after that. Sonoka called the flower store on the morning of October 2 and asked for time off. She was all ready to quit if they said no. Luckily, they agreed to her request, so she packed her bag and went around to Nae's apartment. Nae had made all the necessary preparations and the two of them set out right away. Their destination was Tokyo Station. Sonoka was surprised to learn they would be catching the bullet train. That wasn't what she had been expecting.

"I've got a place where we can lie low," Nae said with a wink.

That was how their life at the apartment in Yuzawa began. Since they hardly ever bumped into other residents and it was Nae who handled all the shopping, Sonoka was confident that the police wouldn't find them.

The question was how long they should stay in hiding. From watching the news, they learned that Uetsuji's body had been found and an investigation had been launched. It was logical to assume that the police must be looking for Sonoka.

Nae didn't ask any questions. She was giving her the chance to speak first, Sonoka realized. Even so, Sonoka found herself completely incapable of doing so. If she revealed that she had passed herself off as a random old woman's granddaughter in order to get money from her, she was convinced that Nae would reproach her and despise her. Perhaps even turn her in to the police.

The days went by. Then suddenly, the situation changed. They had left the Yuzawa apartment and moved to this hotel. Although Nae appeared to be following someone else's orders, she refused to tell Sonoka who that someone else was. Now she guessed that it had probably been Yukawa.

Nae had handed her a piece of paper a few days ago. "You need to call this number right now," she said.

Sonoka went pale. It was Hidemi's cell phone number.

"I'll be right next door," Nae said. She disappeared into the bedroom, shutting the door behind her.

Sonoka felt more bewildered than ever. *What was this all about? Why should Nae know Hidemi's phone number?*

Not quite sure what she was doing, she picked up the receiver of the hotel phone and punched the buttons on the keypad, while placing her other hand flat on her chest.

The phone rang only once before someone picked up. "This is Negishi," said a familiar voice. "Sonoka, is that you?" the voice went on.

Sonoka said nothing. "Uh-huh," she grunted.

"Great. Professor Yukawa delivered on his promise."

The name was not one Sonoka recognized.

"How are you? Are you holding up physically?"

"Yes, I'm fine. I . . . uh . . ."

"No need to say anything. I just wanted to check you were okay. Now I need you to listen to what I am going to say. Can you do that for me?"

"Uh-huh."

"Good. Listen, tomorrow I'm going to go to the police. I'm going to turn myself in."

Sonoka gasped.

"I thought I could get away with it. But that's not how it's worked out. I'm going to throw in the towel. There is something I want to say to you before that. I'm going to tell the police that I fell for you, that I got infatuated with you after happening to bump into you at the Ueno flower shop. I'm not going to breathe a word about you being the daughter of the little baby girl I abandoned. Whatever the police ask you, I want you to stick to exactly the same story. Do you understand?"

"Are you sure it will be . . . okay . . . with a story like that?"

"Sure I'm sure. We'll keep it as our little secret. I really enjoyed these last six months. You have given me so many wonderful memories. In what little of life is left to me, I'm going to treasure them."

"Mrs. Negishi."

"Call me Grandma, won't you?"

"Yes . . . but . . ."

"This is the last time. Come on, call me Grandma."

"Grandma."

There was a giggle at the other end of the line. "Thanks."

A click. The line went dead.

Sonoka was still clutching the receiver as she crumpled and fell to her knees. Tears started streaming down her face and dripped onto the carpet.

19

Dear Ms. Nana Asahi,

Thank you for your note. I got a nice email from Mrs. Fujisaki, your editor at Seho, at the same time.

I am flattered to learn of your interest in my book *If I Ever Met a Monopole*.

To be quite honest, commercially, the book was a complete flop. Since it is now out of print, I am curious to know how you managed to get hold of your copy!

The idea of making the magnetic monopole into the theme of a picture book for children is certainly original!

As someone who is keen to get more young people interested in physics, I would be delighted to do anything I can to help you with your book. Feel free to ask me anything. I will try to couch my answers in simple, jargon-free language. Should you find yourself struggling with any concepts, do not hesitate to say so.

With best regards,

Manabu Yukawa

Physics Dept. Science Faculty

Teito University

Nae was rereading the email, which she'd already read countless times, when the bell rang. She closed her laptop, took a deep breath, and got to her feet.

As she walked toward the door, she pressed her right hand to her chest. Her heart was beating unusually fast and was not going to return to normal anytime soon. Resigned, she took another deep breath and opened the door.

He was standing there. The person she had dreamed of meeting for more than thirty years.

"It's been a while." He—it was Manabu—said. His voice was quiet but friendly.

Nae tried to smile but the skin of her face was so tense that she couldn't do it. Murmuring "Please come in" was the best she could do.

Manabu walked in. He was tall. A good six feet, she reckoned. He couldn't have been that tall the last time she'd seen him. He must have only been in eighth grade then.

He glanced around. "This room is not quite the same as the other one."

"You really didn't need to get a second suite."

"Seeing as we've got a lot of talking to do, we needed a seating area. Anyway, let's sit ourselves down," Manabu said. The room had a single large sofa. Manabu sat down and Nae plunked herself beside him, but a little distance away.

Manabu started inspecting her. Nae dropped her gaze.

"Don't stare at me like that. I'm an old woman."

"Nothing you can do about that. Anyway, look at me. I've more than my share of gray hair."

Nae looked at him admiringly.

"You're so handsome. I managed to find plenty of photos of you online."

"There's no relation between the number of images of a person online and their real-world achievements. . . . Do you search for me often?"

"Sorry. I know it sounds a bit creepy."

"Hardly. I can understand."

"I didn't only want to see what you looked like. I wanted to find out something about you. Even as a boy, you were always writing impenetrable essays stuffed with jargon. That's the sort of thing I was hunting for."

Manabu grimaced self-consciously.

"You mean the pieces I wrote for all those minor science magazines? That was a very long time ago. I'd like to dig a hole, bury them, and pretend none of it ever happened!"

"I remember you wrote this one article about child abuse. It was about how abused children, when they grow up, tend to go on to abuse their own children, because they have no experience of being loved themselves—"

"I wrote the whole thing based on secondary sources. It wasn't a subject I had any great affinity for."

Nae breathed in with a slight hissing sound. She was starting to feel more comfortable.

"The way I treated you was unforgivable."

Manabu drew back his shoulders and tucked his chin into his neck, while his eyes darted from side to side. Nae could see he was struggling for a response.

"Would you like a drink?" he eventually said. "I feel a bit parched myself. I'm going to call room service. Is there anything you want?"

"You decide for us both."

"Are you okay with something alcoholic? How about champagne?"

"Oh . . . That's a nice idea."

Manabu got to his feet, walked over to the desk, and picked up the phone. As she looked at his back, Nae was thinking how much he resembled someone else.

That someone else was Manabu's father.

Having put through his order, Manabu came back and sat down on the sofa. "They'll bring it right up."

"How are your parents?" Nae asked.

Manabu waggled his hand, then said, "My mother isn't doing too well. My father's doing his best to look after her, but she hasn't long left."

"What's wrong with her?"

"Multiple organ failure. Plus advancing dementia."

"I'm sorry to hear that. . . ." Nae lowered her gaze.

"There's something I always wanted to ask you about if I got the chance," Manabu said. "It's to do with my father—my birth father, that is. I checked the family register. It's blank. What my parents told me was that the daughter of a distant relative had me after she got divorced. But there should be a name in the register even in that case."

"That's what you want to know?" Nae nodded. "Your parents probably gave you that explanation because they thought it was easy to understand. It seems to have backfired and only confused you."

"You weren't actually married to my birth father, were you?"

"No, I was not. The two of us were young. He had his whole future in front of him."

"His future?"

"His future as a scientist." Nae looked out of the window at the expansive night sky.

Manabu's birth father was a student. He frequently went to the cafeteria where Nae worked, and that was where they got to know each other. Nae was twenty-one at the time. She had as good as run away from the family home in Obihiro and made her way to Tokyo.

He was renting a tiny room with shared toilet and bathroom facilities. The bookshelves were crammed with difficult books. When she lay beside him on his futon, she always worried about them crashing down on them during an earthquake.

He was good-natured and a hard worker; more than anything, though, he was smart. He could mend anything broken, knew as much about medicine as any doctor, and spoke English well too. He was the kind of person she felt safe with in any situation.

Given all that, his academic record was first class. Thanks to recommendations from his professors in the research lab, he got the opportunity to continue his studies at a research facility in the United States after graduation, a first for the university.

He asked Nae to go with him. "Let's live together in America."

Nae was thrilled. It was a dream come true. Then one night, when she was staying over in his little room, she woke up in the middle of the night to see him sitting at his desk studying furiously. That was when it hit her: *she shouldn't go with him*. This was a man who needed all the time he could get. She shouldn't distract him with anything outside his research. She would only hinder him if she went.

She eventually told him that she'd decided not to go. "I will support you from here in Japan. Go to America and do your very best. I won't wait for you, so find yourself a nice girl over there."

Although it obviously wasn't easy for him either, he didn't try to talk her out of her decision. He was a smart fellow. He must have guessed what her reasons were.

And that was how the two of them parted. Amid her sorrow, Nae tried to assure herself that it was all for the best. Then something happened that stunned her: *she missed her period*. She felt nauseous in a way she had never experienced before. *She was pregnant!* She didn't need to see a doctor to figure that out.

She agonized. What should she do? She certainly couldn't tell him. That would completely derail his studies and distracting him was the last thing she wanted to do. Besides, she didn't know how to reach him in America. She'd also told him that there was no need for him to write her.

Having an abortion never occurred to her. From a rational

perspective, she knew it was the best thing to do, but she was determined to have the baby whatever happened. Because it was *his* child.

Eventually, the manager of the university cafeteria, a woman, realized what was going on. Since Nae lived on campus, concealing the pregnancy was far from easy. The manager contacted Nae's parents. They came straight up to Tokyo and gave her the third degree.

Who is the father? What are you going to do about it? Her father even yelled at her to "just get rid of the damn thing already."

Nae said nothing. When her parents ordered her to abort the baby, she just shook her head.

The cafeteria manager apologized to Nae's parents for failing in her duty of care. She did, however, keep her mouth shut, despite having a good idea of who the father was. Perhaps somewhere inside, she sympathized with Nae.

Nae's parents remained as agitated as ever. In the end, they imposed a condition on her: they would allow her to have the baby, but she would have to give it up for adoption.

They assured her that this would be best for the child. There was no way that a young girl bringing up a child on her own could provide it with a proper education. It would be much better for the child to be entrusted to a respectable family with some financial resources. Of course it would! It was pure selfishness to want to keep the baby and bring it up herself. . . .

All the points her parents made were valid. Unable to rebut them, Nae submitted.

Eventually, she had the baby. It was a boy. She'd come up with the name Manabu months earlier. She hoped it would make him every bit as smart as his dad.

Then the day of mother-son separation came. When Nae met the Yukawas, she was reassured by their seriousness and sincerity. However, the request they had made in advance of the handover irked her. They wanted to be the ones to decide when to tell the child he was adopted, and they didn't want Nae to try to contact him until then. Nae's parents agreed to their terms.

"Sorry, I went off on a bit of a tangent there. Are you interested in what happened next?"

"Only if you don't mind talking about it," Manabu said. He had a champagne glass in his hand. While Nae was reminiscing about the past, the bellboy had brought up a half bottle of champagne and a couple of glasses.

"I'm happy enough to talk about it. I just don't think it's all that interesting. I spent quite a long while living with my parents. Eventually got married and came back to Tokyo. My first husband was a designer and illustrator with a shop where he sold his work. It was while I was working there that I learned to draw and made a few connections in that world. That's how I was able to support myself after our divorce. My husband was a serial adulterer and a violent drunk. That's why I ditched him. See, I told you it wasn't much fun."

"After your divorce, you were on your own again. What did you do then?"

Nae took a deep breath and looked him in the eye.

She knew that he already knew the answer to that question. He only wanted to hear her say it because he wanted to resolve things today, here and now.

"I was in despair so I did something quite outrageous. I tried to get back the son I had given up for adoption," said Nae, spitting out the words. "I went around to the Yukawas' place and I begged them to give me back my boy. It was a shameless, shocking thing to do. I wasn't myself. I was half out of my mind."

"Yes, I could hear you and my parents yelling at each other from up in my bedroom. *Give him back!* No, we won't. *Hand him over!* We'll never do that. You were like children fighting over a toy." Yukawa smiled sardonically. "Of course, you managed to agree on a compromise in the end. You let me make the choice."

Manabu was right. They had gotten him to come downstairs and made him choose a side. That was when Nae had realized she was on a highway to nothing. For all that she was his birth mother, there was no way Manabu would choose a random woman who had suddenly turned up out of nowhere over his adoptive parents. Sure enough, he'd said that he was quite happy where he was.

Manabu's parents did, however, allow Nae to see the boy, so she made the time to see him. Although he never refused to meet, he looked thoroughly miserable whenever they were together.

"When you were in grade eight, I asked you if you regarded the Yukawas as your real family. Do you remember what you said to me?"

"That nothing is real and that all of us are alone in this world," Manabu said promptly, the words tripping off his tongue. "That was a phrase I liked at the time. A pretentious and immature one-liner."

"It had a big impact on me. That was when I realized I was hurting you and decided it would be better for us not to see one another."

"Which is why you vanished from my life."

"Yes. I realized I'd be better off trying to build a new life for myself. Luckily for me, I met my new partner very soon after."

"Goro Matsunaga, you mean? My parents showed me the letter you sent them announcing your marriage to him. It was when I was in tenth grade."

"I meant to put you completely out of my life. I never tried to see you. Not even once. But it was no good. Like I said, ever since I began to come across your name on the internet, I would search for you when I was at a loose end. Then, six years ago, I came across that book of yours, *If I Ever Met a Monopole*. I read it right away. It wasn't easy, but I think I got the gist of it. It gave me a couple of ideas. One was to turn it into a picture book. The other was to contact you on the pretext of research—without revealing my real identity, of course."

"When your editor got in touch, I remember thinking, 'Gosh, some of these children's book authors do have the oddest ideas for stories.' It never occurred to me to wonder about Nana Asahi's true identity."

"When did you figure it out?"

"Only after this whole case began. The detective heading the investigation happens to be a friend of mine. He came to ask me what I knew about the author Nana Asahi. That was when I first discovered that Nana Asahi was you. Feigning indifference in front of him was quite a challenge."

So that's what had happened! Nae had never understood how Manabu had ended up getting involved in this case.

"You didn't tell the police about me?"

"The whole thing was too important to leave it to them. I sensed that the whole situation must be quite complicated and so I decided to get to the bottom of it myself." Manabu smiled as he said this. "Everything suddenly started making sense when I reread the old emails you had sent me. They were full of questions about my childhood and my family."

"I should apologize for that. I never dreamed I'd be able to correspond with you. I suppose I got a bit overexcited and asked too many questions. I didn't mean to trick you."

"I don't feel tricked. When I investigated the past of Nae Matsunaga, I learned that you used to travel around doing traditional storytelling performances with illustrations and that that was how you met Sonoka's mother, Chizuko."

"I'm impressed! You're quite right, though. The two of us immediately clicked. We had chemistry. I admired her as a single mother bringing up a daughter. It was something I hadn't been able to do myself."

"That also explains why you developed such an affection for her daughter, Sonoka."

"Yes, but there isn't the same chemistry I had with Chizuko. There's always going to be a generation gap."

"Regardless, it was Sonoka who reached out to you this time?"

"Yes, that's what happened. When I learned she was aware of the murder of her live-in boyfriend and was desperate to run away, I did what I could. I knew there was no way she could have killed him herself and that she would be fine once the truth came out. But she never told me the whole truth. I was really hoping she would come clean with me at some point."

"She was probably afraid you'd look down on her if she did."

"Look down on her?"

"Because she'd deceived someone. And she's convinced that the murder was committed because of all the lies she told. It's a long story. I'll explain it some other time."

"So that's what was going on. . . . Still, I was really surprised by that first email you sent me."

"I'll bet you were."

The email had arrived while Nae and Sonoka were in the holiday apartment in Yuzawa. The email came from an address Nae had never seen before. This is what it said.

Attn. Nae Matsunaga

If you are in a holiday apartment belonging to a family friend, I strongly urge you to get out of there right away. The police know you are there. I will find somewhere else for you to hide. Come to Tokyo.

Nae initially thought the email was a prank. She changed her mind quickly enough and accepted that someone was warning her of impending danger. Despite having no idea who the someone was, she decided that following their advice was the best course to take. (She did send a return email in which she asked the sender to reveal their identity. No reply was forthcoming.)

"You should have told me who you were from the get-go."

"It would only have made things more difficult for you. You'd have started overthinking things. It would have slowed you down."

He was right. Had the email come from Manabu's regular address, she would have vacillated, suspecting that the police were using his name to entrap her.

A second email arrived when she and Sonoka were already en route to Tokyo. It gave the name of a hotel where a room had been reserved for them. Nae had been startled when she saw the name under which the reservation had been made: Manabu Yukawa. He had appended a couple of lines. "I am sure you have plenty of things you want to ask me. For the time being, it's best if you just follow my instructions."

She'd gotten his third email late that same night. All it contained was a cell phone number and a request for Sonoka Shimauchi to call it.

The fourth email had arrived today. In it, Yukawa said that he would be coming to their room to talk directly to Sonoka Shimauchi and that he wanted Nae to go to another room he'd reserved at the same hotel.

"Why did you decide to help us?"

"It's like I said. I couldn't stand by and let the police handle it. Still—" Manabu tilted his head to one side and shrugged. "That's not much of an excuse really. If I'm honest, I probably wanted to reach my own conclusions about the life of Nae Matsunaga—what you feel about things, the kind of life you've led."

Nae recoiled slightly and eyed him quizzically. "What . . . what did you find out?"

"Not much. Still, I think I understood something about you. The fact that you did storytelling performances for orphans and treated your neighbors' son in Niiza like your own child had to be related to your own life story."

"To call it a penance would probably be an exaggeration. It was my attempt to atone for having abandoned my son. Self-indulgence, really."

Nae giggled wanly.

Manabu's eyes darted from side to side, then he smiled and spoke. "I'm performing a penance of my own."

Nae tipped her head to one side and inspected Manabu. "Why?"

"You remember the house?"

"Which house?"

"The house my parents and I used to live in."

Nae nodded.

"It's a place I'm unlikely ever to forget. That's where I went to try and get you back."

"It was demolished a few years after my parents moved to their new seaside apartment. When I heard it had been knocked down, I realized that the person I was then was a completely different person than the little boy who had tried so hard to be a good and obedient son in that house—that that little boy had died long ago and left his invisible corpse in that old house somewhere."

"That's too sad. . . ."

"The truth is, I couldn't have been more wrong. Decades have passed. Since then, I've met all sorts of people all living life in different ways. Now I can see what a fool I was back then. No one can live their life alone. It's thanks to many other people that I am the person who I am today. I am deeply grateful to my parents for raising me—and I should be equally grateful to the person who gave birth to me and then turned me over to my parents. Now I know . . . now I know what I *should* have said when you told me to choose between one set of parents or the other. 'I can't make that choice. Because all of you are my parents.'" Manabu looked Nae straight in the eye. "I always wanted to apologize, if we met one day. To tell you I was sorry."

Nae felt a surge of emotion roiling her chest. Swallowing in an effort to control it, she managed to hold Manabu's gaze.

"You said something about some other time. That you'd give me a full explanation of this whole episode some other time. Does that mean we can see each other again?"

"Of course it does. You're my mom and I am your little boy." Manabu smiled. "Right, Mom?"

Nae felt the warmth course in her chest. She could hardly breathe.

"Can I give you a hug?"

He nodded.

"Manabu," Nae whispered as she held out her arms.

20

As usual, it was Kusanagi who was sitting waiting for her in the interview room. A female detective was sitting beside him. Hidemi had heard Kusanagi call her Utsumi.

"Sorry to bring you back in again," Kusanagi said once Hidemi sat down.

"I'm okay with it. I just find it hard to believe you've still got questions."

"Not many more. There's something we need you to confirm for us."

Kusanagi slid a number of photographs out of the file at his elbow. He lined them up on the table. There were five photographs, each one showing a different gun.

"Does any one of these guns resemble the gun you used?"

"Yes, this one." Hidemi picked out a picture without a moment's hesitation.

Kusanagi nodded. "Perfect. Thank you. That gives us a little more evidence to work with."

"I threw the gun away. Have you found it?"

"We couldn't find it. That was a major inconvenience. In the end, we decided instead to start looking for the man who gave you the gun to look after. I regret to inform you that he died over ten years ago."

"Why am I not surprised? There was always an air of danger about him. Did someone kill him?"

"No. It was disease. We managed to dig up some information on his handmade gun and concluded it was probably this model. It's one that was manufactured in the Philippines a long time ago. A lot of them were defective. You were lucky it didn't discharge by accident."

"It's because I took good care of it."

Kusanagi pushed all the photographs off to one side of the table, then turned and looked at Hidemi again.

"You don't want to modify your statement?"

"Which part?"

"The part about your motive. You wanted to help Sonoka Shimauchi escape the abuse of Ryota Uetsuji. We get that. What we still don't get is why the girl meant so much to you in the first place."

"I've explained that a thousand times."

"That stuff about your idolizing her, you mean?"

"Yes. Can't you understand that?"

Kusanagi crossed his arms on his chest and groaned feebly. "I find it quite hard to fathom."

"That's your problem, not mine. I'm telling you the truth."

"That you murdered someone for your idol."

"There's plenty of people out there happy to commit murder for chump change. Different things matter to different people."

"I can see that, but . . ."

"Why not ask Sonoka if you don't believe me?"

Kusanagi said nothing. He frowned and the skin above his nose dimpled. Hidemi knew what that expression meant: he'd already checked with Sonoka and she'd stuck to the script Hidemi had given her. Their stories were aligned.

Him too. Hidemi pictured Yukawa, the physicist, in her mind's eye.

She got the impression that he was being sincere when he promised not to reveal the full truth, provided she turned herself in to the police. If Yukawa had told Kusanagi the truth about her and Sonoka's relationship, she was prepared to deny it outright. Clearly, though, she'd judged the man correctly.

It's worked out well, she thought. *This way, everything is safe.*

She could sustain her dream.

Kusanagi was saying something under his breath to Utsumi. He seemed to be suggesting it was time to bring the interview to an end.

Hidemi looked at the pile of photographs at the end of the table. The one she'd picked out was on the top. It was identical to the gun she'd used that day.

When had her doubts started?

At some point, she'd started to wonder if she was wrong about Sonoka's mother being her daughter—that perhaps the whole thing was a monstrous lie. Her doubts felt very fresh; at the same time, perhaps they had been lurking in the back of her mind since her first meeting with Sonoka.

She'd made the conscious choice to ignore the possibility. She'd refused to acknowledge it even existed.

She *wanted* to believe it. She *wanted* to believe that she was spending time with the child of the daughter she had abandoned. Being with her was like being in a dream; it reignited her will to live. Sonoka was a good, openhearted girl who fit right into that dream scenario. Hidemi was determined to believe she truly was her granddaughter.

She couldn't forgive Uetsuji for making her dear Sonoka suffer. When it came to protecting Sonoka, she was ready to do whatever it took.

Going to the police was one option. Otherwise, she could get someone to make him leave her by force. She had connections to plenty of people who would be willing to do the job for her. But what would Uetsuji do *after* she'd forced him to leave Sonoka? Would he turn around and tell her something that she was determined not to acknowledge to be true?

That was the thing she wanted to avoid at all costs.

That was why she was left with no choice in the matter.

She glanced again at the photograph of the gun. She thought back to that day.

As soon as Uetsuji realized she'd led him down a dead-end street with no houses that culminated in a cliff top, he asked her what was going on.

"What is this place? Where's Sonoka?"

Hidemi said nothing. She drew the gun out of her handbag. A look of horror appeared on Uetsuji's face.

"What are you doing?"

"Turn around and face the sea." She only said this because she was too frightened to shoot him while looking him in the eye.

Uetsuji turned around and raised his hands in the air, unbidden.

Hidemi put her finger on the trigger. She couldn't summon the courage to squeeze it.

Uetsuji started speaking.

"Please, wait. It wasn't me. I never said it in so many words. It was Sonoka. It was her. She's the one who li—"

Hidemi had heard enough. She pulled the trigger. Her eyes were clamped shut.

When she gingerly reopened them, Uetsuji had vanished. She walked forward and peered over the edge of the cliff. Uetsuji's body lay on the rocky shoreline, his head and upper body jutting into the water. That at least saved her the trouble of going down to collect his cell phone! What had Uetsuji been trying to say just before she shot him? *"It was Sonoka. It's her. She's the one who li—"*

How was he planning to end that sentence?

Hidemi resolved to put the question out of her mind. That was the best way to keep her dream alive.

EPILOGUE

The funeral hall was at the top of the hill after a long climb. A new, brightly colored building. Kusanagi got out of the taxi in the forecourt and headed for the entrance, fixing his necktie as he did so.

Upon entering the lobby, he saw a table to register the mourners on the right. There was a line of people dressed in funereal black. When Kusanagi reached the front of the line, he took the envelope of condolence money from his breast pocket and placed it on the table. Then he wrote his name and address in the registry.

Someone said his name. Glancing to one side, he saw Yukawa walking toward him.

"I told you that you didn't need to come."

"I couldn't *not* come. Utsumi wanted to come with me. I wouldn't let her, so she sent a telegram of condolence instead."

"I know. I just read it a minute ago." Yukawa glanced at his watch as he said this. "There's still a little time. Shall we go into the family waiting room?"

The door to the family waiting room was next to the reception table. Ten or so people, all dressed in black, sat dotted around the room. Kusanagi noticed Shinichiro Yukawa, Yukawa's father, speaking to another elderly gentleman. Shinichiro must have spotted him, as he made a little bow in his direction. Kusanagi bowed back in silence.

They found a couple of empty seats and sat down side by side.

"How was your mother at the end?" Kusanagi asked.

"She lost consciousness five days ago. They took her to the hospital, where she died yesterday without ever coming around. My father was with her. I was not. It was a peaceful end."

"I see. Well, God rest her soul."

"Honestly, I feel like a heavy load's been lifted from my shoulders. It's probably the same for my father. We'll miss her, but now we can think about ourselves for a change."

"Will you move back to your own place?"

"You bet. I have zero desire to live with my dad. And I want to see my students' faces again. I'm sick of doing all my lectures online."

An elderly woman entered the room. Kusanagi started. It was Nae Matsunaga. She went up to Yukawa's father to greet him. She then looked over at Kusanagi and Yukawa. She made no move to come over and instead sat herself down in a nearby chair.

Kusanagi thought back to his interview with her. From start to finish, Nae Matsunaga had maintained that Sonoka Shimauchi had told her nothing about the murder. She had only said that she needed to lie low and Nae helped her do so.

Nae Matsunaga did acknowledge that it was Yukawa who had warned her to vacate the holiday apartment. He was just someone who had once helped her with a book she'd written, she explained.

So she was clearly taken aback when Kusanagi informed her

that Yukawa had told him about the true nature of their relationship. He went on, "We have been friends since university, but he'd never said a word about you to me before. It was quite a surprise."

"I had no idea. So you . . ." Kusanagi could see the curiosity in her eyes as she looked back at him. He sensed that she was longing to ask him about her son as a young man.

Yukawa consulted his watch again. "It's almost time."

"The murder case . . . ," Kusanagi said. "Hidemi Negishi's trial is scheduled to start next week."

"Is it?"

"Ultimately, she never modified her statement. Personally, I still believe there was something special about her relationship with Sonoka Shimauchi. And I think you know what it is, even though you've opted to say nothing about it." Kusanagi jabbed a finger at Yukawa's chest. "How about this for an idea? After the sentencing, why don't you tell me what you've been keeping secret? For my part, I won't tell a soul. I promise."

"I'll think about it."

Kusanagi's cell phone started vibrating in his pocket. It was a call from Kaoru Utsumi.

"Hey. What's up?"

"A murder victim has been found on the embankment near Senjushin Bridge. It looks like they're going to call us in."

"Roger that."

Kusanagi ended the call and he glanced at Yukawa.

"Another case? Off you trot, then," said the physicist before Kusanagi had even said a word.

"I'm sorry. I'd like to offer some incense. It's the least I can do."

"Don't start feeling guilty. Your professional theater of operations should always be your top priority. I'll be heading back to my own, the research lab, as well."

Yukawa held out a fist.

Kusanagi clenched his right hand.

The two men did a fist bump.

ABOUT THE AUTHOR

Keigo Higashino is one of Japan's bestselling novelists, and his work has been translated into more than twenty languages. He's best known for his Detective Galileo mystery series (*The Devotion of Suspect X*) and his Kyoichiro Kaga series (*Malice* and *Newcomer.*) He lives in Tokyo, Japan.